Two Tickets to Paradise

CARRIE JACOBS

Edited by Court of Spice Editing courtofspice.com
Cover Art from Deposit Photos and/or Canva
Cover Design by Carrie Jacobs
First Edition 2023

WELCOME TO HICKORY HOLLOW!

Each novel in the Hickory Hollow series is a stand-alone, and can be read in any order. There are some character appearances across books, so there may be some very minor spoilers if you read the books out of order.

<u>Hickory Hollow titles</u>:
Drunk on a Plane
Caller Number Nine
The Boy Next Door
Luck of the Draw
Cat Burglar
Mending Fences
Two Tickets to Paradise
Bad Advice
Where There's a Will (novella)

<u>Stand Alone titles</u>:
The Bucket List

For details about all of the Hickory Hollow books, visit my website at carriejacobs.com

For exclusive sneak peeks, behind-the-scenes information, and much more, sign up for my newsletter at carriejacobs.com.

for Cersei and Emma
my furry, judgmental Editorial Assistants

Chapter One

The Hickory Hollow Ladies' Society board meeting convened in their usual corner booth at Sonny's Diner.

Gertie waited until all four ladies had their pie and coffee, and Agnes called the meeting to order.

"Let's start with new business. Anyone?" Agnes asked, already sliding her finger to the next item on the agenda.

"Yes." Gertie pursed her lips as Agnes looked up in surprise. Gertie was the quietest of the group, and it had been months since she'd had a topic to offer.

"Oh?" Agnes's eyebrows were halfway up her forehead. She leaned forward, curious. "What do you have?"

"We have a problem is what we have." Gertie pushed her pie away. Her news was too distressing to be soothed with dessert. "I received a phone call from Erin this morning. We've got quite the monkey wrench thrown into the Two Tickets to Paradise prize." Erin and her now-fiancé, Greg, had been the winners of an international trip for two – the grand prize from last year's Valentine's Day Ball. The trip was the biggest prize they'd ever awarded, sponsored by Phyllis and Toby Warner of Hickory Hollow Travel.

"Is there a problem with their trip?" Millie asked.

Ruth chimed in, "I just spoke with Phyllis a few days ago. She didn't mention anything."

Gertie took just a moment to enjoy the fact that Agnes, Millie, and Ruth were all laser-focused on her for a change. Not that she wanted to be the center of attention too often, but once in a while was quite nice. She looked at each woman in turn–Agnes and Ruth across from her, Millie beside her. "Erin and Greg won't be able to take their trip."

Ruth gasped.

"Why not?" Agnes demanded.

"Greg's father isn't well. He needs a kidney, and Greg is a perfect match."

"Oh, yes," Millie said softly. "I remember hearing he was on dialysis and got on the transplant list a while ago."

Gertie continued. "Greg's having the surgery next week."

"Well, why can't they go after?" Agnes said.

Gertie felt a little smug about having answers at the ready. "Erin told me international travel isn't recommended for the donor for up to twelve months after the surgery."

"And the vouchers will expire before then," Ruth said, nodding in understanding.

"Exactly."

Agnes pinched her lips together and drummed her nails on the table, thinking. "This is unprecedented."

Gertie pulled a manila folder from her bag and opened it. "I took the liberty of making a list of the contestants from last year and how they were partnered up. And since I don't believe that we have a viable candidate in there, I also pulled together the participants from the previous five years."

Ruth leaned forward to look at the list. "Should we award it to the runners-up?"

"The runners-up have already collected very nice prizes.

And aside from that, Mike and Juanita moved to Arizona last fall," Gertie said, pointing to the notation she'd made beside their names.

Agnes said, "We want to keep it local, for sure, and I know Phyllis and Toby would agree." She held out her hand toward the list. "May I?"

"I made copies." Gertie handed each woman a stapled packet of papers.

A few minutes passed as the women studied the lists. "Surely there's something in the bylaws," Agnes said. She raised her hand to catch the waitress's attention.

Corinne came over with the coffeepot and a smile. "Refills?"

"Yes, please, but could you also give me the binder under the counter when you have a moment?"

"Sure."

Corinne refilled their mugs and went to the counter. The Ladies' Society had not only commandeered a booth for their own use, they had a section under the counter that housed their wooden ballot box and business binder.

In exchange for "volunteering" space in his diner, Sonny got a favorable mention as a longtime supporter in every news article, newsletter, or event the Ladies' Society participated in.

Agnes took the binder from Corinne. "Thank you."

Gertie's nerves had sufficiently calmed to take a bite of her strawberry rhubarb pie. She muttered to Ruth, "It's not as good as yours."

Ruth poked at her apple crumb pie and sighed. "It's not terrible, I suppose."

"Here it is." Agnes tapped the page. "Reassigning prizes is at our discretion."

Millie said, "We should make a decision, then run it by Phyllis as a courtesy."

Gertie nodded in agreement. "I agree. We should present it

as a done deal, though. You know how Phyllis likes to take something and run with it."

The ladies all agreed. They studied the lists and discussed each and every couple as they finished their desserts. Corinne refilled their coffees again. And again.

Finally, Agnes sat back and sighed. "Unfortunately, it appears that none of the former participants fit the bill, and we can't hold the prize. I fear creating a new drawing would negatively affect the pool of contestants for next year's ball."

"We don't have time, anyway," Ruth said. "It's already the end of May. Only eight and a half months until next Valentine's Day, so I'm already rounding up sponsors."

"And potential participants," Millie added. "I don't think a whole new contest is feasible or practical."

Gertie could hardly contain her smile. They'd reached exactly the conclusion she'd anticipated. She cleared her throat. "I suggest we select two new singles to take over the prize." She enjoyed the stunned expressions of her friends, then pressed on. "Our goal is to create lasting couples. Rather than choosing former contestants who have already become established couples, we put another suitable pair together."

After a long pause and another deep sigh, Agnes said, "Is that an official motion?"

"Yes."

Ruth nodded. "I second."

"All in favor?"

All four ladies responded in the affirmative. Agnes made notes for the minutes, then said, "I also make a motion to create a more specific policy for such events."

That motion also passed.

Gertie pulled four sheets of paper out of her folder and handed them out. "I suspected we might decide to move in this direction, so I took the liberty of preparing a nominee."

"Noah Spencer. Why does that name sound familiar?" Ruth asked.

"Bill Spencer's his dad," Gertie said. "It's in the notes there. Spencer Roofing is their family's company."

"Oh, yes, that's right. Bill put the new roof on the bakery a few years ago."

"Good family," Agnes added. She read from the dossier. "Forty-one. Divorced." She set the paper down and snapped her fingers. "I remember his situation now. What an awful mess that was with his ex-wife."

Gertie harrumphed. "The way she took off for a whole year, then came back to fight him for their daughter. Shameful."

"Well, we don't know the whole story," Ruth offered, although she sounded as skeptical as Gertie felt. "Anyway, I think Noah would be a great candidate. Did you have a partner in mind for him?"

Gertie shook her head, disappointed that she hadn't had time to do more. "No, I couldn't think of anyone on such short notice."

Millie smacked the tabletop in excitement, sending her fork into a tailspin. "I know *just* the one."

Gertie gasped at the name Millie shared. She should have thought of it herself. No matter, the most important thing was that Project Two Tickets to Paradise was a go.

Chapter Two

"Yeah, sounds great." Becky Reed held the phone away from her ear and made a face. Just hearing the voice of her ex-husband's twenty-seven-year-old fiancée grated on her nerves.

"We wanted to make sure it didn't interfere with any of Wyatt's sports schedules," Veronica said. "My mom's a retired teacher, so she's already planning to help with his big project on the Mayan ruins. I didn't quite get that, since it's summer and he probably doesn't have anything due for school, but whatever floats his boat, right?"

"Sure. Yeah, baseball is over by June 15, so if you're leaving June 25, that's perfect. I appreciate you considering his schedule." She really did appreciate it, but still.

"We also arranged with Joey's parents to watch Wyatt, so he'll never be unsupervised."

"Uh huh." Wyatt had just turned nine in February, so his father had better have planned to have him supervised at all times.

Veronica pressed on. "We'd still love it if you could come. We'll take care of all the expenses."

"Oh, yeah, no, sorry, I have that work thing. Mandatory."

Becky would rather get fifty simultaneous root canals–in her eyeballs and flushed with bleach–than go to her ex-husband's wedding. *Destination* wedding in Cancun, no less. She felt bad for all the negative feelings. Veronica was a lovely person and made so much effort to be good to Wyatt and to include Becky while still trying very hard to stay in her lane with parenting decisions.

Seriously, Veronica scheduled her wedding around her soon-to-be stepson's schedule, made sure the resort was kid-friendly, and even booked excursions to multiple Mayan ruins because Wyatt was obsessed with history. It wasn't Veronica's fault she was sixteen years younger and fifty pounds lighter than Becky. And she'd had absolutely nothing to do with the implosion of Becky's marriage.

"Sooo... do you have another minute? There's something else I'd like to discuss with you."

Becky put a lid on her impatience. Communication with Veronica was a good thing. She kept reminding herself of that fact. "Yeah, of course. And thank you. You've been so thoughtful with including Wyatt, and I really appreciate it. I'm sure I seem weird about it, and I hope you know it's nothing against you. This is all just..." Becky waved her hand, trying to find the word.

"Uncharted waters?" Veronica offered.

"Yes, exactly. You had something else?" This awkward call was never going to end, was it? She went into the living room and waited for Veronica to say whatever she had to say.

There was a long pause. "We're not telling anyone because it's so early, so I'd really appreciate it if this could stay between us."

"Sure." The word came out at the same instant the realization popped into her head. Oh, no.

"Joey and I are expecting a baby. We just found out and

we're only about six weeks along. Of course the timing isn't what we'd planned, but here we are." She gave a little laugh.

"Oh." Becky grabbed the back of the chair and slowly sat down. "Congratulations. That's wonderful."

"I wanted to tell you because I found a class that helps blended families and introducing kids to half-siblings and that sort of thing. I'd really like to sign up and take Wyatt, but of course I wouldn't do it without your permission." Her words came out in a rush. "I'll email you the link so you can see it. I wouldn't expect you to approve without taking a look, of course."

Becky could feel Veronica's nervousness. She swallowed down her own feelings. "That sounds like a great idea. Of course I'll take a look."

"And you can be as involved in the process as you'd like."

How about zero? "Interesting. I'll be sure to look at it."

"You have plenty of time. I wouldn't sign up until we're back from Mexico. By the way, thanks for sending Wyatt's passport over. I'm trying to get all the paperwork gathered up. I can't believe it's less than a month until we leave."

"I can't believe it, either." As soon as it was polite to do so, Becky ended the call and stared across the room, trying to process the idea of a new baby. It was the same old clichéd story – the man adamantly doesn't want more kids, but changes his mind when the shiny new wife comes along.

Her plan was to spend some quality time wallowing with Ben and Jerry, polishing off a pint of chunky monkey. But before she could raid the freezer, her phone rang again with an unfamiliar local number. Thinking it might be one of Wyatt's coaches, she answered. "Hello?"

"Becky? This is Millie VanHouten."

"Millie, how are you?" Why on earth would Millie VanHouten be calling her?

"I'll cut right to the chase. Your friend Erin contacted the Ladies' Society with some very unfortunate news."

"Is she okay?" Becky hadn't talked to her in a few weeks, but if something was wrong, surely she would have called.

"Oh yes, she's fine. The news is regarding the trip she and Gregory won in last year's Valentine's event."

It took a second for Becky to process what Millie said, because it didn't make much sense. "I have to admit I'm a little confused about why you're calling me about it?"

"Erin and Greg are unable to take the trip."

"Um, Millie? I still have no idea what this has to do with me." She suddenly realized that if they weren't taking the trip, that must mean Greg was a match for his dad, who needed a kidney transplant. They wouldn't pass up their prize vacation for anything less. Which still didn't explain why Millie was calling her.

"I'm calling because the Ladies' Society has chosen you to go on the trip in Erin's place."

Becky was glad she was sitting down. "What?"

Millie repeated herself.

Refusal was on her tongue, but she imagined Veronica in her white dress on the beach in Cancun, marrying the man Becky had wasted half her life on. The man who'd done her wrong, but they worked through it. Then one day he decided he didn't want any more kids and the next, he didn't want her anymore, either. The man who was Fun Dad, always taking Wyatt here and there, buying the best video game consoles and streaming services. And now he was taking Wyatt to Cancun for almost a month. With a brand new stepmom.

Ugh. Maybe taking a trip of her own would be a good distraction. Not so much a distraction from Joey getting married. Heaven knew she didn't want him anymore, but she definitely felt some type of way about Veronica's growing relationship with Wyatt.

"Where is the trip? And when?" she heard herself ask. "I can only go if it's while Wyatt is away with his dad."

"I'll have Phyllis give you a call so you can work out all the details. I'm so glad you can go."

Words caught in the back of Becky's throat. She hadn't exactly said she'd go, but she hadn't said no. Which was a huge mistake. Once the Ladies' Society has decided you've agreed, you're stuck.

It's like making a deal with the devil... only scarier and harder to get out of.

Chapter Three

Noah Spencer felt something in the air as soon as he walked into his parents' kitchen. His suspicion only got worse when his mom and dad exchanged a significant look. His mother was full of uncontainable glee, while his dad gave a slow, resigned head shake and looked back at his newspaper.

"What's going on?" Noah dropped his jacket onto the back of a chair.

Sandie couldn't contain her grin. "Gertie Dalton called earlier."

Noah was glad it had nothing to do with him. The Ladies' Society was probably soliciting his dad's business to sponsor their next event, but that didn't explain why his mom was acting so weird. He grabbed a bottle of water from the fridge.

She said, "I know you're probably going to be mad."

That got his attention. What could she have done that might make him mad? The water bottle froze halfway to his lips. Oh, no. "Mom. You didn't sign me up for one of their stupid singles things, did you?" He looked over at his dad, who was suddenly engrossed in the newspaper. Noah reached over and flicked the top of the paper. "Nice try, but you've got it upside down."

Bill groaned and folded the paper. He tossed it on the table and got up, heading for the door. "Good luck."

"Good luck? What's going on? And why is Dad escaping?"

Sandie looked a little guilty as she slowly dried her hands on a kitchen towel. "Noah."

"Mom," he answered sternly.

"An opportunity came up and time is of the essence, so it was either take it or leave it, pretty much."

"An opportunity? From the Ladies' Society? What did you do?" The Ladies were known for two things: philanthropy and matchmaking. And Noah had a feeling there was nothing charitable about this particular "opportunity."

"Maybe you should sit down."

"I'm fine standing here."

She bit her lip and couldn't quite look directly at him. "I kind of signed you up for a trip."

"A trip?" That didn't sound so b— "Wait." He squeezed his eyes shut and gripped the back of the chair. "What kind of trip?"

"It's incredible! A trip to Ireland. All expenses paid. Airfare, hotel, food, everything. There's even a little spending money included. I know you've always wanted to go to Ireland. Obviously your dad is giving you the time off, and we figured with Lilly visiting her mom once school is out…" She trailed off.

Noah's jaw clenched. Lilly spending the entire summer with her mother was a huge sore subject, but she was thirteen and wanted desperately to go, and he couldn't find a good enough reason to refuse. All he could do was cross his fingers and hope his ex-wife would set her selfishness aside enough to keep Lilly safe. "This sounds like a scam."

"No scam."

"Then what's the catch? Free trips don't generally fall out of the sky."

"There's no catch."

He fixed her with a hard look.

"I mean, it's not a *catch*, per se." She dropped the towel on the counter and slid into a chair at the table. "You know the Ladies' Society does the Valentine's Day ball every year."

"Yeah." The word was clipped.

"And you know Erin and Greg won this huge trip last year. Well, they can't go because Greg's donating a kidney to his father, and he's not supposed to do any international travel for up to a year after the operation. Their trip vouchers will be expired before they can go."

Noah sat up straight. "He's a match? I wonder when he found out." He reached for his phone to text Greg, then jerked his hand back to the table. "Nice distraction. What's the catch for this trip?"

Sandie bit her lip.

With his mom's demeanor and the involvement of the Ladies' Society, he put the pieces together pretty easily. "Let me guess. Some poor, desperate, single woman is taking over Erin's place and they want poor, desperate, single me to take over Greg's."

"Something like that," she admitted. "But you'll have your own rooms. It's not like you even have to spend any time together except on the plane."

"No."

"Honey, I know you're annoyed at me, and I know I overstepped by saying you'd go. But I think you need a trip like this. Get out of town, away from all the gossip and opinions and drama. Lilly won't be home, and it won't do you any good to sit in the empty house and be all moody until she gets back.

Everything you do is for her, and I think you need to do something for yourself for a change."

"She's my *daughter*. Of course everything I do is for her. You and dad always did everything for me and Natalie, so it's a little hypocritical to call me out, don't you think?"

She finally leveled her gaze at him. "No, it's not hypocritical. Your dad and I always had each other, so we were able to make time for our own hobbies and interests and friends. You've been doing this all on your own for a very long time."

His irritation deflated. "I'm not on my own. You and dad and Nat have done so much to make sure I've never been in this alone."

"Noah. I really, really want you to take this trip. When are you ever going to have an opportunity like this again? Maybe you'll even make a friend."

Before he could argue his case, he made the mistake of looking over at his mom. Her eyes were rimmed with unshed tears.

She reached across the table and put her hands on his. "I worry about you."

Noah knew he'd lost the battle. "I guess this is why they call it a 'guilt trip.'"

Chapter Four

Becky finished updating Thursday's last patient file in the computer. "I seriously think I'm going to barf."

Sarah's chair squeaked as she leaned back and curled one leg underneath her. "You still don't know who he is?"

"No."

Julie clasped her hands under her chin. "It's so romantic. You'll see each other for the first time on the plane and look into each other's eyes and just know you're meant to be together forever."

Becky and Sarah shared a glance about their hopelessly romantic friend. "Hardly, since I'm meeting him tonight at the travel agency."

"Fine," Julie huffed. "Your eyes will meet across the stacks of brochures and you'll both get dizzy from the overwhelming emotion."

Sarah rolled her eyes. "More likely to get dizzy from Phyllis's cloud of Jean Naté."

Becky laughed. Phyllis was famous for her heavy-handed use of the perfume. "Speaking of Phyllis, I'm feeling a little guilty about springing this short timeline on her. Planning a huge international trip in only four weeks can't be easy."

Sarah waved a hand, dismissing Becky's concern. "I guarantee she had at least half of it planned already since the vouchers only good for another few months anyway. Trust me, Phyllis is in her glory right now. She *lives* for this kind of challenge."

Julie agreed. "I can't believe she's not a bona fide member of the Ladies' Society yet. Maybe when she retires."

"Besides," Sarah continued, "if Phyllis couldn't make it work, she definitely would have said so. She's not one to suffer in silence."

"Okay, that's true. I feel better."

"Are you feeling any better about everything else?" Sarah asked.

"If you're referring to the perfect Barbie doll with the perfect figure and perfect approach and perfect plans and perfect freaking hair, then no. Yes. No. Maybe. I don't know. I really, really want to hate her guts, but she's so genuinely nice that I can't." Becky checked the time and picked up her purse from under the desk. "I'm grateful she's so thoughtful about Wyatt, and she clearly cares about him, which is the most important thing."

"That doesn't mean you can't want her to get a giant zit in the middle of her forehead for the wedding," Sarah said.

Julie snorted. "Maybe on the tip of her nose."

"Full on acne breakout. They'll photoshop it all out so she'll still have perfect pictures, so no long-lasting harm."

Becky laughed. "Thanks, guys. Wish me luck tonight. Hopefully this guy's not a weirdo."

Becky sat in her car outside the Hickory Hollow Travel Agency, where she'd arrived twenty minutes early. She tried playing Candy Crush on her phone, but it didn't hold her attention.

At ten minutes before six, she decided to go inside, but a vehicle pulled in the parking lot and she wanted to wait and see if it was him. Not that she'd know for sure until she went inside, but at this hour, the odds were stacked in favor of it being her travel companion. He got out of his car.

Well, good news. If the guy was a weirdo, at least he was a good-looking weirdo.

He was lanky, tall, and cute in a bit of a dorky sort of way. He vaguely reminded her of Jim from *The Office*. Or maybe Ryan Reynolds. He looked familiar, which was nothing unusual. Growing up and living in Hickory Hollow meant everyone had surely come in contact with everyone else at some point.

She watched him take the handful of cement stairs two at a time and waited until the door swung shut behind him before she hopped out of her car.

The travel agency was a small brick building that at one time was a ranch-style model home for a builder who'd long since gone out of business. Cheerful chimes rang out as Becky pulled the decorative French door open and stepped inside the tiny lobby. Wall racks full of brochures and catalogs filled the room. Colorful signs divided the brochures into three sections of destinations: Local/Pennsylvania, United States, and International.

To her left was a hallway marked "Employees only" and directly ahead was a second French door leading to the biggest room in the building that served as Phyllis and Toby's office. It was propped open, and Phyllis's voice filtered through the doorway.

Becky gingerly stepped into the room, not wanting to interrupt.

"Becky! Come on in." Phyllis stood behind her massive desk and waved to a chair beside the mystery man. The room was full of stacks of papers and brochures and folders on every possible flat surface, from the tops of the filing cabinets down to some antique brown box thing that might have been a humidifier. "Have a seat."

The man looked up and gave her a small, crooked smile.

"Do you two know each other?" Phyllis asked.

"We've met," he answered before Becky could say anything. He looked over at her as she settled into the chair. "It's been a while. Noah Spencer."

She shook his hand, trying to place him. "Becky Reed. Nice to meet you. Again, apparently?" He seemed vaguely familiar in that "seen him around town" sort of way, but she couldn't place him otherwise.

Phyllis drummed her fingers on the table. "Alrighty. So we've chosen Ireland, yes?"

Becky and Noah both nodded.

"Wonderful. What's on your must-do lists?" She looked at them expectantly.

Noah looked over at her. "You first."

"Oh." Becky's fingers tightened around the purse on her lap. "I hadn't really… I thought maybe you'd have some brochures to look through?" She was the one who'd chosen Ireland from the options Phyllis had offered, but hadn't given it any thought beyond *Ireland would be great! Let's do that!* Now she was wondering if Noah had even been given a choice.

"Certainly." Phyllis tapped a stack of magazines on her desk. "But we're in a bit of a time crunch."

Becky felt like she was being admonished in front of the class by the teacher. "Yeah, uh, of course, I mean, I'm good with the usual. Like the Blarney Stone and some famous pubs or something?" The Blarney Stone was literally the only Irish landmark she could think of offhand.

Phyllis's kind smile never wavered, but she did blink a few times. "Noah? Did you have anything in mind?"

"I do." He pulled a paper out of his back pocket and smoothed it on the desk. "I'd really like to do this *Game of Thrones* filming location tour."

Phyllis took his paper and perched her half-glasses on her nose. The beaded chain that hung from the glasses swayed back and forth as she moved her head. "Oh, this sounds lovely. So we're doing Northern Ireland as well as the Republic of Ireland."

"Is that a problem?" He asked.

"No, not at all." She scribbled something on her pad.

Becky's attention was piqued. Filming location tour? "Wait, so you can tour the places the show was filmed? Can you do that for movies, too?"

"Of course," Phyllis said, nodding.

"Oh. Great. Awesome. I'd like to see where *Leap Year* was filmed. It's my favorite movie. Like, ever." That movie was the main reason Ireland had become her number one dream trip if she ever got the chance to travel.

"Do you have any idea where that might be?" Phyllis asked.

Becky sat back in her chair, the excitement turning to embarrassment. "Ireland. I mean, I don't know. They might have filmed it in Hollywood for all I know. Never mind."

Noah pulled his phone out, which only made Becky's face flame hotter. Great. She was clueless, and he was bored and probably regretting everything about this situation.

Phyllis didn't seem concerned. "Don't worry, we can look it up."

"Inishmore," Noah said.

"What?"

"It says here most of the filming for *Leap Year* was on the Aran Islands. In the movie, the setting was supposedly the Dingle Peninsula, but the filming of Declan's Pub and the proposal were actually in Kilmurvey on the Aran Islands."

"Oh." She was surprised that he'd been looking it up. And doubly embarrassed that she hadn't thought to do that herself.

Phyllis made a note. "The Aran Islands are simply stunning. We'll perhaps do a night in Galway, ferry to the island, and we'll be sure to work in the Cliffs of Moher while we're in that area."

Noah added, "It says here it was also filmed at St. Stephen's Green."

Phyllis scribbled some more. "That's in Dublin. You'll want a few days in Dublin and visit St. Stephen's Green anyway. And if we're going to Northern Ireland, a few days in Belfast as well." She chewed on her bottom lip and squinted at her notes. "Let me think, let me think." She suddenly whirled her chair around and stood up.

Becky watched her cross the room. It was only when Phyllis stopped that she realized the wallpaper wasn't just wallpaper. It was a room-sized map covering each wall.

Phyllis tapped her bottom lip, then came back to her desk to pick up a pad of sticky notes. She placed six or seven stickies in seemingly random spots on the map of Ireland, then stood back and tapped her lip again. After several long minutes, she turned around to face them and planted her hands on her hips. "Let's iron out a few important details," she said, crossing back to her desk. "How do we feel about driving? Would you prefer to mostly take bus tours, or stay in the cities and do a lot of walking or use a taxi?"

"I'd kind of like to have a car. Be able to come and go?" Becky said.

Noah nodded. "Me, too."

Phyllis looked at Noah. "Can you drive a stick?"

Noah said, "No," just as Becky said, "Yes."

"Have you ever driven in Europe?" Phyllis asked her.

"No."

"Hmm. The travel vouchers will cover a rental car for your stay, but only the manual sort. The fee for an automatic rental is much more expensive."

"Can we pay the difference?" Noah asked.

"I mean, I just said I can drive a stick," Becky said.

He shrugged. "It's fine with me, but I was figuring we'd share the driving so it's not all on you." He pointed to the map, where sticky notes dotted the whole country. "It looks like we'll be doing a lot of it."

Chapter Five

Noah's head was still spinning. Becky? Becky Reed was his travel companion? Seriously? In no universe did he ever suspect for a single second that she'd be the one he was going to Ireland with.

It stung a little that she had no idea who he was. Sure, it had been almost twenty-five years since high school, but they'd bumped into each other here and there around town from time to time. He supposed it shouldn't surprise him since she hadn't really known him back then, either.

"You make a good point," she was saying.

He noted her clothes were actually scrubs – black pants and a hot pink shirt with butterflies. He wondered if she was a nurse. Come to think of it, he didn't know much about her current life at all.

Phyllis tapped at her keyboard for a moment. "The price difference for an automatic transmission rental car is almost four hundred dollars."

"That's fine," Noah said without hesitation. Seriously, the flight and rooms and even their meals were being paid for, so it was no big deal to cover the rental car.

"We'll split it," Becky said.

Phyllis looked back and forth between them. "Alrighty, if you're sure."

"We're sure," Noah said. At least they were on the same page with driving and not waiting around for bus tours the whole time. That was a good sign, right?

Phyllis went back to her pad of paper. "Now. Do we prefer city or country? Activities or sightseeing? Hotel or bed-and-breakfast?"

Becky glanced over at him. "Um, I think a mix? I'd love to see some old castles and stuff."

Noah agreed. "There are some cool places in Dublin and Belfast I wouldn't mind seeing while we're there. So yeah, I agree. A mix of both."

Phyllis made some notes, nodding her head as she wrote. "A little of this, a little of that. Hmm, okay, I think we can..." she trailed off, talking to herself more than either of them. She flipped through a booklet and typed something into her computer, then scribbled more notes on her pad.

Noah looked over at the map on the wall. He couldn't wrap his head around this situation. Was he really sitting beside Becky, planning a vacation together? It didn't seem real.

Phyllis clapped her hands, startling him. "Okay. You're sure the only must-see items on your list are the Blarney Stone, and the *Game of Thrones* and *Leap Year* filming locations?"

"And a castle?" Becky suggested.

Phyllis waved a hand. "Of course. One doesn't go to Ireland and not see a castle or ten. Would you rather see a lot of things, or stay mainly in one or two places and have leisure time?"

Noah glanced at Becky again. If sitting here was any indication, he guessed lots of unscheduled leisure time would mean lots of awkward silence and trying to figure out what to do. "I think I'd prefer to see as much as we can."

"Definitely. Who knows if I'll ever get back to Ireland, so I'd like to see as many highlights as we can."

A slow grin spread over Phyllis's face. "Does that mean I have carte blanche to fill in the gaps?"

Noah shrugged. "Yeah, I'm up for whatever."

"Sure." Becky seemed a little hesitant.

"There's likely to be a *lot* of driving involved to get you to everything you want to see, plus the things you really must see while you're there. You're okay with that?"

Noah glanced at Becky, who was nodding. He said, "Yes."

Phyllis sat back in her chair and regarded them both. "Alrighty. This is technically a nine-day trip, but the first and last days don't really count. You'll leave Thursday evening, June twenty-seventh, and fly overnight. That counts as Day One. Your last day will be Friday, July fifth, and of course you'll spend the day in the air. That only gives us seven actual days to get everything in. We'll be sure to get a little taste of everything, then you'll see what you enjoyed most and hopefully someday you'll go back to Ireland and get to see more things." She pulled her glasses off and let them hang by the beaded chain. Her chair squeaked as she leaned forward. "Toby and I have been to Ireland five, no, six times. Six times. It's nothing short of magical, and I couldn't be more pleased to have you go there. Now. To practical matters."

Noah half-listened as she talked about avoiding massive international charges on their cell phones, adapters for their chargers, euros and pound sterlings, and the sort of clothing to pack. Part of him knew he should be paying better attention. The last time he'd traveled internationally was a short trip six years earlier, when a good friend from college got married in Greece. He'd gotten to the airport, spent the entire time at the hotel resort, then shuttled back to the airport, so there was no need to worry about any sort of touristy vacation concerns.

Phyllis continued. "We'll have money for you a few days before you leave, with your final itinerary."

He perked up. "Wait, I'm sorry, what do you mean you'll have money for us?"

Phyllis raised an eyebrow. "The travel cash we're providing. It's not a lot, but we'll exchange it to euros and pounds here so you can have it on hand when you get there."

He felt like his question had offended her somehow. "Sorry. I didn't realize the trip included cash, too. That's so generous." Now that she mentioned it, he did recall his mom listing spending money in her hard sell for the trip.

She softened. "I forget you haven't gotten all the details. I put the package together last year, so it's old news to me."

It seemed appropriate to chuckle a little. "This is probably a dumb question, but if we want to take our own money, too, where do we go to exchange it?"

"Believe it or not, our local banks have some of the best exchange rates and can take care of that for you. They just need a few days' notice."

The thought of a bank in Hickory Hollow being able to provide euros was a little hard to wrap his head around.

"Most places also accept credit cards. Only Visa and Mastercard, though. I will have some smaller out of the way places on the itinerary, and many of them only accept cash, so be sure to keep some on hand as you travel."

"And anything we don't use we can exchange back when we get home?" he asked.

"Bingo. Well, except coins. Spend those before you leave." She tapped her nails on the pad. "Your schedule is going to be *very* tight. If you think of anything else you'd really like to do, let me know by end of day tomorrow so I can try to fit it in."

"Sounds good."

"If you don't already have them, I'd get a pair of waterproof hiking shoes because one thing we can guarantee is that it will rain while you're there. Pack layers because it'll probably be nice but chilly. Waterproof lightweight jacket. You'll also have plenty of daylight hours to see everything you want to see." She glanced up at Noah and caught him drifting again. Her brows creased inward.

She paused for a second before continuing. "All of this information will be with your itinerary. A little light reading for the plane." She chuckled and checked her notes again. "I think I have everything I need for now. Like I said, let me know by end of day tomorrow *at the latest* if you want to add anything to your must-do list." She stood, so Noah and Becky stood, too. "This is going to be so much fun."

He followed as Becky moved toward the door. Phyllis followed them and when they'd crossed the threshold, she wished them good night, waved, and locked the door behind them.

Noah shoved his hand in his pocket to retrieve his keys. "Should we exchange numbers or something?"

She looked up from her cell phone. "Yeah, we probably should." She tapped on her screen a few times and handed him her phone.

He entered his name and number and handed it back. "Your turn," he mumbled lamely as he opened a new contact form on his own phone.

Back when they were in high school, and dinosaurs roamed the earth, he'd gotten her number from the phone book and kept it on a slip of paper in his wallet. Which was wholly unnecessary, since he'd memorized it almost immediately. In fact, if he thought about it, he could probably recall it right now.

She typed in her contact info and handed his phone back with a grin.

He looked down and saw she'd added shamrock emojis before and after her name. "I didn't think of that, so mine's just a boring old name."

"I'll fix it." She smiled and slipped her phone into her purse.

He was trying to find something–anything–to say when she beat him to the punch.

"We should probably get together before the trip to talk about expectations and goals and that sort of thing. Like, I want to check out some pubs and stuff, but I don't drink a lot, so it's not really a main focus for me, you know? And I'm pretty anal retentive about being on time. And I like to kind of hit the ground running in the morning. I usually get up at five, but I've been inching my alarm back, so hopefully jetlag won't be an issue since Ireland is five hours ahead of us."

As Noah listened, he realized she must be a little nervous about the trip, too. "I'm usually up at four, so yeah, it shouldn't be awful. There are some pubs I'd like to see, but I agree, definitely don't want to be dealing with a hangover on top of the time shift." He cleared his throat. "Maybe we can grab coffee or something once we get the itinerary from Phyllis. Kind of go over it and see what to expect."

"Sounds great." Her purse buzzed and a panicked expression crossed her face. "I really have to run. We'll talk soon."

He jumped in his car and watched her leave. He was easing off the brake to back out of his spot when he stopped short.

Did his mother know it was Becky when she signed him up for this trip?

Chapter Six

Becky jumped out of the car and jogged up the sidewalk to Joey and Veronica's front door.

Joey answered her knock with a scowl.

"Hey, sorry I'm running a little late."

"Where were you?"

She shot him a look and ignored the question. Her whereabouts were none of his business. Brushing past him, she headed straight toward the kitchen, where she heard Wyatt's voice.

"Hey, buddy, sorry I'm a little late." She kissed the top of his head.

He was perched on a stool at the island, coloring. "Hey, Mommy."

Veronica was on the other side of the island, snapping the lid on a bowl. "Hi, Becky."

"Sorry I'm late," she repeated for the third time.

Veronica shrugged and shook her head. "Barely fifteen minutes. Who cares?"

"I do," Joey answered from the doorway. "We have a schedule."

"Oh, stop being dramatic," Veronica said with an eyeroll. "Where were you?"

Before she could tell him it was none of his business, Wyatt piped up with, "Mom was at the travel agency. That was tonight, wasn't it, Mom?" He was busy putting his crayons back in the box.

"Yup."

Joey crossed his arms. "Travel agency? Anything you need to tell us?"

"No, there isn't anything I need to tell you." Her personal life was exactly zero concern of his, even though he didn't seem to realize that fact.

"Mom's going to Ireland."

"Is that so? And you didn't think you should consult with me about that?"

Consult with him? Her ex-husband? Yeah, no. "Absolutely not."

"What about arrangements for Wyatt?" He crossed his arms, that familiar smug look on his face.

Becky's blood pressure was reaching the boiling point. "He'll be in Mexico with you," she said slowly, enunciating each word.

"So you're just going to leave the country? Were you planning on telling me?"

Becky's eyes squinted as her nose scrunched. "I'll have my phone and my tablet with me, so I can be reached via call or text or email at any time. I'm going to Ireland, not the moon."

"Mom's going to kiss the Blarney Stone. It's in an old castle."

"Is this what all my child support is paying for?"

"Excuse me?!" Her hand fisted around her keys.

"Joey!" Veronica smacked the bowl down onto the counter. "Stop it. What on earth has gotten into you?"

Becky wondered the same thing. Who did he think he was to question her and make comments like this? And in front of Wyatt? "This is completely unacceptable."

"Oh, I would agree. Who are you going with?"

Becky held up a hand. "I'm not participating in whatever you're doing." She lightly touched Wyatt's back. "You ready?"

"Yup." He hopped off the stool and ran over to wrap his arms around Joey's middle. "Love you, Dad."

"Love you, too." Joey ruffled his hair, but his eyes were still shooting daggers at Becky.

Veronica rounded the island. "I'll walk you out."

Wyatt hopped on one foot from tile to tile through the foyer. Becky followed, pausing to pick up Wyatt's backpack from its usual spot on the bottom stair. She slung it over her shoulder as Wyatt opened the door.

Veronica followed them out onto the porch. Wyatt gave her a hug and skipped to the car. He climbed into the back seat and began to buckle himself in.

"I'm really sorry about all that. I think he's stressed about the wedding and the trip and all the details with everything."

Becky looked at her. Really looked at her, this young woman who was about to become Wyatt's stepmom. "A word of advice? Don't start out making apologies for him or excuses for his poor behavior. He's a grown man and should be capable of conducting himself as such."

"I know. I just..." She trailed off, her hand gesturing back and forth between herself and Becky.

"We're good. It's not your fault he's a... Anyway." Becky switched gears. "Did the tux fitting go okay?" Not that she had any interest in any aspect of the wedding, but it was a safer topic than all the things she wanted to say about her ex-husband.

Veronica's face brightened. "Let me show you." She pulled

her phone out of her back pocket and tapped on the screen a few times. "Joey sent me these. Scroll back this way to see them all."

Becky kept her face neutral as she scrolled through a dozen photos of Wyatt and his father and the groomsmen in their tuxes. She stopped on a photo of a man standing with Wyatt sitting on one shoulder and another boy sitting on the other. "Wow."

Veronica gave a little laugh. "My brother Ben and his son Kyle. He's eight, almost nine. Him and Wyatt just love playing together. They're going to be co-ring bearers."

It was so weird, seeing evidence of her son getting a whole new family that she had no part of. Unsettling, even as she was grateful Veronica and her family embraced him with open arms.

She scrolled through the rest of the photos. "Thanks for showing me these. Looks like they had a good time."

"MOM!" Wyatt yelled from the car.

"That's my cue." Thank goodness.

"Oh, I almost forgot. Is it okay if Wyatt's photo is posted on Instagram? Just from the actual wedding."

"Joey's okay with it?" That surprised her. He was the one who had strict rules for posting Wyatt's pictures online. It was one of the few things they mostly agreed on.

"He's fine with posting pictures from the wedding, but not from the beach or anything like that."

"If it's okay with him, it's okay with me."

"Great. Thank you. Our photographer likes to do sneak peeks from weddings and I'm sure he'll be in some of the ones that get posted."

"MOM!"

"Gotta run. You're picking him up Saturday morning?"

"Yup. See you then." Veronica waved to Wyatt. "Have a good last day of school tomorrow!"

Wyatt waved back and said, "Come *on*, Mom."

Becky hurried to the car. "I'm coming, I'm coming. Geez, mister impatient."

"I have to poop."

She half-wanted to send him back inside. Let the kid stink up his dad's bathroom.

It would match his dad's crappy attitude quite nicely.

Chapter Seven

Noah dropped his keys on the kitchen counter. "Lilly? I'm home."

Bass thumped from upstairs, so the odds of her hearing him were slim to none.

"I don't know what you did." Chloe, the seventeen-year-old neighbor kid who babysat, even though Lilly insisted she was old enough to be home alone, shook her head as she stuffed her iPad into her backpack. She warned, "She's *big* mad."

Noah peeled some bills out of his wallet. "I have no idea."

"Good luck." Chloe stuffed the money in the pocket of her shorts and made a quick exit.

Lilly was thirteen. Rainbows and puppies seemed to make her "big mad" these days. The only things that didn't make her mad were the cats and her mother reappearing into her life with promises of an amazing summer with her in Florida. Which Noah was not in favor of. Which Lilly knew. Which made her mad. Big mad.

Lilly's mom, Danae, packed her bags and left when Lilly was four. She went off to California to "find herself." What she found was an alcohol addiction and a string of poor decisions, during which she tried to fight for custody. She lost and vanished from their lives for several years. Three years ago, she moved to Florida with her aunt, got cleaned up, and made herself a nice career in real estate.

Two years ago, she reached out to Noah, asking his permission to reconnect with Lilly. He grudgingly accepted, and Danae began reaching out consistently, taking things slow, following Noah's rules.

One year ago, she'd visited Hickory Hollow and asked to take Lilly home to Florida for a week. Noah had refused. Now, even though he didn't like the idea at all, he was willing to let Lilly visit her mom. Okay, "didn't like the idea" was a weak understatement. He hated the idea. Loathed it.

But he didn't want Lilly to end up resenting him for keeping her away from her mother. Especially now, at the age when girls needed their moms more than ever.

He hoped Ireland would be a little distraction to keep him out of his head, pacing the floors and worrying about Lilly.

He took the stairs two at a time. Lilly's bedroom door was open. She sat on her bed, arms crossed, scowling at the doorway. Both cats, Tormund and Hodor, were curled up at the end of her bed, oblivious to the blaring music.

"Hey. What's up?" he yelled over the noise.

She reached over and flicked the speaker off. Hodor looked up, his floofy Himalayan face confused at the change in the atmosphere. To be fair, Hodor was always confused.

"Did you eat?"

Her eyes narrowed as she glared daggers at him. "Yeah. I had a big ole bowl of Lucky Charms."

"What?" He was pretty sure they didn't have any cereal.

"Yeah, and then I made myself a shamrock shake. And I washed it all down with an *ale* I got from a freaking leprechaun."

Noah leaned against the doorjamb. Apparently Lilly had heard about his trip to Ireland. "I feel like you're trying to tell me something. Like there were some subtle clues in what you just said."

She rolled her eyes like only a teenage girl can.

"You have something on your mind?"

"Yeah," she yelled. "Like what the heck? I have to find out from *Madisyn* that you're running off to Ireland with some hobag? Like were you even going to tell me you grabbed some random skank out of the donation pile? Or were you just going to be all like, 'Welcome home, Lilly, here's your new stepmonster.'?" She angrily crossed her arms across her chest. "Whatever. I don't even care. Like at *all*."

He wasn't sure whether to laugh or be offended. Okay, he knew not to laugh, because that would send Lilly into the stratosphere, but he found her tirade fairly amusing. "Well, where do I begin?"

"I don't care. It doesn't even matter. So whatever."

"First of all, hi. Glad to be home. Nice to see you after a long day."

She *had* to have seen her own brain with an eyeroll that hard.

He walked over and sat on the corner of her bed. "You may have heard that I'm taking a trip to Ireland while you're in Florida with your mom. You know my friend Greg. This was supposed to be his trip, but his dad needs a kidney and Greg's a match, so he can't leave. The Ladies' Society asked Grandma if I might want to go, and she signed me up without even asking me about it because she thought it sounded like a good idea."

It might have been his imagination, but it looked like Lilly softened, just a little.

"I figured I'd go ahead and go because maybe it'll distract me from how much I miss my daughter while she's away."

Another eyeroll, but this one was much less dramatic.

"Since Greg can't go, Erin isn't going. So the Ladies' Society picked a replacement. Her name's Becky. She was a year ahead of me in high school, and tonight we met at the travel agency. This is the first time I've talked to her since high school."

"Ugh. So she's, like, even older than you?"

Nothing like having a teenager to make a person feel older than dirt. "Yes. I have my concerns about her being able to shuffle around Ireland. Hopefully we can rent motorized wheelchairs."

A flicker of a smile played at the corner of her mouth.

"I think we're mostly going to eat pudding and shake our canes at all the young Irish whippersnappers."

She was definitely trying not to smile.

"Reminisce about the good old days, when we had to walk to school uphill both ways in the snow."

"For six miles."

"Seven."

"Even in the summer."

"Especially in the summer." He shook his head and blew out a puff of air. "Those summer blizzards were brutal. You kids don't know how good you have it."

"You're such a dork."

"Guilty. Hey, I guess since you already had a giant bowl of Lucky Charms and a homemade shamrock shake, you probably wouldn't be interested in any of these wings I brought home. Too bad, since they're all garlic parmesan."

She eyed him. "Extra ranch?"

He grabbed his chest. "Ouch. Do you really think I'd show my face around here without extra ranch? Come on now."

She finally smiled.

"Tomorrow's just a half-day, right?" It was the last day of school before summer vacation started.

"Yeah." She hopped off her bed and headed toward the door. "I don't even know why they're making us go. We cleaned out our lockers today and turned in our books and stuff."

He reached out and flicked her ponytail. "Just to annoy you."

"Success." She pushed past him and trotted down the stairs toward the kitchen.

Tormund jumped from the bed and followed her, a few long orange hairs wafting into the air behind him.

Noah glanced over at Hodor, who seemed very, very confused by the activity. He went over and scratched Hodor's head. "You're a sweet boy, aren't you?"

Hodor responded with his loud chainsaw purr, tilting his head into Noah's palm.

"You coming downstairs?"

The cat flopped onto his side and stretched out, hogging half the bed.

"Good call." Noah went downstairs and grabbed a roll of paper towels. He set it on the table and divided the chicken wings—flats for Lilly, drummies for himself.

Lilly eyed him suspiciously. "So you're not dating this *Becky* person?"

It was always his policy to be honest with Lilly, even though that sometimes meant just barely telling the truth. He wasn't about to spill his guts about how he'd loved Becky from afar, how he'd learned to play guitar, and then drums, just to be in the band, then the marching band, for the sole purpose of being near her. How he'd joined the set crew to build props for the theater group while Becky was on stage, acting and singing like she belonged on Broadway. And he darn sure wasn't going to admit that just an hour ago he'd definitely felt a spark of something as they sat in Phyllis's office. So he settled on the technical truth.

"I told you. This is the first time I've spoken to her since high school. We'll go on this trip and hopefully have a nice time. Really, though, I don't see how she can spend a week with me and not fall madly and hopelessly in love. It's a curse, being so handsome and charming."

Lilly made a horrified face. "Do you *want* me to puke up my wings?"

"I would prefer not." He ate a wing. "On a serious note, she seems really nice and if we hit it off on this trip, I probably wouldn't be opposed to seeing her sometimes after we're back home. But that's a whole bridge to cross later."

She dredged a wing through a puddle of ranch dressing. "Promise you won't do something stupid like get married or something?"

Noah laughed. "I promise. We're going to Ireland, not Vegas."

Chapter Eight

"Did you have supper?" Becky glanced in the rear-view mirror.

"Yeah. Dad got pizza after we tried the suits on. And then Veronica made me eat an apple with peanut butter because she said pizza isn't healthy enough."

"Made you, huh?"

"I didn't *say* I didn't like it."

She had to chuckle at his penchant for technicalities. "I haven't eaten, so I'm going to run through Arby's."

"Can I get curly fries?"

The kid could eat his weight in junk food. "I'll get a large and you can have some of mine."

"Get sauce."

She pulled up to the speaker and ordered, then drove around to the window. A few minutes later, they were on their way home, the smell of curly fries filling the car.

"Did you have fun trying on your tux? Veronica showed me some pictures that looked like you were having a good time."

"Yeah, Ben put me and Kyle all the way up on his shoulders. He goes to the gym a lot. I thought I was going to fall, but I didn't."

"Kyle seems nice. Do you see him a lot?" She glanced at him in the rear-view mirror.

He shrugged one shoulder. "Sometimes. He doesn't go to my school."

She pulled in the driveway and hit the button on the visor to open the garage door.

"Mommy?" Wyatt's voice was small and uncertain.

"Yeah?" She eased into the garage.

"Do I have to call Veronica 'Mom' after she marries Dad?"

Becky sucked in a surprised breath. She held it for a few beats and slowly blew it out. Of all the scenarios she'd imagined, she never considered Wyatt calling anyone else Mom. That was her title, and the thought of sharing it didn't sit well. Carefully, she asked, "Is that something you want to do?"

"No. Dad said I should though, but Veronica said it was up to me. She said I can just keep calling her Veronica or we can make a whole new special name. So I said maybe I could call her Vee or VeeVee and I think she liked it, but Dad said it was dumb and then Veronica told him he was rude and it's not his business. It's special between me and Veronica."

They went into the house. Becky was glad for the few minutes to process the conversation. She put a handful of curly fries on a plate for Wyatt. "I think Veronica is right. You should call her something you're both comfortable with."

She was starting to like her ex-husband's soon-to-be wife a whole lot more than she liked her ex-husband. At least she didn't ever have to wonder if she'd made a mistake by getting divorced.

"I'll hate her if you want me to."

Becky choked on a fry. She coughed and pounded on her sternum until it dislodged. "Wyatt, why would you say that? Of course I don't want you to hate her. I don't want you to hate anybody."

Okay, she didn't really want him to love the woman, either, but that was her issue, not his.

He shrugged and dragged a curly fry through barbeque sauce. "I know you don't really like her. So I don't have to either."

Crap. She obviously hadn't been as subtle with the looks and annoyance as she'd thought. "No, sometimes Mommy just has a bad attitude and I shouldn't. Veronica is always nice to you, and that makes me very happy. I want you and Veronica to have a good relationship." As she heard the words she was saying, she knew she was speaking her heart. No matter what insecurities and feelings Veronica stirred up in her, she was good to Wyatt, and that was what mattered.

His somber expression vanished as a big smile took center stage on his sweet face. "Good. Because I like her. She makes really good pancakes. She even lets me put the chocolate chips in."

"Mmm, chocolate chips in pancakes are the best." She finished her last fry and crumpled her trash into a ball. "Okay, kiddo, bath and bed. One more half-day to get through and you'll officially be a fourth-grader."

As he unceremoniously dumped his plate in the sink, sending splatters of barbeque sauce all over the sides, he said, "We met Mrs. Treacle today. She came into our classroom and gave us all a card that said she hopes we have a good summer and she can't wait to be our teacher next year."

Becky followed him back the hall to the bathroom. "That was nice."

"She seems super nice. I told her I'm going to Mexico, and she said she went there a long time ago."

She ran water in the tub for his bath and reminded him to brush his teeth when he was done. "Quick bath tonight, it's already past your bedtime." Technically it was only two minutes past his eight thirty bedtime, but he still had to get his bath.

He managed a quick ten-minute bath, then changed into his pajamas–a t-shirt and shorts set covered in pictures of pizza slices–and hopped into bed while Becky read from his newest book, *The Last Kids on Earth* by Max Brallier. He normally read to her at bedtime, unless they were short on time, like now.

They were more than halfway through the book, and Becky already knew she'd be buying him the rest of the series. Not that she was complaining about the expense. Wyatt loved to read, and that was one habit she was more than happy to indulge.

She finished the chapter and closed the book.

"Aww, Moooooom, one more chapter? I'm not even sleepy yet." His red eyes didn't line up with his claim that he wasn't tired.

"Nope. Tomorrow night we'll read extra chapters to cele-brate the start of summer vacation. How about that?"

"Fine." He yawned and dragged his blanket up to his chin. "Love you. Night."

Becky smoothed a hand over his damp hair, knowing he was going to have a massive cowlick in the morning. She leaned down and kissed his forehead. "Love you, love you. Nighty night."

He was sound asleep before she made it across the room to the door. She pulled it most of the way closed, then tiptoed downstairs to the living room, not that she needed to. Wyatt was out like a light.

She sat down on the chair with her laptop and began researching Ireland. In the two days since she'd agreed to go, she hadn't bothered looking it up. She lived a quiet life, just her and Wyatt, nothing out of the ordinary. International trips didn't just drop into the laps of people like her, so it didn't seem real. Even sitting in Phyllis's office talking about it seemed like they were discussing someone else's vacation. And to be perfectly honest, Wyatt's trip to Mexico was the main thing taking center stage in her mind. It was hard to imagine being without him for three weeks.

Noah was just another part of this imagination gone wild scenario. Really? A random free international trip was outrageous enough, but sharing it with a hot guy? Yeah, this was definitely a dream. Not that it mattered. She had zero intention of getting involved with him. A relationship was a complication she didn't need to add to her life right now.

She scrolled past a zillion sponsored travel agency ads until she came to some links to travel blogs from people who had vacationed in Ireland. Ugh. Most of them were full of sponsored content as well. She skimmed over some posts raving about different pubs in Dublin, then gave up and searched for the filming locations for *Leap Year*.

The Rock of Dunamase. Enniskerry. Inishmore. The Cliffs of Moher. She read a few interesting factoids about the movie being set in the Dingle Peninsula, even though it was actually filmed on the Aran Islands. Then she went down a rabbit hole of other films Amy Adams starred in that were filmed in Ireland.

She made a short list of *Leap Year* filming locations and emailed it to Phyllis, with a note that she didn't need to see them all. Especially since she had no idea how many *Game of Thrones* locations they were going to see. Ugh. That sounded dreadfully boring. Sometimes she felt like the only person on the planet who hadn't seen a single episode of the blockbuster series. In some ways it felt like she had, though. Sarah was a huge fan, and Julie was a casual fan, so she was party to many conversations at work about the increasing madness of Daenerys, and Jon Snow, who apparently knows nothing, and dragons. Oh, and the ominous quote, "Winter is coming," which they bandied about every time it got the least bit chilly outside.

Nope, she was definitely more of a romcom kind of girl. Her dragon knowledge was limited to Puff the Magic Dragon, and the land of Honah Lee.

One thing she knew for sure was that wherever they went, they were likely to have stunning views and scenery. So she fired off another email, this time to her photographer friend Megan, asking for help with the settings on her fancy camera. The Canon Rebel had been a "Happy Divorce" gift to herself. She took decent pictures with it on the automatic settings, but with a little help, she knew her photos of the lush green Irish landscape could be stunning.

That done, she did a little online retail therapy. New swim trunks for Wyatt, some waterproof pants and a raincoat for her. And two new suitcases—one for each of them—since hers had seen much better days. And some more travel-friendly new clothes. And memory cards for the camera. And a European plug adapter for her chargers. And a book on the Mayan ruins for Wyatt. And a few things she'd left in her cart for weeks, because she was on a roll. She closed the laptop with a smirk. The UPS guy would empty half his truck on her front porch come Monday.

Chapter Nine

The next few weeks flew by and before he knew it, it was June eleventh, and Noah was double–and triple–checking that Lilly had everything she needed in her suitcase. "You have all your makeup and girly stuff in here?" He pointed at a zippered black case.

"Don't touch that!" she yelled, effectively answering his question.

"Are you sure you have enough clothes?" The question was mostly sarcastic. Lilly had shoved most of her wardrobe into the oversized suitcase. Which meant he'd be paying a hefty overweight bag fee when they got to the airport. "Electronics? Chargers?"

"Yes, Dad, I have all my stuff. Mom said if there's anything I need, she lives near a huge mall, so it's no big deal."

He patted a spot on her bed. "Come here, Lil."

She came over and sat beside him without even an eyeroll.

He put an arm around her shoulders and pulled her to him. "I'm going to miss you."

Lilly mumbled, "I'm gonna miss you, too."

"This isn't easy for me, letting you go all the way to Florida without me." Understatement of the year.

"I know."

"You know that I have some serious reservations about this trip." He held up a hand before she started to argue. "I believe your mom will do her best or I wouldn't be letting you go. But for my peace of mind, I got you this in case of emergency." He pulled a card out of his back pocket and handed to her.

"You're giving me a credit card?"

"Debit card. I opened a joint account and I'll get an alert every time it's used. So you need to stick to the spending budget I gave you. And if there's an emergency, like if you need a plane ticket home, call me and I'll load money into the account so you can get a ticket."

Her eyes were wide as she inspected the card. Then they narrowed. "This is dumb. I'm not going to need some emergency plane ticket home."

"Probably not. But it makes me feel better to know you can get home in a pinch."

She shoved the card into the side pocket of her toiletry bag. "You're being overprotective."

"Sorry, I have to. It's in the job description."

"I'm almost an adult," she snapped.

Almost an adult? He was not ready for this argument. "Not for five more years."

"Five years isn't that long."

"You must be using that new math, because thirteen is definitely not almost an adult."

That earned him a massive eyeroll. "You're just old and mad because I want to spend the summer with my mom instead of you."

Ouch, that did sting a bit. He waited a beat before responding to what he knew deep down was her own nervousness about going. "Old, yes. Mad, no. I'm nervous about not being around to keep you safe. I'm sad because I'm going to miss you like crazy, and I'm excited because I know you're going to have a great time and have lots of stories to tell me when you get home. And I know how important it is for you to spend some time getting to know your mom." Much more important than he wanted it to be.

"What if I want to stay living there?" She picked at a loose thread on her comforter.

Noah studied her neon green glitter nail polish. It wasn't like that thought hadn't crossed his mind a million times. "We'll cross that bridge when we come to it."

"You wouldn't hate me?"

He pulled her close again. "There is nothing in this world that you could do to make me hate you."

She wrapped her arms around his middle and squeezed. "Yeah, right. What if I did something horrible like burn down an orphanage?"

"Rude, but I'd still love you."

"What if I became a serial killer?"

"I think I need to take a closer look at those true crime podcasts you're listening to. But I would still love you."

"What if I ate the last Snickers in that stash you keep in the veggie drawer?"

He sucked a breath through his teeth. "Ooooh, now that's messed up. I'd still love you, but I *would* call the cops."

She giggled. "You'd turn me in?"

"For first degree Snickers theft? You better believe it."

She squeezed him tighter. "Are Grandma and Grandpa going along to the airport?"

"Yup." He checked his watch. "They should be here any time now."

"Dad?"

He kissed the top of her head. "Yeah?"

"I love you."

"I love you, too." He squeezed his eyes shut tight. He hated the idea of this trip. Hated it with every fiber of his being. His daughter belonged right here, at home with him, where she was safe and loved and surrounded by the family who'd been there all along.

He had a bad feeling about this trip, but he knew that was his own past experience with Danae and her issues. She'd straightened out, and had been establishing a track record of responsible behavior.

So this trip was going to be fine, and when Lilly got home in August, he'd make fun of himself for worrying so much.

Right? Right. Of course.

Right?

Noah swallowed the lump in his throat as Lilly snuggled her face in Tormund's orange fur. Hodor sat on top of her suitcase. He was confused, but he knew something was up. He decided to get in on the snuggles and jumped onto the bed and pushed his way across Noah's lap to bump his head against Lilly's arm.

She grabbed him and nuzzled both cats, who were unusually cooperative.

Noah saw the spot on Tormund's fur, wet from Lilly's hidden tears. He cleared his throat. "I put the video calling app on my phone and iPad, so you can chat with the cats any time you want. Me, too, I suppose, but priorities, right?"

She sniffled and nodded.

"Just remember that naptime is from seven in the morning until ten at night, except for that fifteen minute window where they run around all batshit crazy."

She laughed a little.

"Probably have the best luck connecting with them around three AM, but they'll be busy demanding food."

Her voice was muffled. "It's not their fault you starve them. They should never have to see the bottom of their dish."

"I'll keep it filled to the brim while you're away and when you get back, you'll have twenty more pounds of cat to love."

She jerked up suddenly. "Who's taking care of them when you're in Ireland?"

"Lincoln." He reassured her. "And I'll ask Grandma and Grandpa to pop in and check on them."

"Okay." She sighed and reluctantly let the cats down.

"Speaking of Grandma and Grandpa, I think I heard a car door."

Lilly nodded and put on a brave face. She took a look around her room, then said, "I think I have everything."

"If not, all you have to do is let me know and I can put money on your card."

"Okay." She reached for the suitcase.

"I'll carry that for you."

"Okay." She hugged her arms to herself and squeezed her elbows. "I'm nervous about flying by myself."

He didn't tell her he was having a hard time with the idea himself. Instead, he made sure he sounded like it was no big deal. "It's a direct flight, so you'll be fine, no changing planes. We did all the unaccompanied minor paperwork so I can take you all the way to the gate and your mom will be able to go all the way to the gate to meet you when you land in Fort Lauderdale."

"Okay. What about going through security and all that?"

"I'll be right there with you the whole time."

"Okay."

The words were right on his lips to tell her to just stay

home, she didn't have to do this, and he'd cancel the trip to Ireland. But he knew his daughter, and he knew that even though she was nervous, she'd be just fine, and he didn't want to take away the confidence he knew she'd gain. "You ready, Freddy?"

"I think so."

Bill hollered up the stairs, "We're here!"

"Coming," Noah called back. He grabbed the suitcase, and they headed out and piled into the car.

At the airport an hour later, Lilly hugged her grandparents, who would wait in the lobby. Noah had her check her bag herself while he watched, then followed her through security to her gate. He hovered while Lilly introduced herself to the gate agent at the counter. The woman smiled warmly and assured them both that Lilly would board with the first group of passengers, and would be assisted by the flight attendant.

It nearly ripped his heart out when Lilly informed him that she was fine and he could go ahead and leave. On the one hand, he was proud of her. On the other, he was putting his little girl on a plane and sending her hundreds of miles away, into the care of a woman he didn't trust. For the entire summer.

After a giant bear hug, he pretended he was fine and walked away. Of course they didn't leave, not yet. Noah and his parents sat on the observation deck for the next hour until Lilly's plane taxied down the runway and lifted off into the sky. They all waved, even though there was no way Lilly could have seen them.

He let his parents walk him out to the parking garage and tossed his keys to his dad. He shifted awkwardly, then held his arms out, because sometimes even a full grown man just needs a hug from his mom.

Chapter Ten

The end of June sped toward them.

It was Friday afternoon and work was dragging. Wyatt would be leaving on Tuesday, four short days away, which meant they only had this weekend. Becky was still seething at Joey arguing with her about the weekend. According to the visitation schedule, it was technically his weekend, and he didn't want to give it up, even though he was taking Wyatt for three weeks. Three weeks! And he wanted to be a jerk about strictly adhering to the schedule. In the end, Veronica had stepped in, again, telling him to quit being a jerk.

Becky shook her head. Veronica had her hands full dealing with that man-child. She wished her luck.

"TGIF," Sarah groaned, locking the door and drawing the blinds.

Julie nodded in agreement. "I told you guys it was a full moon."

Becky sat heavily in her chair. "Holy crap, that was bananas. Can I just say again how glad I am I didn't end up working in the ER?"

Apparently, everyone in a tri-county region needed MRIs for a variety of injuries. The most interesting of which was a torn rotator cuff resulting from a keg stand gone wrong. Performed by a sixty-eight-year-old grandma of four. You go, granny.

"Did you get this weekend straightened out with Jerky McJerkface?"

Becky snorted. "Only because Veronica told him to quit being an ass."

Julie said, "What is his problem lately? He wasn't this bad up until recently."

"I have no idea. I'm hoping it's just stress over the wedding or this massive trip, and he'll chill out once they get home. Especially since—" she cut herself off. So far, she'd been able to keep the pregnancy a secret, and it wasn't her place to share. "Since there's no reason for him to be acting like this."

"Big plans with the little guy this weekend?" Sarah asked.

"Nope, just getting him packed and all that good stuff. I'll probably take him to Buffalo Wild Wings for a special mommy-son date since I won't be seeing him for three whole weeks." She swallowed hard.

"Aww, don't be sad. He's going to get to see all those ruins and you don't have to stand out in the blistering heat while he takes pictures of every single rock."

She smiled at that.

"Speaking of which. You're less than a week away from your own vacation. How's that going?"

Becky shrugged. "I haven't heard back from Phyllis with the itinerary yet."

"Have you talked to Mr. Hottie again?"

"No. We texted a few times, but it was mostly about weather and links to the charger adapter things."

"Whoa, slow down there. Don't want to scare him off by acting all desperate." Sarah joked.

"Ha, ha, very funny." Becky would have said more, but her phone buzzed with an incoming text message. She scrambled to pull it out as they headed for the door. "Oh, awesome timing. Phyllis says the itinerary is ready and I can pick it up before six."

"Have fun going over it with Mr. Hottie." Sarah winked.

Becky laughed and got into her car. It was just after five thirty. She should have time to swing by the travel agency and pick up the itinerary before she picked Wyatt up from her parents' place.

***

"Becky, come on in. I was just getting ready to lock up." Phyllis reached behind her and flipped the neon sign off.

"Sorry. I thought I'd make it sooner, but there was an accident and I had to go around the back way."

"No problem. You're still in under the wire." Phyllis tapped her gem-studded watch.

Becky's own watch read 5:59. Under the wire indeed. "I just wanted to pick up the itinerary and then get out of your hair." She followed Phyllis to her office.

Phyllis picked up a thick, green, three-ring binder and handed it over. "Here you go. Let me know if you have any questions."

"Oh, I…" she looked at the binder. This was an itinerary?

"Is something wrong?"

"No… I was just expecting a couple sheets of paper. I had no idea you'd go to so much trouble."

Phyllis grinned. "No trouble at all. I love it when I can be so hands-on with planning a trip. Especially when it's to one of my favorite places."

"I don't know how to thank you."

"Just have a wonderful trip. Tag the agency on Instagram. And use my services the next time you travel."

"Deal."

Phyllis's cell phone dinged.

Becky could tell she wanted to get going, so she made short work of saying goodbye. At the door, she said, "Thanks again. I'll call you if we have any questions."

Phyllis waved and disappeared back inside the building.

Becky ran a hand down the front cover of the binder. A sheet of paper had been printed with an outline of Ireland and the trip dates in a fancy font. It felt wrong to open it without Noah seeing it, too, so she contained her curiosity and set it on the passenger seat.

She put the pedal a little harder to the metal. Her parents never minded if she was a few minutes late picking Wyatt up, but she did. Lateness was one of those things that drove her bananas. Especially when they were doing her the massive favor of babysitting for free.

She needn't have worried. As soon as she got into her parents' kitchen, Donna came at her with a plate and pointed to a box on the counter. "Pizza night. Your dad got the mushroom and olive just for you."

"Aww, thanks." One of the perks of mushroom and olive pizza being her favorite was that no one else seemed to like it at all. She had no idea where she'd acquired the taste, since both of her parents were strictly pepperoni and cheese people.

"Chips are in the living room. We just started a movie."

She took a huge bite of the still-hot pizza. "A movie?"

"What's that?" Brian came into the kitchen and pointed at the binder.

"The itinerary for this Ireland trip. Phyllis went all out."

"Oooh." He reached for it, but Becky smacked his hand away.

"No, I don't want to look at it without Noah. Doesn't seem fair."

Her dad grumbled a little, but went to the fridge to refill his cup with lemonade. "I'm not crazy about this trip to Ireland with someone you don't even know."

"Apparently I do know him. He was a year behind me in high school. He recognized me, but for the life of me, I can't place him."

"What's his name?"

"Noah Spencer. Sarah said he works with his dad. Roofing or construction or something."

Brian's eyebrows went up. "Oh, he's probably Bill Spencer's boy. Good family, at least."

Wyatt came into the kitchen. "*Pleeeeeeeease* can we start the movie?"

Her mom popped the last bite of crust in her mouth and wiped her hands on the kitchen towel beside the sink. "Yup, let's get it rolling."

Wyatt ran back into the living room.

"Wait, I was going to head home and maybe see if Noah's around and see if he wants to look over this."

Her mom suddenly looked like she might cry. "Yeah, that's fine. I just thought... I mean, we won't be seeing him for weeks..."

Becky hadn't stopped to consider how much her parents were going to miss him. Sometimes she was so worried about taking advantage of their help that she forgot how much time they *wanted* to spend with Wyatt. "How about I try texting Noah. If he wants, I can meet up with him while you guys watch the movie and take Wyatt home after?"

Her mom's relieved smile was all she needed. She pulled out her phone and sent Noah a picture of the binder.

Phyllis went a little overboard. Wanna see it?

Chapter Eleven

Noah's phone vibrated on the kitchen table. He snatched it up, hoping it was Lilly. He sighed when he saw the message and tossed his phone back onto the table.

"Who's that?" His mom sat across from him.

"Becky. She got the itinerary from Phyllis. Wants to know if I want to see it. I think I'll pass." He started to type out his reply, declining her suggestion.

"For Pete's sake, go and look at the itinerary. It'll do you good to get out of the house."

He snapped, "I've been out of the house every day."

She snapped right back. "You go to work, you come here, you go home. That's it. You need to quit moping about Lilly being away and go do something."

He grumbled, "I've been to the store, too."

"Noah."

"Mom."

She fixed him with The Look, and he backed down.

"Fine." He sent a one-word response.

Sure.

After a few back and forth texts, they agreed to meet at Sonny's Diner at seven o'clock. "You happy now?"

"Yes. You've been grumpy and moody ever since Lilly left."

He went on the defensive. "You're kind of judgy here. You miss her almost as much as I do. Maybe this whole thing is just a big mistake."

"Yes. It's driving me crazy having her so far away. But she's having a good time and her mother finally seems to be doing right by her. You should relax a little and try looking forward to your trip to Ireland. Which, by the way, is *not* a mistake. I wish we'd gone to Ireland when we went overseas. I'm a little jealous you'll get a whole week there."

He relaxed a little in his chair, even though he saw through her attempt to change the subject. "Where'd you go?" he asked, already knowing the answer.

"England, Scotland, and Wales on one trip, and then later we went to France, Germany, and Switzerland. I'd love to see Ireland, but I think your dad is more interested in someplace tropical."

"You've been to tropical places, too."

"Aruba and Jamaica. Wonderful trips, except for that hurricane."

He zoned out as his mom reminisced for the millionth time about the warnings and the crazy clouds that rolled in. They'd had to cut their vacation short and thankfully were able to get on the last flight out of Montego Bay before the island was shut down. He'd heard the story so many times he could recall it as if he'd been right there with them, abandoning luggage at the hotel, racing to the airport, and finally sitting on the plane, praying for the takeoff to beat the storm even as rain pelted the runway.

"You should get going." Her words cut through the fog of his wandering mind.

He sat upright and checked his watch. A quarter til. "Yeah, I'll head out." He got up and leaned down to plant a kiss on her cheek.

"Let me know how it goes."

Noah slid into a corner booth at Sonny's Diner. He ignored the way his heart skipped a little beat when the bells on the door jingled and Becky came in. It was ridiculous. He hadn't seen her for so long, it wasn't like he even *knew* her as a person, so whatever infatuation he'd had when he was a teenager should be over and done.

She scooted into the booth across from him and dropped a binder onto the table.

"What's that?"

"This," she began dramatically, "is our itinerary. Phyllis went a little overboard."

He stared. The three-ring binder was thick with paper. Color-coded tabs stuck out in uniform increments along the sides of the pages. "What all did she put in there?"

"I have no idea. I didn't open it, even though I'm dying of curiosity. I thought it would be rude to go through it without you."

Corinne, their waitress, came over to the table. "What can I get you two?"

Noah ordered a club sandwich and French fries. "And a Pepsi."

"And for you?"

Becky shook her head. "I already had supper, but if there's any of that apple crumb pie, you could probably twist my arm."

"No, but I have fresh coconut cream."

"Sold. And an iced tea, please."

Corinne went around the counter and handed the slip through to the kitchen. A moment later, she came back with their drinks.

Becky turned the binder so they could both look at it, but a second later, she frowned. "We're going to get cricks in our necks if we try it this way. Scoot over."

Noah swallowed hard and slid closer to the window while Becky moved to sit beside him. As she moved, he caught a faint floral smell of her subtle perfume.

She put a hand on the binder and looked over at him. "You ready? I feel like we should have a drum roll or something."

He tapped his fingers on the edge of the table.

"Here we go." She flipped the binder open to the first page.

"This thing needs a table of contents?" Noah raised an eyebrow. Well, if nothing else, there wouldn't be any mystery about what was happening on this trip.

"She has each day under its own tab. My goodness. I feel like a slacker now with Wyatt's trip. I barely made a list of contact information for him."

"Wyatt?" Noah assumed it was her kid, but he wasn't sure.

"My son. He's getting ready to go to Mexico with his dad, which is the only reason I could take this trip on such short notice. He leaves early Tuesday morning. Then after we get back from Ireland he'll still be gone another two weeks." Her smile seemed forced.

"I can relate. Lilly, my daughter, is visiting her mom in Florida for the summer."

Her eyes went wide. "The whole summer?"

He studied the binder. "Yeah. First time she's been away from me for more than a few days."

"I feel for you. I haven't been away from Wyatt, either. It's so weird to even think about."

Well, at least they had that in common. "How'd you get roped into this trip?"

She wore a wry smile. "Millie. Her nephew Rowan is engaged to my friend Sarah, so that's how I ended up on her radar."

"Ah. Gertie for me. She cornered my mom, who signed me up because apparently I need a distraction from Lilly being gone." He had to admit, maybe his mom wasn't wrong.

"I swear those old ladies have bugs in everyone's house or something. Millie called me literally two minutes after I got off the phone with my ex's fiancée, wherein she dropped a news bomb on me. So Millie offered me the trip out of the blue and I was too distracted to decline. They're like some geriatric mafia."

Noah laughed. "Geriatric mafia. That is the best description for the Ladies' Society that I've ever heard." The nosy part of him really wanted to ask about the news bomb and ex's fiancée, but he stopped himself from asking. "They swoop in and get you when you're weak."

"Or go through your family, apparently," Becky said with a laugh.

Corinne brought their food and set it on the table away from the binder. "Geriatric mafia? You *must* be talking about the Ladies' Society."

Becky snickered. "Yeah, they roped us into taking Erin and Greg's prize vacation."

"They can't go?" She sucked in a breath. "That means Greg's a match? For his dad? That's wonderful."

Noah knew he shouldn't be surprised that Corinne knew about Greg's dad's kidney failure. There were lots of benefits to living in a small town like Hickory Hollow, but privacy was definitely not one of them.

"Where are you going, if you don't mind my asking?"

Becky flipped the binder shut to show Corinne the cover. "Ireland."

"Oooooh, jealous! I love the binder. Phyllis's work, I assume?"

Noah watched the women chat about Phyllis's attention to detail, and speculation that she would join the Ladies' Mafia… er, Society, when she retired from the travel agency. He tried to subtly inch his plate around the binder so he could eat. He was halfway through his club sandwich when Corinne finally walked away.

"Sorry," Becky said.

He waved his hand, dismissing her apology, and pointed to his sandwich. He swallowed, then said, "Gave me a chance to inhale my food."

She laughed and flipped the binder open again. "My goodness, but this is thorough." She ran a finger down the table of contents. "Info about the US Embassies, roadside assistance, petrol station locations, maps, rental car confirmation, travel insurance…"

"Wow. I wouldn't have even thought about the embassy."

"Me, either. Or this. Blank pages to put in the 800-numbers for our credit card companies in case they get stolen or lost." She glanced over at him. "That's actually super smart. The odds of losing a card aren't small."

Noah popped a fry into his mouth. "Do you think she goes this extra mile for every trip she plans?"

"I bet she does." She flipped to the Day One tab. "Notes about the rental car pickup, a schedule broken down in half-hour increments. Oh, look. She even has this stop labeled as '*Leap Year* filming location.'"

"Hotel confirmation, directions, estimated travel times, restaurant and pub recommendations…"

Becky shook her head. "I wonder if I can hire Phyllis to organize my entire life."

"Be careful what you wish for."

"Good point. That could go very bad, very fast."

They went quiet as they ate their food and skimmed over the notes Phyllis had made for their first day in Ireland.

Noah glanced over at Becky. Her brows were pinched inward.

"Something wrong?"

She slowly shook her head. "No, it's just overwhelming. I don't know where any of this stuff is or have any context for the places she's recommending. Maybe this whole thing was a mistake."

He pushed his plate to the other side of the table and leaned forward, turning toward her. Hadn't he said the same exact thing to his mom only an hour ago? So why was he about to argue with her?

Chapter Twelve

"I don't think it's a mistake at all."

Becky watched as he reached over and closed the binder.

"It sounds like we both need a distraction from our kids being away, right? So we go to Ireland, and every day we take a look at what Phyllis has planned and we either do it or we don't."

"Just that simple, huh?"

"Just that simple."

Becky looked down at the binder and back up at Noah. It was driving her bananas that she couldn't remember him from high school. "You're probably right. I think I just feel unprepared because it's a really big trip on such short notice. And to be honest, I haven't looked into much of anything because all I'm thinking about is Wyatt being gone for almost a month."

He smiled a crooked half-smile. "Believe me, I get it. Lilly's been with me or my parents every day since she was born and now she's hundreds of miles away for three whole months. It sucks."

"How old is she?"

"Thirteen going on thirty. She's funny and sweet and too

smart for my own good. Her mom hasn't been around much, so letting her go has been a real struggle." He smirked. "Of course, I'm sure Millie could fill you in on all the details."

She knew exactly what he meant. "Oh my gosh, *how* do they know everything? I swear she knew I was getting divorced before I did."

"Maybe they're witches."

Becky barked out a loud laugh and covered her mouth. "That would explain so much. SO much. Geriatric mafia witches."

Noah laughed along with her. "Agnes for sure. She's gotta be the godmother."

"One hundred percent."

After they paid the check, they walked out to the parking lot. Becky held the binder. "You're sure this is a good idea?"

"Nope. But I still think we ought to go."

"I appreciate the honesty."

They stopped at her car. Noah tapped the top of the binder. "Take it home, throw it in your suitcase, and don't give it another thought until we're there."

"Okay." That shouldn't be hard. This weekend was all about Wyatt. She'd worry about Ireland after he left on Tuesday.

Tuesday came a lot faster than she'd anticipated. She was up at four, double checking Wyatt's suitcase and the backpack he was using for his carry-on. She didn't love the idea of a nine-year-old having a cell phone, but she'd gotten him one to have in case of emergency. She'd loaded it with games for on the plane. Might as well, right?

At four thirty, she set his bags by the front door and tiptoed back upstairs to peek in on him. He looked so peaceful, curled up with his little hand tucked under his chin. She wanted to enjoy it for a moment, because Wyatt was not a morning person, and waking him this early was not going to be pleasant.

He surprised her by stretching and slowly opening his eyes.

"Hey, buddy."

"Is it time?"

"Yup."

He flung his cover off and jumped out of bed. She didn't even have to tell him to brush his teeth. He was dressed and ready to go in fifteen minutes. A new personal record. He sprinkled some food in the fish tank. "Make sure you feed them every day," he warned.

"I will. And Grandma and Grandpa are coming to feed them every day when I'm away."

He leaned forward and kissed the glass of the tank. "Love you, Cheeto. Love you, Dorito."

The goldfish swam toward him, then looped around and swam upward to catch food flakes.

He was bouncing off the walls, but she convinced him to eat a bowl of cereal.

At four fifty-five, she answered the door and let Joey in.

"Got everything, buddy?"

"Yup." Wyatt bounded off his chair and raced for the door.

"Freeze, mister," Becky called after him.

He ran back, grinning. "Love you, Mom." He flung himself into her arms and squeezed as hard as he could.

She dropped down to her knees, eye-level with him. "Be good. Listen to your dad and Veronica. Don't go anywhere by yourself."

"Yeah, I know."

Joey rolled his eyes. "He'll be fine, Bec. I'll be right there."

She hugged Wyatt again and stood up. It was hard to keep the annoyance out of her voice. "You'll be busy."

"Let's get going." He turned to head for the door.

Becky followed, grabbing Wyatt's backpack while Joey grabbed his suitcase.

He stopped abruptly, looking into the living room, his head cocked curiously. "You painted? Why?"

Was he serious right now? "Because I like the color." The walls had been white, and were now a soft sage green.

"You should have—"

"My walls aren't anything we need to discuss." She put a hand on Wyatt's back and walked him to the car. "Let's get you buckled in."

Veronica sat in the passenger seat. "Good morning." Of *course* she was a morning person. Chipper and cheerful and smiling from ear to ear.

"Good morning." She buckled Wyatt into his seat and gave him a ridiculous amount of kisses.

"Have a great trip to Ireland."

Becky still felt a little bad for lying about her reason for missing the wedding, but there was no way that would go well. "I'm sure I will. Your wedding is going to be perfect and the weather will cooperate and everything will go smoothly." Seeing Veronica's excited, beaming face, she couldn't wish for the giant zits.

Veronica grinned. "From your lips to God's ears."

She turned her attention back to Wyatt. "I love you, love you. Have so much fun and take tons of pictures and I want to hear every detail when you get home, okay? Love you."

Joey cleared his throat.

Wyatt's chin quivered a little.

Becky wanted to head that off, so she piled on the excitedness. "I'm going to miss you so, so much, but we are going to have SO MUCH to share when you get home. I can't wait to hear all about the Mayan ruins that are like a hundred years old. That's crazy." She deliberately got the timeline very wrong to distract him.

It worked. "Over a *thousand* years old."

"Whoa, that's even crazier."

He reached up and pulled her in for a tight hug. "Miss you, Mommy." He let go and said, "Have fun in the castles. Love you, love you."

Joey huffed an annoyed sigh. Veronica scowled at him.

Becky pulled back and closed Wyatt's door. She waved with a big smile and kept waving and smiling until the car was out of the driveway and down the street, even though her heart was hurting. She tried to talk herself out of being sad, but it wasn't working. She'd never been away from Wyatt for more than a few days, and even then, he was at his dad's house just a few minutes away.

Back inside, she moped around for a few minutes, then got in the shower to get her day started. At just after seven, Veronica texted her a picture of Wyatt on the airplane next to the window, giving the camera a cheesy grin and double thumbs up.

Becky texted back.

Thank you!

That was it, she vowed. The last straw. No more grudge or ill will toward Veronica. She'd never done anything wrong, anyway. All the internal drama had been rooted in Becky's insecurities. It wasn't Veronica's fault she was younger and skinnier and taller and it wasn't a bad thing that Wyatt loved her. In fact, it was the opposite of a bad thing. No more.

She sighed and put her suitcase on the bed. She had

unopened packages with clothes she'd ordered for the trip. Hopefully they all fit, because it was too late to exchange or reorder them now.

After she opened the packages and tossed the items into the suitcase to be tried on later, she remembered that Megan was coming over after work to show her how to change the settings on her camera.

She snapped the battery into the charger. The little red light indicating the battery was completely dead was no surprise. It had been a while since she'd used anything but her phone for pictures.

She checked the clock again and reluctantly headed to work. It was hard to focus on anything other than missing Wyatt.

The house felt so empty when Becky got home. Even though there were many times Wyatt was at his dad's house when she got home, this felt different. Thankfully, she didn't have much time to dwell before the doorbell rang.

"Come on in." Becky held the door open to let Megan into the house. "I'm so glad you could come over. This camera is like operating a space shuttle or something."

Megan laughed. "Don't worry. I'll get you set up and you won't have to touch a thing except the power button."

"Perfect. I'm not even sure why I'm taking it along. It's so big and bulky and I do have my phone."

Megan shook her head and pointed to herself. "I am not the right person to talk you out of taking your DSLR. Phone cameras nowadays are amazing, but they still can't compete with a DSLR."

They went into the kitchen. Megan opened her camera bag and pulled out a ring of laminated business-card sized cards.

"What's that?"

"My cheat sheet. I like to keep track of my favorite settings for the places we've visited." She flipped through the cards. "Here we go."

"Every place has different settings?" Dang, this was going to be more complicated than she'd thought.

Megan reassured her, "It's not something you need to worry about at all. When I'm taking pictures I want to sell, I need to be really precise with the details. But for Ireland, I'll get you set up and you'll be good to go for the entire trip, getting amazing shots every step of the way."

That was a relief. "Maybe when I get back I'll get you to help me learn some of this stuff. I'd really like to do more photography as a hobby, but I feel like there's so much I need to learn first."

"Photography is amazing, and I promise, you can learn a little at a time. The automatic settings on your Rebel are fantastic. Definitely give me a call when you get back. I'll be teaching my Intro to Photography class later in the summer." She leaned in and lowered her voice. "I also have it on good authority that a bribe of tea and good conversation might score you some private lessons."

"You're the best." She handed over her camera to let Megan work her setting magic.

"Canon's instruction manual is actually really thorough. Don't worry about it now, but when you get back, start reading through it and play with everything. You can't hurt it." She turned a wheel on the top of the camera and then pushed buttons. A few times she stopped and looked through the eyepiece, then pushed the buttons again.

"Where are you off to next?"

Megan beamed. "Eric and I are going back to Egypt. We're staying in the same place we stayed at for our honeymoon. A new pharaoh's tomb has been discovered, and it's got some artwork on the walls and ceiling that is unbelievably well preserved. We had to get some special permissions and some high level visa to get in to see it."

"That's exciting."

"Beyond exciting." She had a dreamy look on her face. She shook her head. "But back to Ireland. What are you seeing?"

"I actually don't know. Phyllis gave us a whole binder with our itinerary, but it was so detailed that I got overwhelmed and Noah told me I should just put it away until we get there and we'll either do what's on the list, or we won't."

"Nice. That's a good strategy. Takes some of the pressure off."

"That's what Noah said."

"Speaking of Noah, how's it going with the two of you?"

"I mean, it's not going anywhere except to Ireland."

"If you say so."

"Just because I'm single and he's single doesn't mean we're going to end up dating or something."

Megan handed her camera back. "Just saying. The Ladies' Society rarely gets it wrong." She made kissy noises.

"Oh hush. The only thing I'm kissing in Ireland is the Blarney Stone."

Megan laughed and said, "I'll stop. Do you want some recommendations of places to see? We've been to Ireland a few times."

"Sure."

"Can I take a look at your binder?"

"Of course." She slid it to Megan and refilled their glasses while Megan flipped through the pages.

"This is great. You're hitting a lot of highlights. We've been to a lot of these places, or close to them. I'll check with Eric about his favorites tonight and text you a list."

"Hopefully we can fit them in."

"Please don't feel obligated. It's not going to hurt my feelings if you don't stop at any of them. Has Noah been to Ireland?"

"I don't think so."

"Are you renting a car?"

"Yeah."

Megan shared some of her stories from their experience in Ireland. She held her hands about two feet apart. "I swear, some of the roads are only this wide. It's a little nerve-wracking, but you're going to love it."

"I hope so." After talking with Megan, she was way more excited about the trip, but still nervous about going with Noah. What if he wasn't a morning person? Or if he was a crabby traveler?

Or worse. What if he had bought into the Ladies' Society's intentions for this trip?

Chapter Thirteen

Thursday dragged. Noah worked until noon, at which point he couldn't take another question from his dad about his "relationship" with Becky. No matter how many times he explained there wasn't one, his dad refused to believe it. With tenacity like that, he'd be a great candidate for the Ladies' Society.

He put his suitcase by the front door just as a car pulled in the driveway.

"Hey, good afternoon."

Lincoln came in with an apology. "Sorry I'm running a little late. Aunt Midge asked me to help load some shelves at the store, and she got to talking." Lincoln's aunt owned For Pet's Sake, Hickory Hollow's pet store.

"Yeah, I couldn't get away from Dad today, either. Must be something in the air."

Tormund came down the stairs to investigate the newcomer, with Hodor close behind.

"Hey, there's my boys." Lincoln bent down, waiting for the cats to approach. He gave them both head scratches and accepted their purrs in return.

"Everything's in the pantry. There's plenty of food and

treats. Tormund likes the ones in the blue bag, Hodor prefers the pink."

"Sounds good. I'll stop by twice a day, morning and evening, feed them and do a little playtime. Looks like Tormund will need to be brushed, too."

The long-haired orange cat wound around Lincoln's legs, leaving fur on his jeans.

"I didn't really think about that."

"No problem. I have a ton of different brushes for these floofy cats I watch. Gets the mats out of their undercoats."

Tormund eyed him suspiciously.

"Yeah, you."

Hodor meowed loudly, demanding equal attention.

"You, too, buddy."

They moved into the kitchen. Even though he'd pet-sit before, Noah showed Lincoln the pantry and pointed out the food and water station in the corner of the kitchen while the cats tried their best to trip them.

Lincoln gave each cat a treat. "You'll be back the fifth, right?"

"Yeah, we get in around lunchtime, so you'll only need to do one stop that morning. I'll text you if we get delayed or anything."

"Sounds good." He handed out more treats and head scratches.

"Hopefully they don't give you too much trouble." Noah gave Lincoln a key to the front door. "You sure you're okay checking on them on the Fourth of July? I can have my parents come over if you've got something going on for the holiday."

"No, I'm also watching a skittish dog who's afraid of fireworks, so the Fourth is definitely a workday."

"Aww, poor pup. Does anything help?"

"Thunder shirt, white noise machine, and snuggles. His

owner didn't want to be away over the Fourth, but he had this work trip he couldn't get out of."

"That sucks. At least you'll be there." Noah was always impressed with Lincoln. He was Hickory Hollow's animal whisperer, which is why there was a waitlist a mile long for his pet sitting services. Noah was lucky to have him squeeze the cats into his schedule.

"Yeah, and it's better for him to be at home than boarded. Poor old guy would really be stressed." He reached out to shake Noah's hand. "Have a good trip."

Noah clasped his hand firmly. "It'll be an adventure, I'm sure."

After Lincoln left, Noah took a final trip around the house, checking the windows, setting the air conditioning, and turning off lights. He knew his parents would come by a few times to check on things while he was gone.

He paused in Lilly's doorway and sighed. According to her texts from this morning, she was having a blast, spending a lot of time on the beach and shopping with her mother. So far, she'd even been under budget with her debit card. Hopefully that meant her mom was making up for some lost time financially, too. Not that she'd ever come close to making a dent in her massive arrears, but he was willing to let that go if she could manage to have a healthy relationship with Lilly.

The cats knew something was up. They followed him around the downstairs, watching his every move.

"Sorry, guys, I have to get going." He tossed treats on the floor. Tormund flounced away from his, while Hodor ate his, then snagged the abandoned treat, too.

One last look around, then Noah grabbed his suitcase and his backpack and headed out the door.

Harrisburg International Airport was busy, but not overwhelmingly so. He went through security and headed down the hallway to his gate. The seats were filled with other passengers, most of whom were on their phones or tablets. A little boy sat in the seat closest to the window, his feet swinging under his chair as he watched a plane speed down the runway and lift off into the sky.

Noah settled into one of the plastic seats and scanned the hallway for a sign of Becky. It was just after six. Their seven o'clock flight would likely begin boarding before long.

Laughter and chatter filled the waiting area, the volume increasing as more passengers arrived.

The gate agent arrived and did whatever gate agents do behind the counter and eventually announced the first round of boarding over the intercom. A handful of first-class passengers headed into the hallway to the plane.

Noah checked his watch.

Six fifteen.

Six twenty.

Six thirty.

He wondered where she was. Then he wondered if he was really going to go to Ireland alone.

Six forty.

Noah's group had been called, but he stayed back, waiting.

Six fifty.

Everyone else had gotten in line to board.

He grabbed his backpack and took a step toward the gate. Looking back, there was no one in the hallway.

The attendant scanned his boarding pass. He took one last glance over his shoulder and entered the hallway to the plane. It bounced a little as he walked. He slowed, considering turning around and going home. What the heck was he going to do in Ireland for a week by himself? With no Becky. And no itinerary. Crap. He'd have to call Phyllis and ask her to maybe email him the details, at least for the rental car.

He stepped over the gap, onto the plane. A flight attendant smiled and greeted him as he took his spot at the end of the line of people getting to their seats. At his row near the back of the plane, he settled onto his aisle seat and shoved his backpack under the seat in front of him. The window seat was occupied by a woman engrossed in a book, and Becky's middle seat was empty.

He checked his watch again.

Six fifty-nine.

Seven.

Seven oh two.

All the passengers were seated now, clicks of seatbelts popping.

The pilot came over the intercom, announcing a slight delay, five or ten minutes at most.

Noah looked past the woman to the outside, where workers loaded suitcases into the belly of the plane next to theirs.

Disappointment settled in his gut. He hadn't realized how much he wanted to take this trip.

Correction—how much he'd wanted to take this trip with her.

Chapter Fourteen

Becky tapped her foot. The large clock on the wall mocked her. Seven oh three. Her heart pounded. Was she seriously going to miss her flight?

The TSA agent waved a wand over her and stepped aside. "Good to go."

She grabbed her backpack and shoes and sprinted down the hallway in her socks. Two other people were just ahead of her, running in the same direction.

Panting, she reached the gate with the same couple. Her hands shook as she tried to pull her boarding pass up on her phone to be scanned. The phone tipped out of her hand and dropped to the floor.

"Crap!" She bent over to pick it up, dropping one of her shoes in the process.

Thankfully, her screen didn't crack from the fall. She swiped again, pulling up her boarding pass.

The agent scanned it while she tried to balance on one leg to shove a foot into one shoe, then the other.

Finally, she followed the other two passengers into the

hallway and onto the plane. Her breathing was mostly back to normal as she pushed into the narrow aisle.

The flight attendant slammed the plane's door closed. A few seconds later, she grabbed the back of a seat to keep from falling as the plane rolled backwards, away from the gate.

The two people finally found their seats and got out of her way. She made her way down the aisle, looking for her row number. A second later, Noah leaned into the aisle. His expression was pure surprise, closely followed by a big grin.

He unfastened his seatbelt and jumped up to let her get into her seat.

They worked together to shove her backpack in the overhead compartment, then hurried to get seated and fasten their seatbelts. "That was crazy," she said.

"What happened?"

She settled back into the seat, trying to ignore her twisted sock. She'd fix it after they were in the air. "I was here in plenty of time. We were stuck in the security line for forty-five minutes because the body scanner thing went on the fritz. Some guy was like three people in front of me. He set it off, and then he started yelling at the TSA person because it was showing up that his entire body was made of metal. It was ridiculous. It was so clearly an issue with the machine, but then he went off screaming and carrying on, so they hauled him away and of course the rest of us were stuck in line forever because they had to scan everyone by hand, and then there was something jammed up in the bag scanner. Ugh. And then I had to run. Like, literally *run* through the airport just praying I'd make it. Thankfully, those other two people were held up, too. I doubt they would have held the plane for just one person."

Two of the flight attendants took their spots in the aisle and began the safety instructions.

Becky leaned her head back against the seat.

"I'm glad you made it."

"Me, too. I'm glad they waited."

The pilot came over the intercom, announcing they were next in line for takeoff.

"I hate this part," Noah said.

"Really? This is my favorite part. There's something so cool about rolling along, faster and faster, and then all of a sudden you're off the ground and in the air."

"Yup." He looked a little green.

"You okay?"

The plane picked up speed. He squeezed his eyes shut and didn't answer. The armrests were being put to the test by his grip. She patted his hand to reassure him.

Becky watched out the window as the scenery blurred and then fell away. Her stomach did a little flip-flop as they lurched into the evening sky. She let herself enjoy the feeling. When they finally leveled off several minutes later, she looked over to check on Noah.

He was still clutching the armrests with his eyes closed, but his pinched expression had relaxed and he didn't look nearly as queasy.

She felt bad for him. This flight was barely half an hour and they'd be landing in Philly to catch the plane to Dublin and have to take off all over again.

Thankfully, the plane leaving Philly was much larger, and the takeoff was less dramatic. The older gentleman in the window seat in their aisle had also been on the flight from Harrisburg. What were the odds?

"Doing okay?" she asked Noah.

He nodded slightly.

"Still getting used to it?"

Another nod.

"Let me know when you're good."

Nod.

She glanced at the man in the window seat. He was already dozing. Since there was nothing else to do, she relaxed and watched the general nothingness of the darkening sky.

A little while later, Noah cleared his throat. "I'm alive, FYI."

"Good to know." She smiled at him. "Did you want to look through the binder now and see what we're doing, or after we get some sleep?"

"Since it's barely eight o'clock, I don't think I'm sleeping anytime soon."

A few other passengers were up, rooting around in the overhead compartment, pulling down tablets and books and whatever else they needed to pass the time.

"Want me to grab it?" he asked.

"Yes, please."

He stood and dragged her backpack down to his seat. He eyed it skeptically. "How'd you fit it in here?"

She leaned over and unzipped the main zipper. "I know. I had to sacrifice bringing my blanket, so hopefully my hoodie is enough to keep me warm." She pulled the hoodie and the binder out of the backpack.

"I can put it in mine, if you want."

Becky shrugged. "It'll go in the carry-on for the trip home, so it doesn't matter at this point." She nudged his mostly-flat backpack with her foot. "Did you even put anything in yours?"

"Change of clothes, papers, chargers, and something I think you'll be happy to see."

She couldn't imagine what he might mean.

"A blanket. I might even be willing to share, for a small fee." He settled back into his seat and put his tray down.

"What sort of fee?"

"It's a sliding scale. Right now I'm thinking five bucks, but if you get really cold, the price goes up."

She gaped at him. He was definitely teasing, but holding a straight face. Impressive. She could never look serious when she wasn't.

"It's just basic business. Supply and demand." His mouth twitched as he turned away from her.

She played along. "I mean, we can certainly operate that way. In fact, yes. Let's."

His brow creased a little as he smirked. "I suddenly feel like I've made a grave error."

"Not at all. It simply occurred to me that the rental car is in my name. This supply and demand strategy could be quite lucrative for me."

"Crap." He nodded his head. "Well played."

They both chuckled and quickly quieted themselves as a few disapproving glares were aimed in their direction.

Becky nudged his arm with her elbow. "You're going to get us in trouble."

"Me?"

"Yes, you. Now shhhh." She put a finger to her lips.

They'd just opened the binder when the flight attendants came around with food. Even though she wasn't particularly hungry, Becky ate a sandwich and some chips because she knew their entire eating schedule was about to be thrown off-kilter for the next week, and nobody wanted to have Hangry Becky come out.

The man at the window roused enough to get some food, smiled pleasantly at them, then settled into his seat and went back to sleep.

They kept their voices low. Noah said, "As soon as we get the rental car we'll head to Enniskerry, it looks like."

"Yes, but I don't want to rush. I'll need a minute to freshen up when we get to the airport."

"Sure. And who knows how long it'll take to get through Customs."

Becky asked, "You've never been to Ireland, either, right?"

"Right."

"Have you been anywhere in Europe?"

"I went to Greece for a long weekend a few years ago when a friend got married. And I went to Italy after college. How about you?"

She shook her head. "Never Europe. I've been to the Bahamas, Jamaica, and Mexico a few times."

"Ah, a tropical traveler."

"Oh, and Canada. Which is definitely not tropical. But yes, if I'm going on vacation I generally want it to be someplace warm." In fact, she wondered why she'd chosen Ireland when Tahiti had been one of the options. Oh, yeah. Bathing suits. She wasn't in the right frame of mind to wear a bathing suit when she was bound to see pictures of perfect Veronica in a bathing suit. She pushed the thought out of her mind. No, she'd picked Ireland because Ireland was somewhere she'd always dreamed of going someday. The bathing suit thing was a nasty afterthought from that obnoxious insecure voice in her head. Jerk.

Noah was saying, "I've also been to Canada and Mexico. And Japan."

"Oooh, what was that like?" Japan was on her bucket list of places she'd like to travel. No bathing suit required.

"Amazing, except I felt like a giant freak of nature the whole time. Japan's just not built for guys who are six-two."

"I bet that made for some awkward moments."

"More than a few. I had people stop me on the street to take a picture with me. It was the weirdest thing."

She could imagine him patiently smiling for photos. "You were a celebrity."

He snickered. "More like a sideshow. It's all good."

"Were you there on vacation?"

"Work trip. It was my first grownup job after college. Japan was nice, but I was in way over my head. I quit that job not long after I got back home. I'm not cut out for corporate schmoozing."

"So you went from Japan to Hickory Hollow. That's quite a difference."

"Suits me better."

"You work for your dad, right?"

"Technically I work *with* the family. I'm quarter-owner along with my sister and both my parents. Mom's mostly retired. She did the bulk of the behind-the-scenes stuff, especially with the expansion and franchising."

"Franchising? I had no idea that was a thing for… it's a construction business, isn't it?" She thought franchising was mainly for restaurants.

"Close. Roofing. It's definitely a thing. We started doing the franchising twelve years ago and now we have about a hundred franchisees all over the east coast with plans to expand to the Midwest over the next few years."

"That's incredible."

"I pretty much took over Mom's role in overseeing the franchise side of the business. Dad still runs the original roofing company, although he thankfully quit crawling up ladders himself. He talks about retiring, but I'm not holding my breath. My sister is head of sales and marketing."

"What's your dad think of the changes?" It must have been

drastic, going from a small independent operation to a franchise model.

He thought about it for a minute. "I think it's one of those good and bad situations. He loves that we've grown the small family business into something huge that means we're set for life, but I think he's afraid of losing the heart of the business if it gets too big."

Becky nodded, understanding. "Which is why the franchising was such a great option. It's lots of hometown small businesses under one umbrella."

"Pretty much. Now tell me about what you do."

"I'm an MRI technician," she told him, then explained what she did on a daily basis. "Lots of injuries with athletes." She thought of the granny doing a keg stand. "And people doing… athletic sorts of things."

When she was done, they turned their attention back to the binder. "Rental car, Enniskerry, then on to Waterford. We're hitting the ground running, that's for sure."

Noah nodded. "We should probably try to get some sleep."

Becky closed the binder and put it on the floor under the seat in front of her. Most of the other passengers had turned their lights off and were settling in.

Noah spread the blanket over both their laps. "No charge," he whispered.

She tried not to laugh as she popped her earbuds in. A few taps on her phone and the white noise sleep app filled her ears with gentle ocean sounds.

Despite her excitement, it wasn't long before she drifted to sleep.

Chapter Fifteen

Noah woke, disoriented for a moment, until he remembered he was on a plane somewhere over the Atlantic Ocean.

Becky was still asleep with her head resting on his shoulder. She stirred and sat up, dragging most of the blanket with her.

The flight attendants were at the front of the aisle, starting to wake passengers and serve breakfast and drinks. He judged the distance, guessing whether or not he could make it to the bathroom and back out before the cart blocked his way back to his seat. Sure, he could make it.

He got up and just before he reached the tiny bathroom, someone else jumped up and went in.

Noah awkwardly stood in a growing queue, waiting until the other man came out. They did that weird little getting-around-you shuffle dance to get past each other. A few minutes later, he felt much better. Of course, in the time he was relieving himself and washing his hands, the cart had moved past the bathroom door. Which meant he was stuck inching along behind the flight attendants for fifteen rows.

When he got back to his seat, Becky was standing. She'd

gotten her bag down and had it on his seat, putting her sleep mask and headphones away.

"Hey. Good morning." She sat down and pulled her backpack onto her lap.

"Did you need out to use the restroom?"

She looked at him curiously. "Already did."

He was confused. "When? How?"

"Like a minute ago. They're right there." She pointed over her shoulder to a curtain a few rows behind their seats.

Noah shook his head. "For Pete's sake. I went the whole way up there."

"I wondered where you were."

The man in the window seat stirred and gestured to the aisle. "May I?"

"Of course." Becky jumped up to let him out of the row.

Noah moved backwards to let her out.

He paused and kindly asked Becky, "Would you like the window for the landing?"

"Oh, yes, please. That would be amazing."

While he was in the restroom, Noah crammed their bags in the overhead while Becky got settled at the window seat. He situated himself into the middle and ate his breakfast. He hoped Becky would be game to eat breakfast again after they landed, because this sad egg sandwich and barely-cold cup of yogurt weren't going to cut it.

The flight attendants were already working their way back up the aisle to collect the trash when the man came back and sat in the aisle seat. "Where are you folks headed?" he asked.

"Ireland."

The man chuckled. "I mean, we're all headed to Ireland, aren't we? Anywhere in particular?"

Becky leaned forward to answer him. "A little bit of everywhere. We're heading to Waterford tonight."

"Ooh, do be sure to visit the Waterford Crystal factory. Their wares are a little too rich for my blood, but the tour is really something to see."

"I do remember seeing it on our itinerary, thanks. How about you? Going anywhere special?"

He positively beamed. "Oh, yes. I'm going to Enniskerry. My son and his wife just had their third daughter two weeks ago and I'm going to meet her." He pulled his phone out of his pocket and showed them half a dozen pictures.

They gave him the appropriate oohs and aahs.

Becky said, "She's beautiful." Then she continued, "Enniskerry is our first stop. We're going to see the bench."

He looked confused. "Bench?"

Noah watched the conversation ping pong back and forth across him.

"It's from a movie that was filmed there. *Leap Year*. We're going to see a bunch of different movie locations all over Ireland."

"How fun. I didn't even know we had a famous bench in Enniskerry."

The loudspeaker crackled, and the pilot announced the plane was approaching Dublin. The fasten seatbelts sign dinged as he spoke.

Noah fumbled to find the two ends of his belt and fasten it. Apparently everyone on board was doing the same. A few brave souls jumped up to shove bags in the overhead compartments, earning disapproving looks from the flight attendants who were bustling up and down the aisles, checking seatbelts and trays and grabbing any stray bits of trash.

He leaned toward Becky, who was intently watching out the window.

She touched the glass with her fingertips. "Noah, look. It's so green. I mean, you know it's going to be green, but you don't realize how green."

Noah saw exactly what she meant. Green fields and grassy knolls filled their view.

The pilot came back over the intercom. "We are now approaching Dublin International Airport. Local time is 8:22 AM. Temperature is 17° Celsius, 62° Fahrenheit. Right now, it's sunny and clear. Enjoy it while it lasts and have a nice stay in Ireland."

Noah felt the plane drop and lean. His chest tightened. He hated this part. Hated, hated, hated it. He glanced at Becky, who was happily watching out the window like they weren't about to plummet to the ground.

The plane bumped and dropped again, so he squeezed his eyes shut and gripped the armrests, using all of his will to keep them from crashing. He appreciated it when Becky patted his hand again. For a split second he considered grabbing her hand to hold it while they landed, but he wasn't willing to let go of his armrest, and he didn't want to crush the bones in her hand.

Finally, the wheels hit the tarmac and the plane bounced a little, then gradually slowed. As it rolled toward the gate, the flight attendants unbuckled themselves and prepared to usher the passengers off the plane.

As soon as they were stopped, even before the fasten seatbelts light was off, there was a mad rush to retrieve bags from the overhead compartments.

Becky said, "Might as well let it clear out a bit."

Noah was content to sit for a few minutes and let the adrenaline work its way out of his system. Flying sucked. Well, flying was okay. Taking off and landing sucked. And since they were seated toward the back of the plane, they were in for a wait whether they jumped up and started shoving or not, so they waited.

The man beside them waited, too, until there was room for him to maneuver himself up. He pulled down his tiny suitcase. "Have a wonderful time in Ireland."

Noah reached over to shake his hand. "Enjoy meeting that new grandbaby."

Becky leaned over Noah to also shake his hand. "Take care. Give her lots of snuggles."

He beamed. "I certainly will."

A moment later, he was swallowed up by the crowd flowing toward the exit.

"Shall we?" Noah got up and stretched. He pulled down both their bags while Becky retrieved the binder from under the seat.

He stepped back and helped Becky put the binder in her backpack and put it on. He slung his over his back and worked his arms through the straps as they inched toward the front of the plane.

A few minutes later, they spilled out into the building.

Becky said, "I was reading that it's best to stop at the second set of bathrooms because they won't be as crowded."

"Makes sense." He soon discovered her tip was spot on. The first set of bathrooms had a long line, while the second had no line at all. He popped into the men's room while Becky went to the women's.

When he was done, he sat on a bench nearby to wait for her. Sun streamed through the walls of windows. He'd expected nothing but rain. Instead, there were clear blue skies.

This was a good sign, right?

Chapter Sixteen

In the restroom, Becky picked one of the large stalls and hurried to change into the fresh clothes she'd put in her carry-on bag. Yoga pants were perfect for flying, but she changed into jeans, which would be a little warmer for the day. Bonus, the clothes she'd worn on the plane now took up less room in her backpack.

As much as she hated the idea, she brushed her teeth in the restroom sink, because she hated the nasty mouth gunk more. A finger-comb of her hair and twist into a messy bun and she called it good enough. It's not like she was trying to impress anyone, right?

Best not to think too much about that.

She put her backpack on and went out to find Noah. He was sitting on a bench nearby, squinting at a paper in his hand.

"What's up?" She sat beside him, dropping her pack to the ground at her feet.

"Just trying to figure out this SIM card thing."

"Oh, good idea." She fished her own SIM card out of the pocket of her backpack and in a minute had the old one out and the new one in.

"How the heck did you do that? I can't figure out where it even goes."

She held up the tiny tool with the needle-like point on the end. "Do you have one of these?"

"No."

"Here." She took his phone and poked the tool into a tiny round hole. The SIM card popped out.

"How'd you do that?"

She winked at him. "Magic."

They tested their phones, then set out to find Customs. The line moved quickly, and before long, they had their Irish passport stamps and were on their way to baggage claim.

"I feel bad we didn't get that guy's name," Becky said.

They hopped on the escalator.

"I didn't think of it."

She thought about him living in the US while his son and his family were in Ireland. "I hope he has a nice trip. I think my parents would be heartbroken if their grandkids were on a different continent."

"Same. My mom and Lilly are super close."

She remembered him mentioning that his sister was part-owner of their company. "Does your sister have kids?"

"Natalie? No, she doesn't have any."

They stepped off the rolling escalator.

Becky took in the crowd. And the crowds of luggage. And the ridiculous amount of luggage conveyors. "Yeush, you could fit a small city in here."

He agreed. "This is not going to be fun."

It took half an hour before they managed to find their luggage in the sea of suitcases and finally wheeled toward the rental car area.

"Even with a hot pink suitcase, that was awful."

"Yeah, my neon green luggage tag didn't help much. Hey, is that the guy?" He pointed his chin toward a row of benches.

Sure enough, the man who'd shared the flight with them was sitting on a bench, his tiny carry-on suitcase beside him on the bench, a larger suitcase at his feet.

Becky slowed. Something didn't seem quite right. "Is it just me, or does he look upset?"

"Maybe?"

She made an abrupt turn toward the bench, cutting across the flow of traffic. "Sorry, excuse me, sorry," she repeated until she came to a stop in front of the man. "Hi. I was just telling Noah that we should have gotten your name, and here you are. I'm Becky."

The creases on his face crinkled as he smiled. "Becky. Nice to meet you. I'm Thomas."

Noah shook hands with him. "Noah."

She cut to the chase. "Is everything okay?"

Thomas let out a heavy sigh. "Yes, I just have an unexpected doozy of a wait ahead of me." His smile seemed tired and forced.

She sat on the bench beside him and put a hand on his arm. "Why?"

"My son's car. It wouldn't start, and the roadside assistance people can't come until two o'clock."

"Two? That's like—" she looked around for a clock. "Five hours just until they get to his place? And then however long to fix it and then his drive to here? That really stinks."

He nodded. "That it does. Thank you for checking on me. I'll be fine. There's plenty to do. I'll grab a bite and maybe catch a nap."

"Well..." she stopped herself and looked up at Noah, questioning.

He gave her a slight shrug, which she took as a go-ahead. "Didn't you say you're going to Enniskerry?"

"Yes."

"I mean, that's where we're going, so why don't you come with us?" Not that she made a habit of picking up strangers, but there was something about him she liked.

He brightened, then pulled back. "I couldn't. It's such an imposition. They live a little outside of town, it'd be out of your way."

Noah asked, "How far out of town?"

"About ten minutes."

Becky made the decision. "We'd be glad to take you that far. It beats sitting in the airport for six or seven hours."

He hesitated, seeming to consider their offer.

She added, "Please. I'll worry all day."

"I don't want to be an inconvenience. You have such a full schedule."

She shook her head. "We're here for an adventure. The itinerary is just a guide."

"You put so much work into it."

Laughing, she said, "Actually, that was our travel agent. She finds joy in the details."

Noah shifted. "I totally understand if you don't want to get in a car with two complete strangers, but we'd both be glad to get you to your son's place."

"We really would," Becky agreed.

"Will you let me pay you?"

"Of course not," she said.

Noah said, "You can get some gas or lunch if you'd like."

Thomas immediately grinned and seemed to relax. "I know just the spot."

"Let's figure out where to get the rental car." Noah waited for Thomas and Becky to stand and get their things ready.

Becky scanned the posted signs and finally spotted it. She pointed. "Car rental, this way." She led them through the crowd, back to a set of escalators, and finally to a tunnel-shaped hallway that funneled them to the rental car counter.

Thomas called his son while Becky filled out the rental paperwork and she and Noah had their passports and licenses copied. While they waited, they gave their phone numbers to Thomas, to give to his son, to reassure him they weren't kidnapping his dad.

Half an hour later, they were on a shuttle that delivered them to the lot where the rental cars waited for pickup.

"I hope we can all fit." She stood and stared at the adorable little car. Emphasis on *little*. The two-door hatchback Volkswagen was cherry red and small. So very, very small. She popped the hatch. The split backseat allowed her to lay half of the back seat down so they could pile their luggage and still give Thomas a spot to sit. A cramped spot, to be sure.

She took a deep breath and headed for the driver's side. Nope, that's the passenger side. She walked around the front of the car and got behind the wheel.

Noah and Thomas got situated and everyone buckled up.

She started the car. At least the gas pedal was still on the right and the brake on the left. She was so glad they'd opted to pay extra for the automatic transmission. Just getting acclimated to the backwards layout was complicated enough without shifting gears.

She set the GPS and eased out of the parking spot. Her heart pounded as signs and roads and cars and pedestrians filled every spot in her vision.

Crap.

This was going to be harder than she'd anticipated.

Chapter Seventeen

Noah could feel Becky's nervousness as she maneuvered their clown car out of the parking lot. He'd been prepared for a *small* car. He hadn't been prepared to spend a week with his knees wedged against the dash. Okay, that was a slight exaggeration, but it seemed even smaller with Thomas mushed into the back seat.

"Good job," he said.

She breathed a nervous laugh.

"You're doing great. We're going to turn left up here." He wanted to find the sweet spot between being helpful and being obnoxious, but for now, he'd err on the side of helping too much. "Yup, good job. Stay to the left."

She sat, tense, clutching the steering wheel and hyper-focused on the road in front of them. "Okay."

The GPS directed them through an intersection.

"I hope this guy's going the same way, because I'm following him."

"Yup, that's the way."

"Ugh, roundabout." She eased the car around the curve.

"You've got it. Just stay with him. Good job." He watched

the map on the GPS screen. "We'll be on M50 for about fifteen miles, so you can breathe."

"You're doing great," Thomas offered. "I never can get the hang of driving on the wrong side of the road when I'm over here."

The GPS informed them to stay on M50 for twenty-five kilometers.

Becky relaxed a little and flexed her fingers on the wheel.

"Doing okay?"

"I'm really, really, really, really glad we got the automatic. I don't think I could do this and try shifting gears, too." She kept her eyes glued to the road. "Sorry, I know I'm probably going too slow."

Thomas said, "Another hour and you'll be zipping around like you've been driving on the left your whole life."

She smiled and relaxed a little more. "I don't know about that."

"So, where are you folks from?" he asked.

Noah jumped in so she could concentrate on getting more comfortable with the car. "Hickory Hollow. It's—"

"No kidding! I live just outside of Newport."

"Really?" Noah said at the same time Becky exclaimed, "No way!"

"How did your son get from Newport to Ireland?"

Thomas sighed. "My wife, Grace, God rest her soul, was originally from Ireland. Her parents moved to America when she was a teenager and opened a bakery. That's how we met. I had a job delivering newspapers, so I saw her every morning on my route. Prettiest thing I ever did see. By some miracle, we got married and had Tommy Jr and Jamie. Jamie's the younger. One of our trips here to visit Grace's family, he met the neighbor girl and they fell in love."

The GPS dinged and instructed them to get off the highway.

"Oh crap, another roundabout."

Noah said, "I hope you end up liking them because it looks like we've got three in a row."

"Ugh."

Thomas chuckled from the backseat. "They're everywhere over here."

"At least Hickory Hollow only has one. I can deal with that."

Becky slowed to make the turn. "Yeah, but the roundabout in Hickory Hollow goes the opposite way."

They passed the next twenty minutes or so with polite random chitchat. Thomas told them about the bakery he and his wife ran after her parents retired and moved back to Ireland. "I just couldn't keep it after Grace passed. I sure do miss her baking."

"You should go to Ruth's bakery in Hickory Hollow. Sounds like she has a lot of similar things your wife made."

"Ruth? Not Ruth Ackerly?"

Noah glanced back at the man. "Yeah, that's her. She's in the Ladies' Society. They set us up on this trip."

"No kidding." Thomas looked wistfully out the window. "Ruth Ackerly. I didn't know she was still in the area."

Noah suggested, "Maybe you should give her a call." Hey, if the ladies could meddle and matchmake, they were fair game for a little turnabout.

"Maybe I will." Thomas pointed out the low stone walls bordering the sides of the road. "We're getting close."

A minute later, Becky leaned forward and pointed to a sign. "Ooh, I think this is it."

The stone wall ended, opening up to a residential area. A

couple of joggers ran on the sidewalk along the right side of the road.

Becky sucked in a sharp breath as a double-decker bus sped toward them in the opposite lane.

A second later, they crossed an ancient-looking tiny stone bridge.

Noah pointed, just in case she missed it. "Stop sign."

"Yup." She slowed the car to a stop.

"This is it!" Thomas said excitedly. "The clock is right up there. That'll be where your famous bench is, I'm sure of it."

Noah watched her check every direction a dozen times before easing the car forward. He wasn't sure if she noticed where to park, so he gestured. "You can park right along there."

Becky pulled into a parking space right at the base of the tiny town square, which was basically a round, raised stone patio with a clock tower in the middle. It looked like something that would exist in Hickory Hollow's downtown.

They got out of the car and stretched.

"That's where I'd get something to eat, if I were you," Thomas said, pointing to a white building framed with a cheerful bright red window and door.

A couple of bistro tables and chairs sat in front of the huge window. Gold letters announced, "POPPIES Country Cooking" under a flag proclaiming the same.

Noah stole a look at Becky. She was staring at the café, grinning.

She told them, "That's the place. They called it Emilia's in the movie, but that's definitely it. Anna went in there and got coffee while Declan was asleep on the bench and he thought she got on the bus and left."

Noah shrugged at Thomas. Neither of them really had any

idea what she was talking about, beyond it being a scene in *Leap Year*.

Thomas startled, then pulled his phone out of his jacket. A smile spread across his face. "Good news. Jamie's car's all sorted, so he'll be around to get me in a little bit."

"I bet he's glad," Noah said.

Becky was staring up at the clock.

Noah asked her, "Well? Are you going to show us the famous bench?"

They started toward the steps to the patio.

"Oh, hang on, I need my camera." Becky jogged back to the car and got her camera from the hatch.

A minute later, Noah watched her take a million pictures of a regular old park bench, then a million more pictures of the area around them.

"Here. You sit." He held out his hand for her camera.

She handed it to him and sat on the bench while he took a few pictures of her.

"You need one of both of you." Thomas reached for the camera.

Noah wasn't sure how close to sit, or whether to put his arm around her. So he put several inches between them and compromised by resting his arm across the back of the bench.

"And now one in front of the café," Thomas insisted.

They went down the steps from the monument to the café. Thomas took a picture of them, then Becky grabbed the camera and took a picture of Thomas with Noah.

As soon as he opened the door to the café, Noah breathed in the delicious scent of freshly baked goods. "This smells amazing."

Becky inhaled deeply and nodded her head. "I want one of everything."

It was eleven thirty local time, which was only six thirty as far as their bodies were concerned. They were halfway through their breakfast-for-lunches when Thomas waved toward the door. "Here comes my son."

A moment later, a harried young man bustled through the door, smiling and shaking his head.

Thomas jumped up to hug him.

Then the man leaned over to shake hands with Becky, then Noah. "Jamie, nice to meet you. Thank you so much for going to all the trouble of bringing Dad here."

Becky waved his concern away. "No trouble at all. This was our first stop, and we figured a ride with us was a step up from spending the whole day in the airport."

"No doubt." He patted his back pocket. "Listen, let me buy your meal. And a few pastries for the road."

Before Noah could object, Jamie was already paying for their food.

He came back to the table with a lemon cake in a box. "Thank you so much. I can't even tell you how much I appreciate this."

"It was our pleasure," Noah said. "Turns out your dad lives just down the road from where we are."

Thomas added, "They're from Hickory Hollow."

"No kidding. Small world, eh?"

"It sure is." He noticed Jamie glance toward the door, probably anxious to get back home. "Well, let's grab your dad's luggage."

A few minutes later, they had the lemon cake and delicious fresh-brewed coffee in to-go cups and were standing at the back of the car. Noah got Thomas's suitcases out.

Jamie said, "You'll want to go see Powerscourt Waterfall. It's only ten minutes from here and it'll take your breath away. We love to go there and picnic." He took the handle of his dad's suitcase and held out his other hand to Noah. "Thanks again."

Noah shook his hand. "No problem. Congratulations on the new baby."

His face broke into a grin. "Thank you. If you need anything while you're here, give us a call. We'll do all we can to help." He texted them his number and his dad's.

Becky hugged Thomas. "We'll stay in touch. Enjoy your trip and your new grandbaby."

Thomas was a little misty-eyed. "I can't tell you… It's been such a pleasure to meet you both. Drive safely, stop often, and enjoy the views."

"We will."

Noah accepted a one-armed hug as he balanced the cake box in the other.

Becky shifted their suitcases so she could put the back seat into its upright position, where they put the cake for the next leg of the trip.

Thomas and Jamie got into a small sedan and drove away.

"Let's go sit on your bench to see what our next move is."

She grinned and grabbed the binder from the car.

While she thumbed through the binder, Noah studied the base of the monument. "Hey. Did you notice this?" He pointed to the curves of the edges.

"What?"

"It's a shamrock."

Her gaze snapped to the concrete outline surrounding them. She jumped up and followed it all the way around the clocktower. "How did I not notice this?"

"I'm not sure how I *did*."

"That's so cool." She held her arms out and looked up to the sky. "This is amazing. I can't believe how great this trip has already been."

Noah grinned at her enthusiasm. "It's been a pretty great day so far."

She sat down again and picked up the binder. "Okay. It looks like our next stop is the Rock of Dunamase, and then on to the hotel in Waterford."

"Did you want to check out the waterfall? Is it on the way?"

She seemed reluctant. "Probably not. We have to go back up toward Dublin and then west. The waterfall is south of here."

He checked the GPS on his phone and showed it to her. "We'd be twenty minutes out of our way, basically. That's fine with me. I'd kind of like to see it."

"Megan did say it was one of her favorite spots. With two recommendations, we have to go, don't we?"

"I believe that's the rule. Is there anything else you'd like to see here?"

"No. Wait. Yes. Is that a phone booth?"

He followed the direction she was pointing. "I think it is."

They walked over and marveled at the antique phone booth.

"I wonder where Superman changes now that all the phone booths are gone." Becky said.

"Probably in his car. I wonder where kids make prank calls from these days." Not that he'd ever done such at thing when he was young.

Next, she spotted a green letterbox.

A few dozen photos later, they made their way back to the car.

Even with Becky driving cautiously, they arrived at the waterfall parking area less than twenty minutes later. A stone wall and wrought-iron gate guarded the entrance. They followed the signs toward a little chateau-looking building where an employee stood, handling ticket sales.

"I didn't realize there was a fee," Becky whispered under her breath as the woman waited for her credit card device to register the transaction.

He shrugged. "Me either."

The pleasant woman handed Becky their tickets and pointed toward the parking area.

They parked in a lot with at least two dozen other cars. Picnic tables were full of families eating and laughing. A stone building offered a concession area as well as restrooms.

Before they got out, he asked, "You okay with the driving?"

"Yeah. I'm just tense trying to get used to being on the wrong side of the road." She laughed a little. "And the wrong side of the car."

"I'll take a turn whenever you want."

"I'm good. But thanks." Her tone was firm.

He was still struggling to find the line between being helpful and overstepping. It felt like he was getting pretty darn close to that line, so for now, he'd stop offering to help and wait for her to ask.

They got out of the car and followed a paved path around the building.

Becky came to a dead stop. Noah bumped into her, putting his hand up against her back as he stopped.

"Look at that." Her words were a reverent whisper. Before them lay the greenest, brightest, most stunning landscape he'd ever seen. In front of them was a tall ridge covered with bright green trees and bushes. In the midst of it was a stone formation with water cascading down its surface.

His hand rested on her back until she started moving again.

A large sign with a giant red "X" and the word "DANGER" greeted them with a warning not to climb the waterfall because a slip could be fatal.

He noted the sternness of the warning. "They're not

kidding around, are they?"

She shook her head. "It's so steep. What kind of moron would even try it?"

"Eh, me at seventeen?" To be honest, probably him at twenty seven, too. But definitely not now.

She seemed to consider it. "Okay, fair. I probably would have tried it too, back when I thought I was immortal."

They walked on, passing a handful of picnic tables set along the trail in the lush green lawn.

The roar of the water covered the sounds of the people all around them, talking and walking and laughing.

The path looped around on itself. A well-worn dirt area lined by boulders and bushes served as a barrier to the waterfall.

Becky snapped pictures with her camera. "This is amazing."

"It is."

They stood, looking up at the waterfall, just watching the white water rush down over the rock face. Droplets sprayed gently over them.

He nudged her arm. "I guess it was worth the six bucks."

She chuckled. "Totally."

Children raced past, squealing and shrieking at each other. A harried mother called after them to stay away from the rocks. An older couple with a dog wearing a raincoat strolled by.

He waited, watching as she let her eyes drift shut and pulled in one deep breath after another. A moment later, her blue eyes fixed on his. "I'm glad we made the detour. This is beyond beautiful."

"Yeah." He barely choked the word out. It was beautiful, to be sure, but somehow it felt like it was only a backdrop to frame her. Tiny water droplets clung to her hair. He stared a little too much, a little too long.

Chapter Eighteen

Becky pointed skyward. "We should probably head back. It looks like our good weather isn't going to last much longer."

The sun still shone, but gathering clouds inched across the sky.

Noah nodded and turned back to the paved walkway.

Becky took a long look back at the waterfall. It really was spectacular. She supposed all of the scenery had been, but she hadn't been able to look around much. Driving on the "wrong" side of the road took a lot more concentration than she'd expected. She fell into step beside Noah. "I wonder what the Rock of Dunamase looks like in person. I was reading that most of the location in the movie was CGI."

"A lot of the *Game of Thrones* locations will be like that, too. I'm trying to keep my expectations low."

"Same. On the upside, I can't remember a lot about that scene beyond them walking along a stone pathway. If nothing else, it'll be cool to share the pictures with Wyatt. He's a huge history buff. Old rocks and ruins are right up his alley."

Noah grimaced. "Lilly used to like history. Now it's all boys and makeup."

"Oh, yeah. I remember that age." Boys and makeup pretty much summed it up. Big hair and little skirts were all the rage when she was in middle school at the tail end of the 80s influence.

The clouds overtook the sun as they reached the car.

"Okay, I need to find the wiper switch before anything." Becky started the car and examined the switches on the gear shift. "This looks like it." She toggled the switch to its various settings, getting a feel for how to set the wiper speed.

Noah got their raincoats out of the trunk and set the GPS while she got her console situated.

"Rock of Dunamase, here we come."

Once they were on the road, Becky said, "I'm glad we took the detour. The waterfall was spectacular."

"I can't believe Phyllis didn't have it on the list since it was so close to Enniskerry."

"It's a wonder."

The GPS estimated they would reach their destination in one hour and four minutes. It was off by half an hour, thanks to a heavy downpour that made the sharp curves of the narrow roads even more intimidating to navigate.

Becky's shoulders ached with tension from clenching the steering wheel.

"That's it, right up there." Noah pointed to a parking lot just ahead.

The rain had slowed to a steady drizzle that showed no signs of letting up.

Suddenly, the ruins came into view, rising up before them, massive, reaching into the thick clouds. Becky had to force herself to keep her eyes on the parking lot as she eased into a parking space.

"Wow," Noah said.

She parked and turned the car off. "Why'd they bother to

cover it all up with CGI? It's amazing as it is. I can't wait to see it up close."

They put their raincoats on and walked up a set of steps that took them to a gravel path similar to the one at the waterfall. A historical marker told some of the history of the Dunamase Castle. Even though the trail was smooth, it was steep and winding. About a dozen people dotted the pathway, some walking toward the ruins, a few walking toward the parking lot.

"My calves will be screaming later," Noah said.

Becky laughed. "You're not kidding." She tried not to huff and puff as they climbed. The main entrance archway loomed ahead of them. It was a tower-shaped structure with an arched doorway, made of stacked stones and simply oozed centuries of tales and secrets it would forever keep.

She put her hand on the stones. "I feel like it could tell the wildest stories."

They hiked up the path to the main castle ruins. Narrow pathways and long-abandoned rooms surrounded them. Moss and wispy grasses grew in crevices that once held opulence and splendor. Echoes of history itself whispered on the wind, breezing through the decaying windows. As if the structure itself wasn't breathtaking enough, Becky gasped when she turned a corner and saw the view. The castle was set high on a hill, with a panoramic view of the farmlands below.

She quickly forgot it was raining, captivated by the ruins. She snapped a few pictures. "I hope Wyatt's ruins are as beautiful as this."

Noah made a questioning noise.

She explained, "Chichen Itza. They're going to see the Mayan pyramid while they're in Mexico."

"If he's a history buff, he's going to absolutely love it."

"He will. He's been reading about it for months. Veronica's

mom is a retired history teacher, so I think the two of them are more excited about the ruins than the wedding."

"Veronica?"

"She's my… oh, heck, I don't even know what to call her. My ex's new wife. My son's new stepmom."

"That's a lot."

She stared out over the farmland. "Yeah. I don't know what to think. I'm trying to be good about it for Wyatt, but I definitely have a whole range of emotions with the whole deal." She wondered how long she'd struggle with all the conflicting feelings, or if they'd last forever.

"It's not easy to let other people into our kids' lives. I mean, I'm struggling with Lilly being with her own mother."

She didn't know the whole story, but she'd heard rumors suggesting his ex wasn't the greatest mom. Not that she had any intention of asking him to fill in the blanks. It was clearly a sore subject. "I'm sorry. That's a mess."

"At least Wyatt's with his dad, too, right?"

She snorted. "Honestly, I'm to the point where I feel better about him being with Veronica. Don't get me wrong, Joey's a good dad, but we just don't see eye to eye on a lot of things. Like he had the audacity to question me about this trip. And not just a simple 'how can we reach you' thing. We've been divorced for six years, but he still thinks he has some kind of say in what I do. Even stupid stuff like repainting my living room." She immediately felt like she probably didn't need to add that last part.

"Whoa. That's overstepping a bit."

"Anyway, as much as I don't want to like Veronica, she's so good to Wyatt. It was her idea to do the excursion to the ruins just for him, and she always consults me about anything she wants to buy him or do with him."

"Why don't you want to like her?"

Becky sucked in a deep breath. "You want me to be totally honest?"

"I mean, you can lie if you want to," he joked.

"She's bad for my ego. She's twenty-seven. Tall. Blonde. Gorgeous. Skinny. So sweet that one conversation can rot your teeth. Next to her, I feel like a bridge troll. Who can compete with that?" She had no idea why she'd just word-vomited all her insecurities.

And now he was looking at her like she had three heads.

What a way to kick off the trip.

Noah looked out over the green farmland, then back at her and said, "That's one of the most asinine things I've ever heard."

As she always did when she was the least bit uncomfortable, she deflected. "Yeah, well, you've never met Veronica." She turned to head back to the ruins, but Noah's hand lightly touched her elbow.

He looked down at her. "I don't need to."

Chapter Nineteen

Uh oh.

It took everything Noah had to not take her face in his hands and kiss her. Unfortunately… no, correction, *fortunately*, the weather saved him from himself by choosing that exact moment to send a downpour. Fat drops of rain pelted them as they ran to the castle, seeking shelter in the first arched doorway they came to.

"Holy crap!" Becky shook the water off her pink raincoat and inspected her camera to make sure it hadn't gotten drenched. "There was no warning at all."

As quickly as it came, the rain slowed to a drizzle. Noah took it as a sign from the universe that he was definitely not supposed to kiss her.

"Should we make a run for the car?" he asked.

"Probably." She gingerly made her way over the slick ancient stones. "Careful, these are really slippery."

They made their way back through the castle, dodging puddles and taking care not to lose their footing on the wet path.

Noah's phone vibrated in his pocket. As soon as they got

settled in the car, he checked it and couldn't help but smile. Lilly had sent him a selfie in a huge shopping mall with one of her favorite clothing stores behind her. Before he could respond, another photo popped up of Lilly holding two large bags from said store aloft. She was grinning like a Cheshire cat.

"My daughter is definitely having a good time." He showed the pictures to Becky.

"Oooh, she certainly is."

He texted her back,

> Looks like fun. Try not to bankrupt me. LOL

She responded with a rolling-eye emoji.

> We're going to a fancy French restaurant for lunch.

> Awesome. Try the escargot.

> What's that?

> Snails.

> It is not.

She must have looked it up, because her next text said,

> EEEEW that's gross.

He replied with a string of laughing faces.

> Miss you bunches.

Miss you too. How's Ireland? And Beeeeeecccckyyyyy. Did you kiss yet?

He ignored her sarcasm.

Ireland is nice. We just saw the Rock of Dunamase.

He sent her a picture.

Looks boring.

Definitely not as exciting as snails for lunch.

Gotta go love you

Love you too.

Becky drove back down the lane, toward the road.

Noah realized she'd set the GPS while he was texting with Lilly, and he hadn't even noticed. "Sorry, I'm slacking on my navigational duties."

"I know. I think it's only fair I get an extra slice of the lemon cake."

"Sneaky. I think you had that planned all along."

She shrugged. "Maybe I did, maybe I didn't."

The GPS informed them it was one hour and twenty-five minutes to their destination.

Noah checked his watch and said, "That gets us to the hotel around seven, give or take. What were you thinking of doing this evening?"

"My plan is find the hotel, get food, check in with Wyatt and my parents, and go to bed. Unless you've got some better options."

He was relieved she didn't want to go to pubs or clubs or whatever kind of nightlife was available in Waterford. "Nope, that's exactly what I was thinking. It's been a really long day and I don't know about you, but I didn't get much sleep on the plane."

"Definitely not."

"I'm not sure if I'll actually be able to fall asleep when my body still thinks it's mid-afternoon, either."

The GPS interrupted with their next turn.

"I know. I'm afraid it'll think I'm just taking a nap and I'll be wide awake two hours later."

The misting rain decided to ramp up again, sending fat drops splattering and wiggling across the windshield. This time, though, it didn't let up.

Noah stayed quiet and attentive, trying to keep an eye on the road and on Becky. She was perfectly calm, but her hands were tense on the steering wheel and she sat ramrod straight. He briefly considered finding out what was on Irish radio, but figured Becky didn't need the distraction.

They'd been on the road for an hour and a half when the rain finally let up and he could see her relax a little. "Doing okay?"

"Yeah, just having to chant 'stay to the left' in my head the whole time."

"It looks like we're only twenty-five minutes from the hotel."

"Great. I slowed us down by half an hour." She sounded disappointed.

It felt like they were making decent time to him. "What, you have an appointment somewhere?"

She took her eyes off the road long enough to shoot him a look.

"I'm just saying. We're making good time."

The GPS alerted them to an upcoming turn. It had been quiet for so long it was a little jarring to have its mechanical voice fill the car.

"See?"

"Hmm." She followed the instructions, and twenty-seven minutes later, at two minutes after seven, she pulled the car into a parking space at their hotel.

The rain had let up completely, and the clouds were breaking up.

The friendly clerk behind the counter smiled and processed the rooms. She explained that the rooms were on different floors. One with a view of the River Suir, and one with a view of downtown Waterford.

Noah said, "The only thing I plan on looking at are the backs of my eyelids. Take the room with the river view."

The clerk gave Becky her key and then repeated the process to get Noah's room. Becky asked her, "What's the best way to McLeary's Restaurant? Is it far?"

"Oh, not far at all. You'll be walking, and on the way you'll want to stop and see the Dragon Slayer Sword. Don't want to miss that." She whisked a local street map onto the counter and showed them where they were, where McLeary's was, and where they simply must stop to see the sword.

While Becky talked with the clerk, he glanced at a brochure with the hotel's amenities. In the elevator, he held one out to her. "You could get a massage. Get those knots out after all that driving."

"A massage would be amazing, but at this point all I want is food and a good night's sleep."

The elevator dinged on Noah's floor. "Meet you back in the lobby? Ten minutes?"

"Perfect."

He dumped his suitcase in his room and went back down

to the lobby in closer to five minutes. He sat on a plush sofa, waiting for Becky to come back down.

She hustled from the elevator to where he was sitting. "Sorry, I hope you weren't waiting long."

"Not at all." He held his phone out for her to see a picture. "The dragon sword thing does look really cool."

"It really does."

They strolled along the sidewalk, following the simple route the clerk had given them. She wasn't kidding when she said it was a quick walk.

McLeary's was a sleek restaurant positioned between a pub and what appeared to be a shuttered travel agency. They went inside, and the inviting smell made Noah's stomach rumble.

When they were seated, a look at the menu only made him hungrier. "Everything looks amazing."

"I know. I want one of everything."

"We're on vacation, right? So it wouldn't be wrong to splurge on this steak Diane, would it?" He didn't want to blow the food budget too soon into the trip, but he was really, really hungry.

"I hope not, because I'm seriously considering getting two appetizers on top of my meal."

Appetizers? He flipped the page to study those selections. "Anything in particular?"

"The breaded garlic mushrooms and/or the fresh garlic prawns."

"I'm sensing a garlic theme."

"At least you know I'm not a vampire because I love garlic."

He narrowed his eyes and stared at her over the menu. "I hadn't suspected you were. Until now, because that seems like something a vampire would say just to avoid suspicion."

She met his playful glare with one of her own. "You seem to know a lot about what a vampire would say."

His stomach growled, forcing his attention back to the menu. "If you want to share, I could go for both of those appetizers, too."

"Perfect. And don't think I didn't notice you changing the subject."

A few minutes later, they'd ordered both appetizers, a steak Diane for Noah, and traditional fish and chips for Becky, and not long after that, both appetizers were delivered and rapidly demolished.

"So good." Becky wiped the buttered garlic sauce from the last shrimp off her fingers.

Noah nodded as he swallowed the last bite of mushroom. "The best."

"Good call on getting both appetizers."

Their entrees were similarly devoured, and it wasn't long before they were back on the sidewalk, heading back to the hotel.

"Ugh, I ate way too much."

"Same. Totally worth it, though." He pointed out across the river. "Check it out."

"Looks like a riverboat cruise. Want to go look at the water?"

"Sure." They crossed the street and found themselves in a little paved area with a semi-circle of Viking thrones under a canopy. He guessed it was an art installment.

Becky snapped photos of the intricate details, as well as photos of boats on the river, while Noah checked his phone. "This is the William Vincent Wallace Plaza. He was an Irish composer. He was a *double virtuoso*, brilliant on both the violin and the piano."

"I take it he's from around here?"

"Born at Colbeck Street. According to Google maps, it's just back that way." He pointed toward a side street.

"Nice."

A sculpture that popped up on the maps caught his attention. He took a closer look. "Colbeck Street is also close to a set of sculptures I think you're going to want to see."

"Now?"

He assured her, "It's only a five minute walk. We can make a loop around back to the hotel and also see the dragon sword thing. If you want."

"Sure." She snapped another photo of a massive white sculpture and they headed down a narrow side street.

A few minutes later, Noah pointed. "Right up there."

"What is it?" She sounded interested.

As they got closer to the pair of people-shaped-throne sculptures, he read from his phone. "This is Strongbow and Aoife. Strongbow invaded Waterford at the behest of Aoife's father, on the eve of the feast of St. Bartholomew on August 24th, 1170, and was married to Aoife the very next day."

She groaned and rolled her eyes. "Nice. You invade these lands for me, and I'll give you my daughter."

"According to Brehon law, an Irish woman could not be forced into marriage, so it is presumed she agreed to the arrangement," he read.

"Look at the detail of the hands. That's amazing."

They, of course, took a handful of selfies with the sculptures before heading down another side street and finally onto Bailey's New Street, a narrow, gray, brick street that led to a massive stone cathedral.

"Whoa."

Noah almost ran into Becky as she took in a massive wooden sword that stretched nearly half the block.

She reached out and grabbed his forearm. "That's incredible."

Again, he paraphrased from his phone, trying not to read

too much into a casual touch that had only lasted a few seconds. "The sculpture is the largest wood sculpture in the world, at 23 meters long. It was carved by John Hayes and installed here in 2017. It says here it was carved from a single tree."

"This is just… Wow."

Noah glanced skyward. "You might want to get your pictures. Looks like we're in for another shower."

"Figures. I just want to take in every inch of this. It's amazing." She snapped pictures of every intricate detail. "I can see why the clerk recommended seeing it."

He watched her move, angling this way and that to get a better shot. She'd just straightened and turned to look at him when the light rain started. She made a face.

He chuckled. "Don't be sick of it already. We've got another week to go."

"I know, I know. Let me grab a quick shot with my phone so I can send it to Wyatt. He'll love this."

The two-minute walk back to the hotel was increasingly wet. Their shoes squeaked across the lobby.

In the elevator, Noah said, "I think there's a lesson in this."

"Yeah. From now on, always, always, always wear the rain jacket, no matter what."

"Bingo."

The elevator stopped at his floor. "What time should we meet?"

"Shoot. I don't know what's in the binder."

"I'll dry off and come up," he managed to say before the doors slid shut. And before he had a chance to question the wisdom of hanging out in Becky's hotel room.

Chapter Twenty

Becky ducked into the bathroom to change into a dry sweatshirt and yoga pants before she toweled her damp hair. From now on, she would definitely, absolutely, positively, not go outdoors in Ireland without her raincoat. Or an umbrella. Or both. She would also take care to dress in layers. "Summer weather" meant very different things in Ireland versus Pennsylvania.

Her room had a small table with two chairs by the window. She put the binder on the table and flipped it open to Day Two.

The knock on the door startled her even though she'd fully expected it.

"Come on in." She moved aside to let him in.

Noah crossed the room and peeked out her curtains. "You really did get a better view than me."

"Not that we'll be here long enough for me to enjoy it." The light outside was fading to twilight. Boats on the river had turned into shadowy figures gliding along the surface.

"What's on the agenda for tomorrow?" He settled onto one of the chairs at the tiny table and leaned over the binder.

"I haven't looked yet." She sat beside him and glanced down over the page. "Is that axe throwing? Seriously?"

"That sounds fun. Crystal factory tour, not so much."

"Megan said the crystal work is amazing, and the tour is really informative, but don't even think about getting a crystal souvenir because they're very expensive."

"Good to know." He tapped his finger on the paper. "It looks like the Waterford factory is right down the block. I'll see where Axe Junkies is located."

Becky waited while he found the route on his phone.

"Sweet. We can walk there, too. Looks like we should be able to get breakfast, get to the axe throwing, then back for the factory tour. After that, we'll head to Blarney." He slid his phone over in front of her.

She looked at the map, then gave his phone back. "Breakfast starts at 6:30, so if we get there by seven, we can eat and then head out. How long is it to Blarney?"

He entered the directions to the Blarney castle. "According to this, one hour and forty-two minutes. I think we can safely estimate two hours."

Becky caught their reflection in the window, their heads close together as they looked at his phone and the binder. It was cozy. Comfortable. Nice.

Very nice. It had been a long, long, long, long, long, long time since she'd spent any time with a man. Alone with a man. Alone with a man in a hotel room. Alone with a very attractive, available man in a hotel room. Alone with a very attractive, available man in a hotel room in a foreign country where no one would ever see or know or find out what they were up to.

"Bec?"

She jolted nearly out of her skin. "What?!"

He sat back, leaning away from her. "You okay?"

"Yes! Why wouldn't I be okay?"

"Why are you yelling?"

"I'm not yelling!"

He stared at her for a moment, amusement playing at the corners of his lips.

They were really nice lips.

Dang it!

She got up and walked over to the mini coffee maker. "Do you want coffee?"

"Nah. It'll keep me awake."

"Oh. Yeah, that's probably true." Her face was finally starting to cool down from the inferno of embarrassment that she'd just endured.

"Sooo… I was asking if you want me to drive tomorrow? We can trade off days if you want."

She slid back onto her chair, subtly inching it away from Noah. She bristled a little. "I don't mind driving. And I know we didn't make great time today—"

He held up a hand to stop her. "No, hang on. I'm sorry if I'm overstepping. I appreciate all the driving you did today, and if you love it and want to do it all, have at it. I was just thinking it's a big job and I'm letting you know I'm happy to do my share so you don't miss all the scenery."

"I didn't really think about that." Having a conversation with a reasonable man was so different than talking to Joey, whose "suggestions" were usually thinly veiled insults.

"We're in this together. And if we switch off day by day, we only have to adjust the seat once a day."

She laughed at that. "Okay, that's the most compelling argument I think you could have come up with."

"Excellent. Cut me a little slack when we first start out. I've never driven on the left."

"It definitely got easier as the day went on, but still pretty nerve-wracking when we got into the city here. Of course, I don't much care for city driving anyway."

"You did great."

"Thanks."

They looked at each other for a moment. The moment stretched out a little too long.

Oh, boy. Why did she have to start noticing the little crinkles around his brown eyes when he smiled?

Noah finally cleared his throat and pushed back from the table. His knee bumped hers.

"Sorry. Meet in the lobby at seven?"

"Perfect," she squeaked out.

"We should probably get to bed then. Uh, I, uh, I mean I should go. To get some sleep. It's late."

"Yeah. I'm beat." That was a bald-faced lie. Something was crackling in the air between them and she was wide awake.

"So… seven." He stepped toward the door. "Good night."

"Good night."

He didn't look back as he hustled out the door.

Oh, crap. Crap, crap, crap, crap. It was only the first night of their trip and all of a sudden there was this physical attraction she hadn't been prepared for. Not that she *hadn't* been attracted to Noah on some basic level. That was a no-brainer. He was tall, good-looking, funny, smart, single, and had all but admitted he'd had a crush on her back in the day.

This was going to be a long, long week.

<h1 style="text-align:center">Chapter Twenty-One</h1>

Noah huffed out a breath as the elevator doors slid shut. What the heck was happening right now? Something had just happened there, right? That hadn't been his imagination. She'd definitely been zoning out and from her reaction–and that flaming red blush–he guessed it had something to do with him.

Or was that just wishful thinking?

Probably wishful thinking.

She was probably thinking about her ex-husband and Veronica. Ugh, Joey.

Noah remembered him from high school, too. He'd been captain of the football team, captain of the basketball team, captain of the track team. He'd had girls falling all over him, all the time, from the time he hit puberty. Eventually, Becky had fallen for him, too, and they'd been inseparable from their junior year. Noah had been a sophomore, watching his dreams of Becky noticing him evaporate with every wave of her pompoms.

After that, he'd waited for them to break up, but it never

happened. Even after Joey got caught with another girl. And another.

Noah hoped he straightened up–grew up–after high school, and then college, but judging from the fact they were divorced, he kind of doubted it. At least she'd wised up at some point.

The guy had been an idiot back then, and if he was dumb enough to let Becky go, he clearly still was.

Saturday was a whirlwind, from the time they got up and indulged in a full Irish breakfast (Becky loved the grilled tomatoes), walked to Axe Junkies for their axe throwing activity (Noah almost threw his shoulder out), and went through the Waterford Crystal Factory tour (fascinating tour, but they were both terrified of breaking something in the gift shop).

"I can't believe some of those prices." Becky shook her head. "I know Waterford Crystal is super high end, but holy cow."

They turned down the sidewalk, back to the car.

"No kidding. That's some amazing skill that goes into making it, but it's a little out of my league pricewise."

"I guess it's basically fine art. I can't afford that, either," she said with a laugh.

He chuckled at a memory she'd jarred. "Speaking of fine art. Natalie and I used to have this thing where we'd buy each other the ugliest, tackiest art we could find. One year for Christmas, she gave me a painting she'd found at a yard sale. It was supposed to be a horse."

"Supposed to be?"

They got in the car.

"Yeah. It looked like a sort of watercolor stick figure horse with penciled-in teeth and really creepy eyes that looked in different directions, created by someone who had never seen a real horse or even a picture of a horse and never touched a paintbrush. It was bad." He chuckled at the memory. "Our grandmother read us the riot act for ruining Christmas. Boy was she *mad*. Everyone else thought it was hilarious, but that was the last time we exchanged art."

"That's a shame."

"It is. I should surprise her with 'art' this year." He started the car. "Okay, now where's the wiper switch?" He took a few minutes to get familiar with the console while Becky set the GPS.

She sighed and leaned back in her seat. "I feel like this whole trip is going to be me wishing we had more time at every stop. I would have loved to spend more time checking out all the Viking history here."

Noah nodded. "We're getting the sampler platter. Little bit of everything." He eased out of the parking lot and intently followed the GPS's instructions. When they reached the highway and he could relax a little, he said, "You're right. Driving on the opposite side is harder than you think it ought to be."

"Told you so."

Just as he felt like he was getting the hang of it, traffic came to a screeching halt to avoid running into a farm tractor puttering along the road, and a few miles later, an intersection that resembled an asphalt octopus with turns and lanes in every possible direction. He was grateful Becky helped navigate him through that mess.

They drove through a million tiny villages and past another million green fields until they finally came to Cork.

A sign marker caught his attention. "Wait, what happened to N25?"

Becky checked the GPS. "Looks like it just magically turned into N8. We're good. Another roundabout coming up."

"Great," he grumbled.

"Hey, I had about a thousand of them yesterday," she teased.

"You're right, I've been pretty lucky so far."

"Looks like we're only about twenty minutes away."

He didn't admit it out loud, but he was glad. His shoulders were tight with tension and he'd be glad to park the car and get out to walk for a while. He followed the instructions to turn onto R635, and then N20. As soon as they got outside the city and the traffic thinned, he was able to relax a little. The clear blue skies helped a lot, too. He was glad she'd agreed to let him share the driving, because it was definitely too much for one person to handle it all.

A few more turns, and Becky read from the sign, "Welcome to Blarney Castle and Gardens."

The GPS gave up, insisting they had arrived at their destination and its job was done.

Becky pointed to the left. "Arrow's pointing that way."

He slowed to a crawl, probably annoying the driver of the car behind him. "Is this right?"

"Keep going. There's a gift shop, so I bet the parking is up ahead."

She'd barely finished her sentence when he saw the parking lot. He turned right into the crowded lot and drove up and down the rows until he found a vacant space.

"Good job. Now you can relax."

They got out of the car and headed along the paved walking path to the castle. Picnic tables dotted a lush green lawn with a picture-perfect creek flowing through it. They crossed a wrought iron walking bridge while Becky snapped a few pictures.

"Wow," she breathed as they got their first full view of the castle. The huge square center structure rose out of the greenery, with a tall round tower to its side, and the remains of supporting walls surrounding it.

A sign pointed the way to the castle, a river bank walk, a fern garden, and caves. Noah paused. "Caves? I had no idea there were caves."

"Me, either. We'll have to check it out."

They walked around the perimeter of the castle, taking in the sheer imposing size of the castle. And then the imposing line to the entrance to go inside to get to the stone.

"Look," Noah pointed upward to the top of the castle. "You can see someone kissing the stone."

"Holy crap that's high. Those two little bars don't seem like enough to keep someone from falling through."

They inched their way forward as the line moved, going up the ninety-nine skinny, steep, stone stairs that circled up to the tower. The stairs were narrow enough that they had to place their feet sideways for a lot of the trip. By the time the line finally spilled out onto the rooftop, Noah's calves ached. The pain was forgotten as soon as he saw the breathtaking views of the green countryside that awaited them.

Becky nudged his arm. "Worth the trip?"

"For sure."

A sign warned them to remove hats, sunglasses, and any loose items from their pockets. A few more steep steps, and they were on a walkway leading to the famous stone.

A chatty gentleman with a thick accent sat by the opening, instructing visitors to sit on a mat, then lean backward over the opening, gripping two bars, and then tip the head back to kiss the stone.

"You're up." He nudged Becky and took her camera. He

snapped a picture as she gingerly leaned backward. Her knuckles were white, gripping the bars.

Then it was his turn. He heard the camera snapping as the blood rushed to his head while he leaned back and kissed the stone. He tried not to think too much about all the other lips-or worse-that had touched the stone before him.

They followed the line back down and out of the castle.

"That was so cool," Becky said. "You could see the whole way down to the ground."

"Yeah. You could see all the hepatitis on the stone, too."

She laughed. "It's best not to think about such things."

Next, they strolled across the grounds to the Poison Garden, where perfectly manicured hedges outlined the homes of toxic and medicinal plants. As they walked, the air cooled as clouds rolled in, covering up the sun. Soon, a light rain fell, darkening the informational signs at each plant.

"Rhubarb is poisonous?" Noah cocked his head as he read the sign explaining about the poison contained in rhubarb leaves but not the stalks. "I had no idea. Wait until I tell Mom I know she's been trying to murder us with her rhubarb pies."

Becky laughed. "I knew there was a reason I didn't like rhubarb pie."

He took a picture of the sign with his phone. "I'm sending this to her with no context."

"For shame, trying to confuse your poor mother."

Laughing, he said, "And I don't feel the least bit guilty. Believe me, she gives better than she gets."

The light rain turned heavier. They both flipped their hoods up over their heads.

The plants were reasonably interesting, but Noah was ready to move on. "Do you want to check out the cave?"

"Sure," she answered, tucking her camera inside her raincoat.

They ventured along the path, around the castle, following the signs to Badgers Cave. Along with everyone else. Including two full bus tour groups.

They stood, waiting for a turn to go into the cave, reading the sign that told a tale of Lord Broghill's foiled siege on Blarney Castle.

Becky looked up at him. "I'm okay with it if you'd rather skip this."

He surveyed the crowd. "Do you mean 'okay with it' like you'd really like to see it, or 'okay with it' like you're being polite in case I really want to see it, but you really want to go."

"Door number two."

"Thank goodness." He spun on his heel. "Let's get out of here before the mass exodus to the parking lot."

They jogged back to the car, dodging puddles.

When they were finally situated back in the car, Becky said, "I'm kind of hungry. You?"

"I could definitely eat something. How long until our next stop?"

She plugged the address of their bed & breakfast in Doolin into the GPS. "Two and a half hours."

Nope, he could not wait that long. "What's around here?"

"I'll check." She pulled out her phone and did a quick search. "There's a restaurant like two minutes away." She muted the GPS on the car and set her phone to take them to the Muskerry Arms restaurant.

A couple minutes later, they were seated at a cozy table next to a couple vacationing from France who were on their way to the castle. With the help of a language translating app, they had a nice conversation until the French couple left for their stop at the Blarney Stone.

"Fish and chips again?"

"Can't get enough." Becky speared the last bite of slaw. "This is the best food ever."

Noah tapped his fork on the bit of roast beef still on his plate. "Nope, this is."

"It does look good."

"I'm a little jealous of your pint." One pint wouldn't get him drunk, or even tipsy, but driving on the left made him too nervous to risk it.

Becky wiggled her eyebrows and took another huge swallow of her Guinness. "You can have a sip if you want."

"Sure." He accepted her glass and took one gulp of the beer. "Mmm. I'm having one when we get to our bed & breakfast."

"And I'm having another."

They headed back to the car. Noah waited for the GPS to recalculate from their new location.

"We should get there around six thirty. Check in, light dinner, Guinness, and then bed." Becky ticked her list off on her fingers.

"Sounds like a good plan to me. Look out, Doolin, couple of party animals headed your way."

Becky's laughter filled the car. "They aren't going to know what hit them."

He glanced over and was struck again by her smile. How this woman thought Veronica could be some sort of upgrade was beyond him.

Chapter Twenty-Two

The weather turned gloomy as they drove. The skies filled with thick gray clouds. The traffic was light, as though everyone had decided to stay home rather than be outside. Even the lush green scenery seemed subdued.

Becky watched out the window. "You know, this kind of weather is perfect for curling up with a good book. It's gloomy, sort of damp, with just enough of a chill in the air to put a fuzzy blanket over your lap."

"That does sound nice. What books do you usually curl up with?"

She relaxed back in her seat. "It's been so long I hardly remember. I like mysteries. My favorite is probably Carl Hiaasen. Lots of humor in his books."

"I've read a few of his. *Bad Monkey* and I think *Tourist* something."

"*Tourist Season.* It's one of my favorites. I also like Darynda Jones. Her Grave series is so good. The main character is a private investigator and a grim reaper. I think I'm on book six in that series, so I need to get caught up. I think she's up to twelve or thirteen now. And Nora Roberts. I love her stuff."

"Have you ever read James Rollins? His Sigma series is fantastic. Sort of mystery adventure with a secret military investigative team. Lots of history and action."

"No, I'll have to check it out."

"I think he's got a new one out. Maybe two. I haven't sat down to read a book for a while either."

"There aren't enough hours in the day to do everything I want to do."

"Like what?"

She stared out the window and thought about it. "Like… anything. I go to work, I come home, I do stuff with Wyatt, I cook and clean. And that's about it. I have lunch with friends every once in a blue moon, but I don't really have any hobbies or go out and do anything. Except grocery shopping or a trip to Target, but those hardly count."

"I get it. Ditto everything you just said, with Lilly instead of Wyatt."

"Is Lilly in a lot of activities? It seems like Wyatt has something going on all the time. One sport or club no more than ends than another one starts. Sometimes they even overlap and I feel like a shuttle service."

"Let's see. She's in field hockey in the fall, basketball in the winter, and softball in the spring. Luckily, we seem to have the summers off."

"Wyatt does baseball in the spring. He played basketball for one season but hated it. He plays soccer in the fall and then he's in an indoor soccer league over the winter. He also does a chess club that's year-round, but they started doing a lot of their meetings online, which is definitely more convenient for me."

"That's a lot."

"It is. And I try not to complain, because it's so much better than being on his computer or Xbox 24/7."

"Very true. I swear Lilly's phone has grafted to her hand. She's always texting or snapchatting or whatever the kids do on their phones these days that vacillates between making them happy and making them cry hysterical tears."

"I did that, and we didn't have cellphones. It comes with the age." Some things never changed, did they?

"Okay, good point."

"Just wait until she starts dating," Becky teased.

He grinned. "It'll be fine, because she'll be thirty-five and living in her own place."

She laughed. "That's exactly what my dad used to say, right down to being thirty-five. It must be ingrained in the male DNA, like corny dad jokes and tugging on straps to make sure they're secure."

"Hey, if you don't give them one last tug, you're just asking for things to go flying." He glanced at her. "Was your dad okay with you dating pretty seriously when you were so young? I mean, you and what's-his-face got together junior year, right?"

"He wasn't thrilled, that's for sure. Especially since he didn't like Joey from the beginning." That was an understatement. Her dad made no bones about his dislike for Joey, but he stood back and let her make her own choices.

"Oh?"

She didn't miss how that perked him up. "I think he was relieved when we broke up, and I have no idea how he managed to keep from blowing his lid when we got back together after college."

"I assumed you'd been together the whole time. From high school up until the divorce."

He wasn't the only person in Hickory Hollow to make that assumption. "No. We split up right after graduation and didn't really communicate for several years. He'd fooled around on me and I finally had enough. I think I was twenty-six when we ran into each other again, and I assumed we'd both grown up in the interim. So we started from scratch, as much as that was possible. We didn't get married until I was thirty because I wanted to make sure it was the right thing. Spoiler alert, it clearly wasn't."

"But you have Wyatt, so it wasn't a complete mistake."

"Wyatt is literally the only good thing to come out of that marriage. I also got a crippling mortgage and crushing self-doubt as consolation prizes. His bonuses were a 100-point increase in his credit rating and almost no debt, thanks to my money management during the marriage."

"Are things better for you now? It's been a while, right?"

"Six years since the divorce. And yes, I'm doing great now. I'm maybe the *slightest* bit bitter." She held her index finger and thumb an inch apart.

"What if he called and wanted to get back together? Would you?"

Becky sputtered. She definitely had not expected that question. "No! Absolutely, unequivocally, one hundred percent, no. I should have left the past in the past. It's not a mistake I would ever make again. *Ever.*"

Noah held up a hand. "Sorry. I didn't mean to offend you, and it's none of my business anyway. I was just curious about why you had so many feelings about Veronica if you're really done with Joey."

She sucked in a sharp breath, but the GPS cut her off before she could snap that it wasn't about Joey, it was about Wyatt. The screen showed a large intersection with several loops. "I think we just stay left. The exit's right up here."

"Right?"

"Sorry, the exit is immediately ahead of us. Stay left." She watched the screen while Noah watched the road. "You got it."

They rode a few miles in silence.

"Looks like the clouds are breaking up," Noah said.

"Good. Hopefully it stays clear since you have a dozen roundabouts coming up."

"A dozen? Please tell me you're exaggerating."

"Slightly. There's like six of them." She relaxed a little, trying to put the conversation out of her mind.

"Why doesn't that sound any better than a dozen?"

"You really don't like the roundabouts, do you?"

"Nope."

She chuckled. "Hey, I don't think we're far from the coffee place Megan raved about. I'll look it up." She checked her phone where there was a massive list of places Megan recommended they stop if they got the chance. "Yup, here it is. Route 85 Coffee Drive Thru. She said their iced coffee is the best anywhere, ever."

"Then we'll have to stop."

Half an hour later, they were parked across from the drive thru coffee shop that looked like a modified shipping container. Becky sipped her iced coffee. "Would it be wrong to get another one for this evening? I'll even skip my Guinness."

Noah loudly sucked the last slurp of his iced coffee from the bottom of the plastic cup. "Wrong? I think it would be wrong *not* to get another one. I mean, we want to do all we can to support the local economy as we travel, right?"

"Yes. And we should probably support them by purchasing a few of those caramel squares I regret not getting."

"You read my mind. I feel good about getting the granola pots, but I think I would regret skipping the caramel squares for the rest of my life."

"We don't want that."

A few minutes later, they had fresh iced coffees, caramel squares, and brownies, and were back on the road to Doolin.

Only half an hour later, they pulled into the driveway of the bed & breakfast that would be their home for the night.

Their bubbly mom and daughter hostesses helped them carry their bags to their rooms, insisting they *must* visit Gus O'Connor's Pub, which was only a three-minute walk away, and had the best traditional Irish music anywhere in the world.

Even though Becky had been looking forward to a quiet evening, the pub experience sounded like a lot of fun.

Noah leaned in her doorway. "What do you think?"

"I think it sounds like a blast." She checked her watch. "Freshen up and leave at seven thirty?" That would give them almost half an hour to relax and get ready to go.

"Perfect." He gave her a wink and disappeared into his own room.

Becky used the ensuite bathroom to freshen up, then piled her pillows against the headboard and sat on the bed. She scrolled through social media and her heart nearly stopped in her chest. She'd been tagged in posts on Instagram.

Wedding pictures.

Veronica was beyond stunning in her simple white gown, with her hair loosely pulled back, deliberate loose curls dangling to frame her face.

But Veronica wasn't what made tears sting the backs of her eyes.

It was Wyatt.

Wyatt, in his little tuxedo, beaming up at his brand new stepmother like she hung the moon.

She scrolled through photo after photo. Wyatt hugging Veronica. Veronica whispering something in his ear as he laughed. Wyatt holding Veronica's hand. Veronica leaning down to kiss Wyatt's cheek.

Every swipe stabbed another arrow into her heart but she

couldn't make herself stop until she got to the end. Her hands shook as she closed out of social media and tapped into her contacts to call Sarah.

"How's the Emerald Isle?" Sarah's bubbly voice came over the line.

Becky choked on a sob.

"Hey, hey, hey, what's going on?"

She sniffled and wiped her wet cheeks. "I... I just had to hear I'm not crazy."

"What on earth is going on? Did something happen with Noah?"

"No, Noah's great, it's been fine. I just... I got tagged in wedding pictures and..." A gurgling sob caught in her throat.

"Wedd—oh. Oh, are they really bad?"

"They're horrible. Horribly perfect. She's gorgeous and ridiculous and I want to hate her so bad." She squeezed her eyes shut. "No, I don't. It just sucker punched me."

"Honey, I love you, but I have no idea what you're talking about."

She sat up and pulled the pink wool blanket over her lap. "Wyatt. Wyatt and Veronica. It's just getting to me since I got tagged in all these amazing dream sunset beach..." She wiped her face again. "I know I'm being ridiculous and petty and jealous, but these wedding pictures are getting the best of me. I can't take it, the way he's looking at her like he just loves her so much."

"Aww, hey. Breathe. You know Wyatt loves you more than anyone in the whole world. No matter what, you're his mom and nobody can ever change that. Okay?"

She sniffled. "I know, you're right."

"No more social media while you're on vacation. That's an order," Sarah said sternly.

"Aye aye, captain."

"What are you doing this afternoon?"

"The afternoon is over. It's–oh, crap, it's just after seven thirty. Noah and I are going to a pub our b&b hostess recommended. I gotta run but I'll call you again."

"Fill me in when you get home. Go have a pint and enjoy yourself."

"I will."

Chapter Twenty-Three

Noah raised his hand to knock on Becky's door when he heard her say, "I know I'm being ridiculous and petty and jealous, but these wedding pictures are getting the best of me. I can't take it, the way he's looking at her like he just loves her so much."

So much for him having a shot. Despite what she'd said, obviously she was still hung up on her douchebag ex.

Noah tamped down his disappointment and tiptoed away from her door. He found the living room and sat on the plush sofa, waiting for Becky.

"Are the rooms to your liking?" The elder of the hostesses, Kate, asked with a warm smile.

"Yes, definitely. I had to get off the bed before I fell asleep. Very comfortable."

"Oh, good. Too bad you're only here for one night. Where are you headed tomorrow?" Her accent was thick, and it took him a few seconds to process the question in his head.

"Inishmore."

She blinked a few times and he figured he'd butchered the pronunciation.

After a beat, she asked, "Oh, you'll be taking the ferry then?"

"Yeah. We're hoping to see the Cliffs of Moher in the morning, then head to the ferry."

She clucked her tongue. "Not giving yourselves much time, then."

"Unfortunately, no. The whole trip is pretty rushed. The good part is that we're getting to see a lot of different places."

"You'll have to come back and spend more time. Ireland should be savored."

"Sorry, I had to make a quick call." Becky came into the living room. Her cheeks were pink.

"No problem." He stood.

Kate pointed them in the direction of Gus's, so they set off into the tiny village that looked like it was straight off a postcard. Surrounded by rolling green hills dotted with sheep, they walked along the road, past a couple of bed and breakfasts and O'Brien Knitwear before coming to Gus's, a stone building with smart black trim and gold lettering.

Even on the sidewalk, they could hear music. Noah held open the door, and they stepped into what felt like a movie set. A young woman was doing Irish dance in the middle of the pub while a table full of musicians played–violins, guitars, a flute, some sort of hand drum, and even an accordion.

They were ushered to a small table. As soon as the song stopped, one of the musicians, an older gentleman, immediately pegged Noah as a tourist and began ribbing him.

Noah threw his hands up and called to their waitress, "A round on me!"

Half the people in the pub cheered, including Becky, who was clapping along with the crowd.

It was too loud for conversation, which suited him fine. He wasn't sure what they'd talk about anyway. He was still stuck on the fact that she was still stuck on Joey and any hopes he'd had of them getting together were effectively quashed.

The first pint of Guinness didn't really help, but the second did lift his spirits, as did the third.

He was halfway through the fourth when the same gentleman ribbed him to sing along with them.

"I don't know the words," he protested.

"Just make 'em up!"

Noah pointed to the guitar the man held. "How about you sing and I'll play?"

The man guffawed. "Play *and* sing!" he boomed as he handed over his guitar.

Noah strummed the guitar a few times. The man began singing, his loud voice surprisingly pleasant. The other musicians joined in as he sang a raunchy song that rhymed quite a few dirty words that didn't really rhyme outside of his song.

By the time the song ended, his fingers hurt from the guitar strings, and his stomach hurt from laughing. He handed the guitar back and ordered another round.

"I didn't know you could play the guitar. I'm impressed."

"I could do a lot of things that would impress you," the Guinness said before he could stop it.

She simply cocked an eyebrow and let the comment pass. Probably thought he was drunk. Which was just as well. Actually, now that he thought about the pleasantly warm buzzing in his head, he either was drunk, or he was about to be.

"We should get food," he said.

Becky agreed. She ended up getting a salad, while he ordered a massive burger and fries. Food definitely helped balance the excessive amount of Guinness sloshing around in his gut.

"I'm trying the O'Connor's Warm Apple Crumble," Becky informed him, pointing at the dessert menu.

Despite the brownies he'd already consumed from their stop on the way to Doolin, Noah ordered the Warm Chocolate Brownie, which came with vanilla ice cream.

He'd gotten halfway through it when he stopped himself. One more bite and he'd probably end up on the barfing tourist wall of shame, because he just knew there was such a wall somewhere around here. He pushed the plate away and sat back, tapping his fingers along with the music.

"You're not going to finish that?"

He shook his head. "If you want it, go ahead."

She took it, polishing off every last bite. "I'm going to gain fifty pounds on this trip."

His head swiveled to look at her. "Go ahead. You'll still be beautiful."

"Noah." Her eyes widened. A smile faltered on her lips, like she wasn't sure whether or not he was joking.

He let the Guinness do the talking. "What? You are. You're so beautiful and I have no fricking idea why you think that Veronica person is anything better. She's not. And I have no fricking idea why you're still hung up on some asshole who can't see how amazing you are, but hey, if you want to waste your time, go ahead. Be my guest."

"What are you talking about?"

"It's getting late." He pushed back from the table. "Big day tomorrow." He grabbed the mostly full glass of Guinness–his sixth–and chugged it down in only a few gulps. He waved goodbye to the musicians.

Becky gave him some kind of look he couldn't quite decipher, but she got up and followed him out to the street.

As soon as the door closed behind them, the quiet enveloped them. They walked in silence, the only sound their footsteps crunching on the loose gravel.

"Sorry. It's none of my business."

She stopped walking and planted her hands on her hips. "What are you even talking about?"

"The pictures." His loud words echoed off the buildings.

"What?"

"I heard you talking about the pictures. About how you can't stand the way he looks at her. How it just guts you to see he loves her." He threw his hands up. "I don't get it. He was a jerk to you in high school. Then he was a jerk to you long after he should have wised up. But somehow you're still stuck on this loser? I don't get it. I. Do. Not. Get. It." He poked a finger in the air to punctuate each word.

"Are you done?" She sounded furious.

He met her angry gaze. "Sure."

"You were right about one thing. It's none of your business."

"Great. Fiiiiiiine." He crossed his arms, unable to come up with a better argument.

"I don't know why you were eavesdropping on my conversation, but you're clearly lacking context."

He was also lacking his common sense filters and he knew it. But that didn't stop him. "You know what? If you're just going to use big words, then fine. You just... *conceptualize* it then."

"What?" She was definitely annoyed now. "Are you even going to remember this conversation in the morning, or am I wasting my breath?"

"Pssssht. Whatever. Fine. Great. Let's go."

"I was talking about my *son*, Noah. The pictures of Wyatt and Veronica. I couldn't care less about Joey. It was seeing my son looking at his brand new stepmother like he absolutely adores her. That's what got to me."

He stumbled a step and sat on the low stone wall separating the road from the Allie River, which was more of a creek, as far as he was concerned. "Oh."

"Think about it. If Lilly had a new stepdad and she thought he was amazing, how would you feel?"

He blinked heavily. "I would feel… like shit."

"Exactly." She sat on the wall next to him.

"Sorry." He reached over and put an arm around her back. She didn't slug him, so he took it as a good sign. "I'm really shorry." Even he heard the slurring. "Sorry," he enunciated carefully.

"You're going to be so hung over tomorrow."

Probably. But tonight, he was going to muster up his own courage and supplement it with the supercourage the Guinness was suddenly providing. This was it. He was going to kiss her. After all this time, he was going to lean over and he was going to kiss Becky.

He reached over with his free hand and lightly touched her chin, turning her face toward him.

"Noah."

"Shhh," he managed, then leaned forward.

The Guinness turned on him then, rushing upward from his gut. He spun away from her, barfing his burger, brownie, ice cream, and lots and lots of Guinness across the wall into the grass. He heaved over and over until there was nothing left to come up.

When he felt confident he was done retching, he straightened. Becky stood a few yards away, pinching the bridge of her nose. Two of the musicians from the pub were on the sidewalk, pointing and guffawing so hard one of them was doubled over and the other was leaning on the building.

One of them shouted across the street, "We knew ye was a lightweight!"

Noah lifted a hand in a wave of surrender. Thank goodness

the B&B was close. He wanted nothing more than to brush his teeth and crawl into bed. No more taking advice from a delicious stout.

He was pretty sure she was mad as they walked back to the house, but she didn't say anything. Instead, she opened the door for him and steered him to the right room. She flipped the light on in the bathroom.

He was pretty sure he'd already apologized, but he wanted to apologize again. Trouble was, he wasn't sure which part he should apologize for this time, so he didn't.

"Are you okay on your own?"

What would she do if he said no? Would she stay with him? He shoved the thought aside. "Yeah," he croaked.

"Where's your phone?"

He dragged it out of his pocket and handed it to her. She fished the charger out of his backpack and plugged it in, then set the alarm.

"I'll see you in the morning. Good night."

He just nodded, anxious to use the bathroom.

She closed the door behind her with a quiet click.

He grabbed a quick cold shower, hoping to sober himself up. At least most of the booze had exited his system. The downside was that he was pretty embarrassed. He hadn't been drunk for many years, probably since college, and he knew it hadn't done anything to endear himself to her.

He got dressed and climbed into bed, vowing to redeem himself in the morning.

Chapter Twenty-Four

Becky woke up before her alarm. The bed was so comfortable and cozy she stayed there, curled up under the covers, thinking over the events of last evening. She wasn't sure what to think. Noah's old crush was flattering, to be sure, but on the other hand, she was getting annoyed. High school was a long time ago. A whole lifetime ago.

Ugh. They were going to have to have an actual conversation about it at some point. While they were stuck in Ireland together. Great.

Finally, the urge to pee was stronger than her will to stay in bed. She got up and showered and dressed.

It was barely six, a full hour before they'd planned to eat and head out to the Cliffs of Moher. The cozy bed beckoned her to crawl back under the covers, but she resisted. Instead, she pulled on her hoodie and shoes, planning to take a brisk walk around the property. She crept out of her room and tiptoed toward the front door, though she needn't have bothered being so quiet.

The hostesses were busy in the kitchen, preparing breakfast.

"Good morning." Kate and Mary cheerfully greeted her in unison.

"Good morning."

"Would you like some tea?" Kate asked.

Mary added, "Perfect morning to take tea in the garden."

That sounded wonderful. "Sure. I was going to take a walk, but that sounds better." She took the steaming mug of tea and a wool blanket they suggested, and sat outside at a small table on the patio, watching brown cows graze in a neighboring field.

"Hey."

She jerked her head toward his voice. "Hey. How are you feeling?"

He sat down at the opposite side of the table with his own mug of tea. "A little headache, a bit tired, and a lot embarrassed."

"Yeah, that was a pretty impressive display."

He grimaced. "I don't drink very often, and I never drink that much."

She believed him. "That was probably a good reminder as to why."

"For sure."

"I think breakfast was about ready. We should probably eat and hit the road."

"Okay," he said meekly.

"Lucky for you it's my turn to drive."

He grimaced as he nodded.

She folded the blanket and finished the last of her tea. Inside, they piled plates full from the buffet of yogurt, cereal, fruit salad, and granola. Four more people, two men and two women, joined them at the large dining table.

"I didn't even know there were other guests," she whispered to Noah.

He shrugged. "I had no idea."

They were almost done when Mary presented them with more food–full traditional Irish breakfasts with eggs, grilled tomatoes, sauteed mushrooms, beans, sausage links, fresh bread and homemade marmalade.

"I'm going to burst," one of their tablemates said.

Becky agreed. "Me, too. Everything is delicious."

"Where are you from?" one of the women asked in an accent Becky was pretty sure was German.

"We're from the United States. How about you?"

"Austria," she said, pointing to herself and the man beside her. Then she pointed to the other couple. "Our friends are from Sweden."

The Swedish man smiled and asked, "What is your plan for today?"

Noah answered, "We're going to see the Cliffs of Moher, and then take the ferry to Inishmore. We're going to see the pub where Becky's favorite movie *Leap Year* was filmed. Maybe get some lunch there."

Mary froze in the middle of filling a water glass. "You mean Declan's Pub?"

"Yeah," Becky said excitedly. "You've been there?"

She set the water pitcher down with a sympathetic expression. "I'm afraid not. It's been closed for years. All boarded up, last I heard."

Her face must have reflected her disappointment because Mary rushed to say, "I'm so sorry. It's a beautiful island, lots else to see. Maybe I shouldn't have said."

Becky straightened the napkin in her lap. "I'm really glad you told me. That would have been such a bummer to get there expecting to visit a pub." She felt all the eyes of her tablemates on her, so she put a smile on her face and asked, "What's everyone else doing today?"

As it turned out, the rest of the group was also starting their day at the Cliffs of Moher. From there, they were planning to visit several ruins in the area.

After breakfast, Becky and Noah got their things gathered up and packed into the car. They said their goodbyes and set out on the fifteen minute drive to the Cliffs of Moher.

The sky was clear and bright blue, the most perfect sort of weather she could have possibly hoped for.

At the visitor's center, there were already a ton of tour busses with people swarming the center.

Becky nudged Noah's arm. "It looks like everyone's going up to the north side."

He watched for a moment. "South side, here we come."

They set out along the "unsupervised" dirt trail that ran along the edge of the cliffs. A little too close to the edge for comfort. "I'm not sure I love this," she said, gingerly inching along the path.

"Here," he said, tugging her toward the low stone wall that ran along the trail. "There's another path on the other side of the wall. Do you want to use that?"

"Yeah." She wasn't normally afraid of heights, but the prospect of falling over seven hundred feet into the ocean was making her a little antsy.

Noah easily hopped over the wall, then lifted Becky over. "Better?"

She nodded, holding onto his wrists. "Better. Thanks."

They'd only walked for ten minutes when she turned and gasped. "Look. That's exactly what's on the postcards."

The sun cast rays onto the rock wall, bright green and brown, making a beautiful contrast to the brilliant blue sky and deep blue ocean.

Noah pointed. "You can see O'Brien's Tower from here, too."

Becky took a million pictures, give or take. "This is so perfect. When I went out this morning, it was sort of foggy, so I was afraid we wouldn't get a decent view."

"It couldn't be any better than this, that's for sure."

They walked farther along the trail. Becky spotted a little grassy hill with a perfect view of the cliffs. She walked over and sat down, patting the ground beside her to invite Noah to join her.

They sat in silence for a few minutes. She closed her eyes, just breathing in the sea air and enjoying the calming roar of the ocean far below them. The breeze played with the loose ends of her hair.

"I could sit here all day," she said.

"It's peaceful."

"What would you say if I suggested we skip the island?" She wasn't sure how he'd feel about making a drastic change to the itinerary.

He paused before carefully answering. "I'd say, do you *want* to skip the island?"

She stared out over the ocean. "I had this big idea in my head of seeing the pub and going in and having chicken."

"No fish and chips?"

She laughed. "No. Anna orders chicken at the end of the movie and then sends it back, saying it's too dry because she knows that drives Declan completely insane when customers say his chicken is dry. So she knows it'll get his attention."

"Ah."

"I know it's silly to be this disappointed. I mean, even the whole CGI Rock of Dunamase didn't disappoint me."

"I don't think it's silly."

"I think I'd rather just keep the image in my head than go spend a whole day where the highlight is a boarded up. I know there's a lot more to see, but the pub really, *really* bums me out."

"Look, I'm still kind of queasy, so I'm definitely not going to complain about skipping a ferry ride, but I want to make sure you're sure. Didn't you also want to visit the Aran Sweater Market on the island?"

"I did, but there are two sweater markets right in Doolin by Gus's." Her mind was made up, so she hoped she'd convince him. "We'll get to Dunguaire Castle early, and then we'll get to Ashford way earlier than planned, so we can see more of it."

"If you're sure…" He didn't sound convinced.

The more she thought about it, the surer she was. "I'm completely sure. One hundred percent. I'd rather have a few more hours in Ashford since it's by far the priciest place we're staying and there's a ton to do there."

"Okay, I'm leaving it entirely up to you."

"Good. Let's head up to see the north side of the cliffs."

They made their way back along the trail–the one closest to the cliff this time. Becky took a ton of stunning photos she couldn't wait to print and frame. Although at this rate, she could probably do an entire wall of photos. Several, in fact. Hopefully she could recruit Megan to help her narrow down the best ones.

O'Brien's Tower was crowded, as was the trail to view the cliffs. Becky nudged Noah. "I think I got what I need on the other side."

He looked down at her in surprise. "Are you sure?"

"Yup."

He shrugged and followed her back toward the visitor's center. They took a few selfies in front of the unique building that was built into a hill to blend into the surroundings, then headed back to the car.

Becky got in the driver's seat. "Back to the village to do some shopping, then on to Dunguaire Castle?"

"Not to beat a dead horse, but are you sure?"

"I am. If it was a regular stop, I'd probably go. But since we're beholden to the ferry schedule, I would rather skip it."

"I mean, if you're sure."

She appreciated that he didn't want her to make a hasty decision she'd regret, but it was time to stop second guessing her. She firmly said, "I am. Now let's go check out that little pink shop."

The adorable little pink building with green trim and a thatched roof was a unique sight. Becky took pictures of it before they went in. From there, they visited the Village Crafts and strolled up the street, past Gus's.

"Did you want to stop in and get a pint?" Becky asked sweetly.

Noah looked a little green at the thought. "I think I'll pass."

"Awww, right over there is where you left your dinner. Want a selfie with that spot? For posterity?"

"I have enough posterity, thanks."

She laughed as she snapped a picture. "You're really leaving a piece of yourself in Doolin, aren't you?"

"Now you're just being mean."

They stopped in at O'Brien's for the last of their souvenirs. As they walked back to the car, Becky took a picture of Gus O'Connor's Pub.

"What'd you do that for?"

"It's a beautiful building, and it was a mostly fun evening. It's not Gus's fault you overshot your limit."

"Yeah, yeah. Are we putting this stuff in the luggage now, or later?"

She popped the back of the car and shoved the bags in. "Later."

Just like the conversation they were going to have to have. It'd be dealt with later. As later as possible.

Chapter Twenty-Five

They arrived at the Dunguaire Castle car park a little after eleven. It only took an hour to stroll around the castle and be back on their way to Ashford. Noah found himself not as interested in this particular castle. It could have been the hangover, but for whatever reason he was indifferent, and had no objection when Becky suggested they leave.

Before two o'clock, they approached the Ashford Castle front gate, a massive stone arch that looked like a castle itself. A green-uniformed employee marked their names off a list and waved them through. The massive green iron gates stood open, imposing in their own right.

The lane to the castle was at least a mile long, winding through perfectly manicured grounds and a golf course.

Becky gasped. "Holy crap, is that it?"

Noah leaned toward the windshield, looking far ahead, where she was pointing. "Looks like it. It's huge."

As they got closer, huge became an understatement. It was the castleyest castle he could have imagined. The lane led to a bridge over a river, complete with a tiny yacht motoring past. Uniformed guards–guards!–stood at the spires that marked the beginning of the bridge. Another imposing arch marked the far side of the bridge. It, too, had heavy iron gates standing open.

The massive stone castle with its arched windows was at once welcoming and intimidating.

Noah said, "There's a spot up there."

"Can we park there?"

"I'm sure they'll tell us if we need to move." He stayed quiet as she squeezed the car into the small space.

They walked across the parking lot slowly, paying the barest attention to where they were going because the scenery in every direction was ridiculously gorgeous.

Another green-uniformed man opened a door leading to the massive, majestic lobby, where they checked in. While one employee retrieved their bags, another arrived to give them a brief tour of the castle, ending at their rooms, which were next to each other. Their bags were already inside.

"Holy efficiency, Batman," Becky said, inviting Noah to see her room. "Look at this. I'm really glad we came early, but I'm pretty sure you're going to have to drag me out of here tomorrow."

"Tell me about it." He peered out her window at the incredible view of the loch. "Let's go see my view."

Where her room was decorated in a silver-gray brocade, his was rich green. His view of the lake was almost identical to hers. "This is amazing."

"Let's walk the grounds before it starts raining," she suggested.

He looked up at the sky, where, as they were getting accustomed to, clouds gathered. "Better take umbrellas."

She went back to her room while Noah fished his umbrella out of his backpack. It was a small, compact thing that fit in his jacket pocket.

They met in the hallway and made their way through the castle to a side door that led to a path that would take them through the gardens.

Suddenly, Becky grabbed at her pocket and pulled her phone out. A beaming smile lit up her face. "It's Wyatt. Sorry, I have to take this."

He held the door open for her and said, "I'll meet up with you in a few minutes."

She nodded as she answered the phone. "Hi, baby, how's Mexico?"

The door closed behind her, and he made a beeline for the reception desk. He'd had an idea, and Wyatt's call had given him the perfect window of opportunity.

A few minutes later, he had a piece of paper in his pocket and a smile on his face. He strolled along the paved walkway until he saw Becky sitting on a bench up ahead. She was still on the phone, smiling and nodding enthusiastically. He didn't want to intrude on her conversation, but her voice carried.

"Right now we're in a castle that was built in the twelve hundreds. It's *huge*. Yes, I'm taking lots of pictures. Are you? ... Wow. ... Oh, Wyatt, that sounds amazing! ... You are? That's so cool. ... Yes, I texted Grandma yesterday. Cheeto and Dorito are doing fine. ... I'm sure they miss you, too. ... Oh, okay. Yup, call me again when you have time. ... I miss you, too. ... I love you, too, Wyatt. Can't wait to see you. ... MWAH! Kisses. ... Have fun! Bye."

Noah walked over and sat on the bench beside her. "How's his trip going?"

"Oh, my. It's like ten o'clock and they're on their way to the ruins. He's over the moon excited. But he was worried about Cheeto and Dorito." She glanced up at him. "His goldfish. He won them at a carnival last year and I expected them to go belly-up overnight, but they didn't. So we went out and bought an actual tank and all the accessories and they're still doing great. He's so good with them. He even sets his alarm clock so he feeds them the same time every morning. My parents are coming over to feed them while we're away."

"Cute names."

"Cheeto is the brightest orange fish I've ever seen. Cool Ranch Dorito–his official name–is more of a yellowish-orange. They were only this big when we got them." She held her thumb and forefinger an inch apart. "And now they're like this." She moved them to about four inches. "I hate the idea of using live goldfish as prizes, but he was at a carnival with a friend and came home with those two."

"Yeah, Lilly came home with a pregnant cat about four years ago, so I understand the surprise pet thing."

"Oh, gosh."

"She was with my parents and someone dumped this cat in a parking lot. Poor thing was terrified. They came home and the original plan was to take her to a shelter, but she started having kittens in the laundry room."

"No way."

"Yup. So Lilly was basically a cat midwife. I thought she'd be grossed out, but nope, she was right there, getting blankets and setting up a whole kitten nursery. We had my friend Lincoln come over–he's got a pet sitting business–and he said it was above his paygrade, so then we called my neighbor, Margo Lewis, who happens to be a veterinarian. She checked them all out and said if we could keep them for a while, it'd be less stressful than going to a shelter. Which is how I ended up with nine cats for a while."

"Nine? That's a lot of cats."

"Tell me about it. She had eight kittens. Four boys, four girls. My parents kept the mom. Lilly and I got attached to two of the kittens in particular, so we still have them. Tormund and

Hodor. When they were a few months old, Margo and Lincoln helped me find good homes for the rest of them."

"Those are interesting names."

"From *Game of Thrones*. Tormund the character is a red-haired Wildling, and Tormund the cat is a bossy orange menace. Hodor is super lovable but not very bright. The cat *and* the character."

"Is your friend Lincoln watching them while you're away?"

"Yup. If you ever need a pet sitter, he's your guy. Right now he just does home visits, but he's wanting to expand and open a doggie day care facility."

"That's really cool."

They got up and walked along the path. After a few minutes of strolling in silence, just taking in the lake and perfectly manicured scenery, Noah worked up the courage to say, "About the other day. I guess it was just last night, wasn't it? Anyway, I'm sorry. I know it got awkward and weird and I was overstepping big time, and I'm sorry."

She looked up at him. "I certainly accept your apology. I feel like there's been some awkwardness underlying the whole trip. Which of course makes sense because we're strangers taking a trip together, but..." she trailed off, staring out over the lake as if she was putting her thoughts together. "I'm not sure how to say this." She stopped walking and looked up at him. "I feel like you think you know me more than you actually do. And I get that you know things *about* me from back when we were kids, but we never even had one conversation. And let's be real, Becky at forty-three is a whole different person than Becky at seventeen."

With her words, Noah had an epiphany. A revelation. One of those heavens-parting, angels-singing, bright-light, instantaneous moments of complete and utter clarity. The crush he'd had on her was no different than having a crush on Kelly on

Saved By the Bell or Topanga on *Boy Meets World*. She was right. He knew things *about* her. He knew she was a cheerleader, that she dated Joey, that she was in the choir and the theater, that she had English for second period, she worked part time at Prescott's grocery, and she drove a powder blue 1987 Acura Integra with the pop up headlights and parked in the lower student lot.

He didn't know where she'd planned to go to school or where she'd wanted to live, if she'd wanted a big or small family, if she'd gotten along with her parents, if she'd had a dog… She was a different person at forty-three, but the truth was, he didn't *know* her at seventeen, either.

She was still talking. "I'm not trying to be… I don't even know. Sorry."

Noah's attention snapped back to her. "Please don't apologize. I know what you're saying, and you're right. Heck, I didn't even know myself in high school, right? How about this?" He held out his hand. "Hi. I'm Noah. I'm forty-one. Divorced. Single dad of one teenage daughter and two cats. I have a job and own my own home. I don't know if you've noticed, but we've been bumping into each other a lot here in Ireland. You seem really nice and I'd like to get to know you."

She smiled, and if he wasn't mistaken, she even blushed a little before she reached out and took his hand, giving it a firm shake. "Hi. I'm Becky. Forty-three. Divorced. Single mom of one son and grandma to two goldfish. I also have a job and a house. I've seen you around quite a bit on this trip. In fact, hmmm…" She squinted and put a finger to her chin. "Are you the guy who was in my car on the way here?"

"Yes! That was me. I'm flattered you recognized me." He put a hand over his heart.

A light, steady rain began to fall. Not enough to chase them back inside, but enough to use the umbrellas. While Becky was popping hers open, Noah fished the slip of paper out of his pocket.

He said, "I know I don't really know what you like or don't like, but I'm hoping you'll like this."

She took the paper and read it. "A massage?" Her gaze sliced up to meet his. "You booked me a massage?"

"Yup."

"Noah, I don't know what to say. Thank you. That's amazing. I haven't had a massage in forever."

He could have wilted with relief that she'd accepted his gift. "Your appointment is at four thirty, so we should head back in."

"What are you going to do?"

"Call Lilly, call my parents, maybe take a nap, maybe look through the binder, maybe just stare out the window at the scenery. I've got plans."

"You didn't want a massage?"

"I wanted a bikini wax, but there weren't any appointments available." He was so serious it took her a second to start laughing.

Chapter Twenty-Six

Becky felt like she was turning to mush. The masseuse was amazing, massaging and using heated stones and crystals and scented oils to relax muscles that hadn't relaxed in… probably never.

All the tension she'd been holding in her shoulders was pounded and smoothed away. Next time, she was just coming here. She entertained a fantasy about mortgaging the house just to take a weeklong trip and never leave the Ashford grounds. As the masseuse worked out a kink in her neck, she wondered if such a trip could be deducted as a medical treatment on her insurance? Probably not.

She also felt lighter after her conversation with Noah. She hadn't even realized she'd been feeling a weird sort of pressure, like on some level she had to live up to an idealized version of herself that never even really existed.

By the time her massage ended, she felt like jelly. The masseuse, a stern-looking German woman with a gruff voice and the hands of an angel, helped her sit up and gave her a glass of water, infused with hints of cucumber and lemon. Her head spun a little.

The dizziness passed, and the masseuse helped her to her feet, then left her alone in the room to change. She pulled her clothes on and went to her room to shower and change for dinner. Since they were in such a swanky castle, she put on the single black dress she'd packed. It was simple and comfortable. She dressed it up a little with a deep blue cardigan and black flats that didn't take up much room in her suitcase.

She felt like a completely new person when she knocked on Noah's door.

"Hey." He let her in. "How was the massage?"

She sat in the chair by the window and propped her elbow on the tiny table. "Aaaahhh-maaaayyyy-zing. When it was over, she gave me this delicious cucumber lemon water that was so good. And a stern warning to drink lots of water this evening."

"When did you want to have dinner?"

She glanced at the clock. It was almost six. "Now would be great."

"I was going through our dinner options, and I think we should go to the Dungeon."

"Sure." She had no idea what the Dungeon was, nor did she care.

<hr>

The Dungeon was aptly located on a lower level of the castle. The room was done in deep red, with black iron bars on the windows and suits of armor guarding the heavy wooden doors. The chairs were plush red with gold designs against dark wood. Candles on the tables gave a soft glow to complement the room's low lighting.

"These cocktails look good, but I'm afraid I'll end up dehydrating after that massage," Becky lamented.

"I'm sticking with water. Still feeling it after last night."

"Serves you right," she teased.

He tapped the menu. "Maybe I'll try the steak tartare prepared tableside. It sounds fancy."

"I'm not brave enough to eat raw meat."

His nose scrunched. "Raw?"

"That's what tartare is. Although the vegan carrot tartare is intriguing. No raw meat there."

They studied the menus a few minutes longer.

Noah asked, "What are you getting?"

"I'm going to try the confit duck with spiced red cabbage."

"And you say you're not brave."

It wasn't long before Becky had a fancy plate with crispy duck placed particularly over red cabbage with a sprig of fennel they billed as a "salad" and a little fancy blob of citrus jam, and Noah had a small, fancy, round, layered carrot tartare in front of him.

"I should have brought my camera." Instead, she used her phone to take pictures of their appetizers, both of which turned out to be delicious.

The main meals were equally fancy. Becky got a perfectly seasoned seafood risotto, while Noah had a glazed salmon.

Then came the dessert.

"This is literally the most gorgeous dessert I have ever seen in my life." Becky took a picture of her apricot trifle with perfect layers of orange custard and a white chocolate cremeux. "I almost hate to put my spoon in it."

Noah paused, glancing at the fork in his hand. "I'm not having that problem." He dug into his lava cake, pausing long enough to let Becky take a picture of the molten center ooze onto the plate. Then he scooped up a generous bite of cake and peppermint ice cream.

The apricot trifle was as delicious as it was beautiful.

Becky's eyes fluttered closed as the flavors combined on her tongue.

"That good, huh?"

She savored the bite, then swallowed. "Better."

The weather had cleared, so after dinner, they went back out to stroll around the grounds.

"Are you excited about the falcons tomorrow?" She hooked her hand around his elbow as they strolled.

"I'm a little nervous, to be honest. I don't want to get my eyes pecked out by a rogue bird or anything."

"I'm pretty sure that doesn't happen."

"I don't want to be the first."

Becky couldn't believe it was July already, and the fourth day of their trip. She was glad they'd settled into an easy, friendly routine. It was nice traveling with someone who had the same sort of vacation energy she did.

After breakfast, they went to the falconry school on the castle grounds. Becky listened with rapt attention as the falconer walked them through their orientation and introduced them to the falcons they would be walking, Sonora and Beckett. A large slate chalkboard listed the falcons and their weights.

When the instructor asked for questions, Becky pointed to the sign and asked, "What's the significance of their weights?"

The falconer answered, "The falcons will show no signs of sickness. So we track their weight to make sure they're not gaining or losing, which could signal an illness." She went on to describe the differences between the birds, with the females being larger and stronger, while the males are smaller and faster.

Finally, they were equipped with long leather gloves and shown how to handle the birds, both of which had leather straps and tags on their legs. Becky couldn't keep the smile off her face as the instructor placed Sonora, the large female bird with rust-colored wings, on her arm.

Sonora cocked her head, regarding her with one bright watchful eye. Her powerful talons gripped the leather glove.

Noah was quiet, doing as he was told and looking rather anxious as Beckett, the smaller male falcon, perched at his wrist.

The falconer then led them out of the barn and out through a wooden gate onto a path that stretched into the woods.

"This is amazing." She was having a hard time keeping her eyes on the path and off the gorgeous bird on her arm.

Sonora was alert, scanning her surroundings.

They reached a little bit of a clearing, where the instructor showed them how to send the birds off and entice them back with bits of meat. Since the birds were occupied, they were able to start taking pictures.

Becky stretched her arm out as instructed, and Sonora soared toward her. The bird's wingspan was massive. As Sonora ate her treat, Beckett landed beside her. Becky gasped, marveling at having both falcons on her arm. A second later, Beckett took off and went back to Noah, where he found his meat reward.

"Does that happen often?" she asked, awestruck.

The instructor beamed at her enthusiasm. "Every now and again."

Too soon, their time was up. Becky held her arm out, but Sonora ignored it. From her perch in a tree, she tilted her head, focused on something on the ground.

Beckett went back to Noah's arm, but still Sonora ignored them. Then, she dove straight for the ground.

Before Becky could ask what was happening, Sonora straightened and revealed her prize–a small snake. She launched herself upward into the tree and made quick work of devouring the snake. A moment later, she decided to return to Becky's arm.

The instructor grabbed the leather strap on Sonora's leg and had Becky hold it tight for the walk back to the barn.

When they left the barn and headed back to the castle, Becky gushed, "That was the most amazing experience of my entire life."

"It was definitely interesting." He sounded less than enthused.

"Didn't you like it?"

He shrugged. "I'm not a big fan of birds that could eat my face off if they wanted to. Those talons were like razor blades. And did you know their beak could exert enough pressure to snap your finger right off?"

"Of course."

His head jerked toward her. "Of course?"

It was only logical. "Well, sure. I mean, they can disassemble a rabbit, so it only makes sense they could take a finger off."

"And that doesn't bother you?"

She held up both hands and wiggled her fingers. "Nope."

He shuddered. "I mean, it was a great experience and I'm glad we did it, but I'm glad it's over."

She nudged his arm with hers. "I'm sorry you didn't have a good time."

"You had a good enough time for both of us. I'm just glad they didn't both land on *me*. I'm pretty sure I would have screamed like a little girl."

Becky laughed. "I'm pretty sure you would have, too."

"I did have my wits about me enough to get a picture when both of the murder birds were on your arm."

"No way!"

He pulled out his phone and showed it to her, then texted her a copy.

It had to be one of her favorite pictures of herself. She was simply radiating wonder and happiness with the two falcons on her arm. She reached over and wrapped her arms around him for a quick hug. "Thank you."

Chapter Twenty-Seven

Yeah, it wasn't a joke. The bird experience had kind of freaked him out. Sure, they were majestic and interesting and blah blah blah, but he would happily live the whole rest of his life without offering a massive bird of prey a perch on his arm, which was pretty darn close to his face. That beady eyed featherball had sized him up and immediately figured out he was nervous. If they had been alone, Noah had no doubt that Beckett would have taken his shot.

He shuddered. Nothing like being judged by a freaking bird and coming up short. At least Becky had a good time. She'd handled the larger bird without a single ounce of fear. He was impressed with her. He was also impressed with himself that he'd had the presence of mind to snap a quick picture when Beckett surprised them all by landing on Becky's arm next to Sonora.

And let's be honest, her friendly hug had made the whole experience worth it.

They parted company at their rooms so they could finish the last of their packing and get back on the road. This would be the longest leg of their trip, with Coleraine being a little more than four hours from Ashford.

He double checked his room, making sure he'd grabbed his phone charger and adapter, and closed the door behind him. He wheeled his suitcase next door and waited for Becky. She was doing her last double check, then met him in the hallway. "I really don't want to leave here. This place is incredible, and there's a lot more to see."

"I think that sums up our entire trip."

"Good point." She started for the lobby. "I was looking at the binder. We've got about a four-hour drive, but I was thinking we should plan ahead for rest stops."

They checked out and went out to the car. It was warm and sunny after a quick downpour that was perfectly timed after their bird adventure was over.

He nearly ran into Becky at the back of the car. She was staring at the sky, so he turned to look.

"Wow."

A bright double rainbow arced over the horizon.

"Grab your camera."

"Oh!" She hurried to get her camera out and snapped some pictures of the rainbow with the castle and lake in perfect balance.

He took a few pictures with his phone. The rainbow faded as they watched. The larger, outer rainbow disappeared first.

"That was the most stunning rainbow I've ever seen."

Noah agreed.

They stashed their bags in the back of the car and he got in the driver's side. He adjusted the seat and mirrors as she got situated.

"I was saying, I think we should plan ahead to stop every hour or hour and a half or so. What do you think?"

"I think that sounds perfect. It's eleven now, we can stop for lunch around twelve thirty. Do you want to check the map and find a place ahead of time, or just wing it?"

"I checked the list Megan gave me and there's a place in a town called Ballymote. It's about an hour and a half from here."

"Sounds good. Plug it in the GPS and we'll make that our first stop."

He waited until the GPS was ready to go, then backed out of their parking space and headed for the bridge that would take them away from the castle. The green-uniformed guard at the main gate gave them a nod as they passed through.

Becky sighed. "I'm conflicted."

"How so?" He asked.

"I'm sad to leave here, but I'm excited to see what we get to do for the rest of our trip. Everything has been better than I could have imagined."

"Except Declan's Pub." He bit his tongue. Probably not the best idea to bring up low points of the trip.

"I mean, it actually worked out for the best. I'm really glad we got here early and had time to explore. Otherwise, we would have gotten here last night after eight and then just had time to eat and go to sleep." She smiled over at him. "I wouldn't have gotten that amazing massage. And who knows if I would have had phone reception to talk to Wyatt out on the island."

He was doubly glad he'd followed the whim and sprung for the massage. "It sounds like he's having fun."

"Oh, my. Veronica sent me a picture last night, and he's grinning from ear to ear. I don't know how they dragged him away from the ruins. Have you talked to Lilly? How's Florida?"

"She texted me last night, which I saw this morning. More

shopping. I'm cautiously optimistic that this trip is a good thing for her."

"Cautious optimism is a good thing."

The GPS interrupted with directions. They passed the time with small talk. Forty minutes into the trip, Noah had to put the car in park and wait out a herd of cows that was strolling across the road from one field to another.

"I expected more sheep and less cows," Becky said.

"Maybe the sheep are more of a Scotland thing."

"There have to be a lot of sheep here, too. Foxford wool is pretty famous, so I'd imagine there are tons of sheep somewhere."

Noah pointed toward a ridge. "Over there. Aren't those sheep?"

White blobs dotted a field in the distance.

"Good timing."

"Maybe the sheep just stay away from the road. Probably dangerous to have them where they could be counted by people driving."

Becky groaned. "You did not just make a really bad joke about counting sheep."

"I'm pretty sure I did."

The farmer followed the last of the cows off the road and gave them a wave. They waved back and Noah put the car back in drive.

"How many pictures did you get?"

"Only a dozen. Cows are cute."

"I had no idea you were into animals. First the killer birds and now the traffic jam cows."

"I can't believe you didn't enjoy the hawks. I'm going to see if there's a falconry place somewhere at home. Wyatt would love it."

"Lilly would probably love it, too. I'm going to pass,

though. I have a strict one scary bird encounter per lifetime limit." Actually, zero was his limit, and he'd exceeded it.

"Scary?"

"He wanted to eat my face off."

She laughed. "He did not."

"He did. And your bird murdered a snake right in front of you, and you seem to think it was cute."

"It was. Do you know how many people get to see something like that? Not many."

"Lucky them," he muttered, mostly teasing her.

Even though the drive was long and tedious, Noah didn't mind. He had to keep reminding himself to stay to the left, especially when they passed through tiny villages with lanes barely wide enough for one car, let alone two. The weather vacillated between cloudy and sunny, but the rain managed to hold off.

They stopped in Ballymote to see the ruins of the Ballymote Castle, and had lunch at the Coach House Hotel restaurant. Both of them got the fish and chips this time.

Their second pit stop was in Donegal, where they spent longer than expected touring the Donegal Castle and then the Donegal Abbey–ruins of an ancient friary overlooking the Donegal Bay.

It was an hour later when Becky grabbed her camera and pointed excitedly. "We're crossing the border."

He glanced in the rear view mirror to make sure there was nothing behind them, then slowed down to park on the gravel pull-off behind the sign.

Five minutes later, they had a ton of pictures of the "Welcome to Northern Ireland, Speed limits in miles per hour" sign. That sign and a slight line on the asphalt were the only indications they'd entered an entirely different country.

It wasn't even an hour from the time they crossed the

border until they arrived at their hotel in Coleraine. Huge letters spelling out "Bushtown Hotel" on a low stone wall marked the entrance to the hotel.

They checked in and took their bags to their rooms. Noah checked the time. Even with the extra time they spent in Donegal, it was still before six o'clock.

He knocked on Becky's door. She let him in and he said, "I had a thought."

"Uh oh." Becky made her eyes go wide and leaned back. "Should I put this on the calendar?"

"Ha, ha. What would you think about going to see Giant's Causeway now instead of in the morning? It's about twenty-five minutes away."

Her brow furrowed. "We do have a ton of stops tomorrow, don't we?" She took the binder out of her backpack and sat on the bed with it. She flipped it open to the next day's section. "Yeah. Seven stops before we head to our hotel."

"I probably shouldn't say this, but the w-e-a-t-h-e-r—"

"Hush, don't finish that sentence."

He gave her a thumbs up and mimed zipping his lips.

"You've already been driving a lot today, are you sure you want to go back out instead of just staying in?"

"It's up to you. If you'd rather stay in, I'm down with that." He was hoping she'd decide to go. It felt too early to just sit in the hotel room for the entire evening.

She looked down at the binder and finally said, "Let's do it."

By six forty-five, they were hiking down to some of the world's most unique rock formations. Hexagonal columns of stone, all of varying height, ran from the cliffs into the ocean, like stepping stones. Depending on who you asked, they were either formed by an underground volcano, or legendary giant Finn McCool. Noah was on board with the scientific explanation until he saw the interlocking stones in person. Then the legend didn't feel quite as farfetched.

Becky stopped and snapped pictures of the surrounding cliffs. "This is stunning."

They spent an hour and a half exploring the stones. Even though it was after eight o'clock, there were still dozens of other tourists climbing on the rocks with them.

Noah's favorite part was the giant's boot, a massive stone shaped like an old fairy tale boot. Legend explained it as the size ninety-three and a half boot Finn McCool lost as he fled from Scottish giant Benandonner.

They learned this information from a ten-year-old girl. Her parents apologized profusely for her incessant chatter as she explained that his proper name is Fionn mac Cumhaill, which she spelled out, and that he was fifty-four feet tall. She also rather proudly shared that it was actually Finn's wife, Oonagh, who saved the day.

"Katie, stop bothering these people," her mother wearily said for the nth time.

Noah shook his head. "No bother at all. I have a daughter just a little older than her."

Becky smiled at the girl. "You know a lot of things. You should be a teacher when you grow up."

Katie wrinkled her nose. "No. I'm going to be a CEO and a horse trainer."

"Also great choices," Becky said. She looked up at the mom. "My son's nine, and he loves sharing the things he's learned, too. I just got an education in the Mayan civilization."

"That's in Mexico, on the Yucatan Peninsula," Katie said.

"Yup. That's where Wyatt is now."

"Why is he in Mexico if you're in Ireland?"

"Katie!"

Becky just chuckled. "He's with his dad."

Noah had to stifle a laugh as Katie gave him an obvious side-eye and Becky explained, "His dad and I are divorced."

Katie's mom pressed her hand to her face and shook her head. "Katie, let's go."

Before she could apologize again, Noah said, "There's the shuttle. I think we're going to grab it instead of hiking back up."

They all piled onto the crowded shuttle. Noah could hear Katie several rows behind them, telling Finn McCool's story again.

"Makes me miss Lilly."

Becky leaned her head on his shoulder. "Tell me about it." She reached up to wipe her eyes.

"Are you okay?"

She nodded, but squeezed her eyes shut. She pulled herself together as the shuttle rumbled to a stop back at the visitor's center.

As they walked to the car, Noah slipped an arm around her waist. He fished in his pocket for the keys and opened her door. "You good?"

Her chin quivered, and she covered her face with her hands. She sniffled and her shoulders shook.

"Hey, hey, hey."

"I miss him so much," she sobbed.

Noah pulled her to his chest and hugged her, letting her cry it out. He rested his chin on the top of her head and stroked her hair for several long minutes until she pulled back and composed herself.

"I've never been away from him this long. I hate it."

"I know." He stroked her hair away from her face and tucked it behind her ear.

She wiped her eyes and leaned back from him, pulling herself together.

He said, "Let's head back to the hotel and get some food. I bet they have fish and chips."

That earned him a smile. She nodded and got in the car.

Noah waited while she set the GPS. They didn't talk on the way back to the hotel. He knew she was miserable without Wyatt, and he didn't feel much better about being away from Lilly. Ireland was a great distraction, but he'd rather be home with her, safe and sound.

Back at the hotel restaurant, they ended up getting a massive "Sharing Platter" of nachos, chicken wings, cheesy garlic bread, and BBQ ribs. They devoured it in silence, both of them anxious to get to their rooms and call home.

Chapter Twenty-Eight

Becky felt like she'd ruined their excursion. Something about Katie's confident lecturing just reminded her so much of Wyatt. She glanced at the clock. It was just before nine, which would be four in Wyatt's time zone. She sat on the edge of her bed, staring at her phone. Should she call? What if he heard the sadness and even a little bit of desperation in her voice and it made him sad? Was it selfish to even try calling?

The last thing she wanted to do was make Wyatt feel bad just to make herself feel better. She debated a while longer, then settled on a text.

> Hey sweet pea! I hope you're having fun! I was just at Giant's Causeway. It was so cool.

She attached a picture to the message and sent it.

A few minutes later, her phone dinged with an incoming message. A picture popped up of a lizard basking in the sun at the ruins. Then a message came in.

> This is Herman.

Herman seems nice.

Can I get an iguana?

Cheeto and Dorito would be jealous. Are you having fun?

She waited several minutes, but no response came. Which suggested to her that he was having a lot more fun doing whatever he was doing than texting with his mom. So she sent one more text.

Talk to you soon. Love you bunches!

She put her phone on the nightstand and got ready for bed.

"Noah, calm down." Becky stabbed at her breakfast.

"What? I'm calm."

"You're practically bouncing off the ceiling." She was trying not to be annoyed by his enthusiasm, but a restless night didn't help her mood at all.

"You're going to love Dunluce Castle."

She doubted it, but she said, "Okay."

He pulled his phone out to show her a picture. "It was used as Pyke Castle, of the House of Greyjoy in the Iron Islands."

"Okay." She had no idea what the words he was babbling meant. All she heard was, "Blah blah blah, *Game of Thrones*, blah blah blah."

"Of course, there was a lot of CGI, but the ruins look incredible on their own."

"Are all the stops today *Game of Thrones* locations?" She'd never seen a single episode, so today would be all about Noah. Hopefully she could just hang back and enjoy the locations without feeling like she was missing something.

He skimmed down over the binder's itinerary page for the day. "Not all of them. Just Dunluce Castle, Cushendun Caves, and the Dark Hedges."

She yawned and speared another grilled tomato. This trip was the first time she'd ever had tomatoes for breakfast, and she was loving it.

"Did you get to talk to Wyatt last night?"

"No." She tamped down the disappointment. "They were off on another excursion, so he was busy. He did send me a picture of a lizard and asked if he could get one."

"I prefer my pets to have fur. No scales, no feathers."

"No scales? What about fish?"

"Okay, fish in a tank are fine. No lizards, no snakes, no reptiles."

"And no birds."

"Absolutely not."

Teasing him lightened her mood a little.

They finished their massive breakfasts and checked out of the hotel.

Becky was glad to see the sun shining. It was her turn to drive, and rain wouldn't have helped her crappy mood at all. As it was, her attitude definitely lifted on the way to Dunluce Castle. Noah spent the twenty-minute drive giving her an in-depth overview of the Greyjoys and the Iron Islands, but she had no idea what he was talking about. Still, she let his enthusiasm buoy her mood, and by the time they reached the castle, she was feeling pretty good.

Much to her delight, the castle was stunning, even from their first sighting of it from the parking lot.

"It's huge." She pointed as they got out of the car. "It looks like two separate buildings."

"It is." Noah could hardly stand still while she got her camera and locked the car.

They followed the marked path to the first cluster of buildings and ruins. Groups of people wearing black cloaks and carrying swords milled all around the grounds.

"Umm, is there something going on? What's with the capes?"

"Cloaks. I bet it's a tour group. They have bus trips and stuff that go to all the filming locations."

"Oh. So it's basically a traveling Ren Faire with everyone in costume." A little weird, but probably a lot of fun.

To reach the main castle, they had to cross a narrow footbridge. A group of cloaked men, probably in their thirties, strode from the opposite side. Becky stepped as far to the right as she could, against the wooden railing, to let them pass. The third man in the group stopped short, barely a foot in front of her, whipped his sword from his waist, held it high over his head, and yelled in her face, "What is dead may never die!"

Becky screamed and stepped backward, trying to turn. She tripped into Noah and fell against the other railing. She pushed back, shoving one of the other cloaked men, scrambling to get away from this lunatic. She ran off the bridge, back up the path, and slipped on wet grass. Her camera swung and smacked the ground, loosening the strap enough for it to fall from her neck.

Noah was only a step behind her. He dropped to his knees beside her. "Hey, hey, hey, it's okay. It's okay. You're okay."

Her hands shook so hard she couldn't pick up her camera.

The cloaked man was a few steps behind, looking horrified. "Are you okay? I'm so sorry."

One of his friends snatched the sword from his hand.

"I'm really sorry."

Becky couldn't help the flood of tears. Somewhere in the melee, she'd smacked her elbow painfully, and her ankle twinged from the fall on the grass.

"Look at me." Noah put his hands on her shoulders. "Beck. Breathe. It's okay." He picked up her camera and popped the lens cap off. He took a couple pictures, and checked them in the viewer. "Your camera's okay."

She nodded, cradling her elbow.

"Did you hurt your arm?"

She heard the caped man whisper, "Oh, shit."

"I think I hit it on the railing." She took a few shaky, deep breaths as the tears slowed. She stretched her arm out and pulled it back. "It's fine."

"I'm so sorry," the man repeated.

Noah helped her to her feet.

Her ankle was a little sore, but seemed fine. She busied herself fixing her camera strap as she got herself under control.

Noah waited until she was steady, then strode the few steps over to the cloaked man. "What is wrong with you? A grown man running up to a woman–on a freaking *bridge*–who is clearly not part of your group, and screaming in her face like an idiot? You're lucky she didn't fall over that railing." He poked his finger in the man's chest. "Seriously, dude, you can't even imagine the self-control it's taking to not punch you in the face."

He took the verbal lashing from Noah without any pushback.

"Don't ever pull a dumbass stunt like that again, you hear me?" Noah slowly put his finger down.

Becky put a hand on Noah's arm.

"I really… I'm so sorry," the man said. "Are you hurt?"

"I'm fine, but you *really* scared me and that's not okay."

"I know, I'm sorry. I truly didn't mean to scare you. I kind of assumed anyone who's here would understand."

It occurred to her then that whatever he'd yelled about being dead must have been some *Game of Thrones* reference.

His buddies flanked him, looking a little sheepish on his behalf.

"Again, I'm so sorry."

"I accept your apology, but for crying out loud, my nine-year-old behaves better. This was a historical site long before it was in your stupid show. Just… use your head and make better choices." If she had a nickel for every time she used that line on Wyatt, she'd be rich. She gave him a curt nod and stepped back toward the bridge.

She heard one of the men say, "You're lucky he didn't pop you one." The other said, "You're not getting this sword back, either. You're lucky you didn't get us all kicked out."

Her legs were a little shaky as she crossed the bridge. It hadn't seemed scary at all a few minutes ago, but now she was keenly aware of how high it was, and how easy it would be to go over the railing.

"You sure you're okay? We can leave."

"No, I'm fine. He just scared the crap out of me, but the camera's fine and I'm fine. Just give me a few minutes to let all that adrenaline work its way out of my system." She walked over to a stone window. "Look at this." She breathed in the ocean air. The castle was built on a pillar of land, with the Atlantic Ocean lapping at its foundation.

Noah stood behind her, his hands on her shoulders. She knew he was half-looking at the scenery, half-keeping an eye on her to make sure she was okay.

She pulled in a deep breath and let it out slowly. "So was this Thon Iron-whatever a good guy or a bad guy?" Not that she cared, but she wanted to distract Noah from worrying about her.

"Theon. Theon Greyjoy. Of the Iron Islands."

"Ah. Well, I was close."

"Theon was a complicated character. He was basically a good guy, but let himself be manipulated in his quest for power and to earn his father's approval. He was kind of a good guy, then a bad guy, then there were some, um, major consequences to his actions, and then he was a good guy again when it counted."

"I've never seen a single episode. Sarah and Julie–who I work with–are both fans, so all I know is 'Winter is Coming,' there are dragons, and Jon Snow knows nothing."

"That pretty much sums it up."

"What that guy yelled in my face, I assume, is a line from the show?"

His fingers tightened on her shoulders a second before he answered. "Yeah. The Greyjoys have a ceremony in the ocean and that's one of the main lines they repeat."

Becky held her hand out the window. "You can feel the mist off the ocean."

Noah leaned against the wall and stuck his hand out. "I'm really sorry that happened to you. I never saw it coming."

Chapter Twenty-Nine

Noah kept going over the scene in his mind. There had been no warning, no clue that idiot was going to brandish a sword and start screaming. Sure, the guy was just a dumbass caught up in his medieval fantasy, but Noah couldn't shake the fact that he could have done some real damage if he'd intended to. It was unsettling.

And on some level, he felt like it was his fault, since this whole day was about visiting film locations he was interested in.

Becky slipped an arm around his waist. "Stop."

"What?"

"Overthinking. This is amazing. Can you just imagine the lords and ladies who traveled here for coronations and balls and political alliances disguised as weddings? The fireplaces blazing, cutting the chill from the ocean air? This place is breathtaking as a ruin. It must have been simply amazing in its prime."

He looked around, relaxing and shoving the earlier unpleasantness to the back of his mind. If she could let it go, he would, too.

"Let's go see the other buildings."

The hour they'd allotted to Dunluce Castle stretched into two hours. Next, they went to Dunseverick Castle, arriving just fifteen minutes later. A set of pillars was all that remained of this castle, so they were back on the road in a few minutes.

Another fifteen minutes later, they arrived at the Carrick-A-Rede rope bridge car park. The sky was blue and clear, but wind viciously whipped in from the ocean. They were able to walk along the trail to the bridge, but the bridge itself was closed, so they got some pictures of the gorgeous landscape and piled back into the car.

A little more than half an hour later, they arrived at the Cushendun Caves. They, along with a busload of tourists, hiked down a hill to the caves. Unlike most of the places they'd visited, this one was not well marked for tourists.

Becky asked, "This is one of the film locations, right?"

"Right."

"What happened here?"

He tried to simplify the complex plot as much as he could. "In season two, Ser Davos brought Melisandre here so she could give birth to a demon shadow smoke baby."

"Oh."

"It's also where Jaime Lannister battled Euron Greyjoy in the last season."

"I can imagine this as a good place for a battle. Not so much for having a baby. Even a demon shadow smoke baby."

Noah pointed out some spots to get pictures of, and soon they were back in the car, on their way to the Dark Hedges.

While she drove, he pulled up the location on his phone. "It says here that it's best to park in the free hotel parking lot and walk to the hedges."

"Okay. Tell me about this place. What was it in the show?"

"King's Road. It's the road where Arya Stark escaped from King's Landing."

As they pulled into the hotel's free parking lot, which was packed full of vehicles, Noah said, "I hope these people are staying at the hotel and aren't at the hedges." Three double-decker buses were parked at the side of the parking lot closest to the road.

It was a quick walk to the hedges, where they discovered that the three tour buses full of people were also visiting. Plus more people who weren't part of the tours.

The hedges were not what Noah expected. He knew they'd been heavily altered for television, but it appeared as though several storms had come through and downed a significant number of the ancient trees. The bright sunshine also made them feel far less creepy and imposing.

"Oh, geez," Becky muttered.

"Hmm?" He followed her gaze. To a group of cloaked men. As they walked closer, he confirmed it was the same group they'd encountered at Dunluce Castle.

"At least they seem to be behaving," she said.

Much to Noah's surprise, the man who'd caused the ruckus spotted them and jogged over. "Hey, hi. I'm glad we ran into you guys again. I still feel really bad about this morning, and the guys have been harassing me nonstop. I'd really like to pay for your dinner, if you'll let me. I know it's not much, but it'd make me feel better, not that it matters how I feel, I know that." He pulled some bills out of his pocket and handed to Becky.

"You don't have to do that. I'm fine, it's water under the bridge."

"I'd really like to."

"Alright. Thank you."

He looked at Noah and gestured to the trees. "Is this what

you expected? I mean, it's cool, but we thought the trees would be thicker or something."

"Yeah, I knew they were heavily photoshopped or something, but this is totally different. The trees are really interesting, but I'm not sure I'd make the trip again."

One of the other men hollered for their friend.

"Gotta run, but I'm glad I saw you again, so I know for sure you're okay. All the same, my wife's going to kill me when she hears the story."

"Maybe I should get her number," Becky said with a laugh. She held up the folded bills. "Thanks for dinner." Then she slipped the money into her pocket.

They got some pictures, mostly full of people, and headed back to the car.

Noah said, "Sorry, that was kind of lame."

"The trees were really interesting. I bet they're super eerie at night, especially on a full moon."

"They're supposedly haunted by the Grey Lady."

"Well, she's not going to find any peace with all those people dropping by, is she?" She got into the driver's seat. "What's next?"

"On to Belfast."

"I hope you're up for an early dinner tonight because I'm already really hungry."

"Megan didn't have any suggestions for a little out of the way pub on the way to Belfast?"

"Unfortunately, no."

"Do you want to check into the hotel and then get dinner, or eat first? We should be getting in around five, maybe a little after."

"Let's reassess when we get there. I knew we should have saved some of that lemon cake from Enniskerry."

"Or the brownies from Route 85 Drive Thru."

She sighed. "Those were the best brownies ever. And the caramel squares. Oh, my. Would it be weird to drive six hours to get more of them?"

"Weird? Yes. But I wouldn't argue about it."

As they got closer to the city, the traffic got heavier and heavier. Noah resumed his job as quiet navigator, pointing out upcoming turns and lane shifts. Becky was doing fine, but he saw the tense way her fingers gripped the steering wheel.

After some stop and go traffic, the GPS directed them into the parking lot of the hotel, the only chain hotel for their trip.

Chapter Thirty

Becky stretched as she got out of the car. "Maybe we should have done dinner first. I'm so hungry."

"Let's get checked in and we can ask where the closest restaurant is."

She nodded, not bothering to say anything. She was past hungry and well into hangry. It wasn't Noah's fault, and she'd feel bad if she snapped at him for no reason.

They unloaded their suitcases and backpacks. She pushed the hatch closed.

Noah held out a granola bar. "A little something to tide you over?"

It didn't look particularly appetizing, but she was too irritable to be picky. "Thank you." She munched on the bar as they crossed the lot and entered the spacious lobby.

The spacious, *full* lobby. The line for the reception desk was six people deep. Yep, good thing she had a granola bar to take the edge off.

They finally got their keys and dumped their suitcases in their rooms.

"Do you want to see what restaurants are nearby or—"

Becky cut him off. "No. There's a restaurant downstairs. I don't care what they have or what it costs, that's where I'm going."

Noah snickered. "I'm right behind you."

"I hope it's not terribly busy. The granola bar was great, but it was a temporary patch at best."

"Yeah, I'm getting a little testy myself."

The restaurant was upscale, serving Mediterranean style dishes. Fortunately, they were ushered directly to a table and their focaccia appetizer came out quickly, and was devoured just as fast.

Noah looked up from the menu. "I can guess what you're getting."

"I'm sure you can."

He was right, snickering as she ordered battered haddock and hand-cut chips.

When their food arrived, she pointed to his rotisserie chicken. "Not really in a position to judge me for not having an adventurous palate, are you?"

They both polished off their meals, then ordered crème brûlée for Becky and panna cotta for Noah for dessert.

Becky pushed her empty plate away. "That was amazing."

"Sorry about the lack of scintillating dinner conversation."

"I wouldn't have noticed, even if you were talking. Lesson learned. Don't skip lunch, even if it's just a quick bite."

"Agreed."

She looked at her watch. "It's six thirty. Do you want to go out and see the river?"

"Yes."

Outside, there were a handful of people taking pictures at a large object near the railing. As they walked closer, she could see it was a massive stained glass window framed and mounted on a concrete base.

"Whoa."

"That's really cool. Must be some historical battle or something," Becky speculated.

Noah made a strangled noise. "No. It's scenes from *Game of Thrones*." He excitedly pointed out Jon Snow, Sansa and Arya Stark, the three-eyed raven, and some other things Becky had no clue about.

The piece itself was stunning, probably ten feet tall and six feet wide, if she had to guess. The glass artwork was stunning and meticulous, whether it was history or fiction.

Noah said, "That is the coolest thing I've ever seen."

An older man walking past stopped and turned to them. "Yanno there are more, don'tya?"

"More of these?" He pointed to the glass.

"Aye. Six of 'em. Only take ya about forty minutes to see them all. Glass of Thrones, they call it. Sure you can find it on your phone there."

A pair of teenage girls ran over to take selfies with the glass while Becky pulled it up on her phone. She showed the route to Noah. "Shall we?"

"Of course."

They walked along the river, toward the bridge, stopping to take photos of an adorable seal sculpture, when a massive blue fish caught their attention. The thirty-plus-foot-long blue and white fish was a mosaic of ceramic tiles that formed a salmon.

Noah looked it up on his phone. "This guy is the Salmon of Knowledge, based on an old legend. It was commissioned in 1999 to celebrate the regeneration of the Lagan River, created by artist John Kindness. Supposedly, if you kiss it, you'll gain all the knowledge of the world."

"What is it with the Irish and kissing things?" Still, Becky went up the two marble stairs to kiss the fish. Because why not? "Noah, check this out. These tiles are from newspaper articles. Here's an old photograph. This is amazing."

They spent a few minutes walking around the salmon, taking pictures and investigating its tiles before heading across the Lagan Weir footbridge. The second glass window was mounted just off the bridge.

"This seems a lot darker," Becky said, looking at the large red woman who dominated the glass.

"This is the red witch. She's the one who gave birth to the shadow baby in the cave." He pointed out the unfortunate moments for House Baratheon depicted in the glass.

"Yikes. They had some bad luck." She was enjoying his enthusiasm.

"They deserved most of it. Except Renley. He was a good guy for the most part."

From there, they strolled to the next window. This one featured dragons. Noah filled her in on Daenerys, the Mother of Dragons, and her story arc across the series. The next window was done in whites and ice blue. A large man with a pained expression seemed to be holding back an army.

"This is Hodor."

"The character you named your cat after."

"Yup." He briefly explained Hodor's impossible task.

"That's so sad."

Even Becky recognized the next window. "The sword throne that everyone was fighting over."

"The Iron Throne," Noah corrected.

This stained glass window had a stool affixed to the base so visitors could get pictures of themselves sitting on the Iron Throne. Clever.

Several regal poses later, they headed for the final window. It was done in vibrant reds and yellows, depicting key moments for House Lannister.

"I'll be interested to look at the pictures closer when we're back home," Noah said. "There are so many little Easter eggs in each of these windows. I know I've missed some of them."

They strolled back the way they came, paying more attention to the scenery this time.

"Now we know where to go for the *Titanic* museum tomorrow."

"That's great that we can just walk to it," Becky said. "I actually didn't realize the *Titanic* was built in Belfast. I assumed it was built in England."

"Me, too. I guess I didn't pay enough attention when I took Lilly to the *Titanic* traveling exhibit a couple of years ago."

"I wanted to go, but we never got around to it."

"It was interesting. They gave out little passports that had a real passenger's information, like the class they were traveling, who they were sailing with, whether they survived. It made it more personal."

They strolled around the hotel and surrounding area until the inevitable raindrops began falling around nine.

"That's our cue," Noah said.

They parted company at their rooms, agreeing to meet at seven the next morning.

At seven on the dot, Becky was up and packed and ready to go. After a nondescript breakfast in the hotel, they walked to the *Titanic* visitor's center. They worked their way through the nine interactive galleries, but decided to skip the guided tour of the shipyard in favor of strolling through the beautiful city of Belfast without an agenda.

"There was a pub Megan recommended that's not too far away, but I'm not sure if they're open for lunch or just dinner."

She pulled out her phone to check. "The Dark Horse. She said the menu is fairly small, but it's a must-see for the ambiance."

"Sounds good to me."

They walked down narrow cobblestone alleys until they reached the charming alley that housed The Dark Horse. Rows of hanging baskets of bright red impatiens covered the walls of the shops, with strings of party lights strung across the alley.

"I bet this looks really cool at night," Noah said.

The Dark Horse itself was warm and charming, with a polished copper ceiling, mirrored walls, and stained glass lights hanging from the ceiling. Everything was dark, but warm and inviting. Becky took a ton of pictures of the décor. "That's really interesting." She snapped a picture of a sculpted wooden door.

Their server was clearing their plates and overheard her. "Lots of people come in just for that. It's the tenth *Game of Thrones* door."

That got Noah's attention. "The what?"

The server smiled and went behind the bar. A moment later, she came back with two little booklets. "There are ten doors all over Northern Ireland. They were all crafted from trees from the Dark Hedges that Storm Gertrude knocked down back in 2016." She handed them the booklets. "Journey of Doors passports. You'll get a stamp in your booklet for each door you visit."

Becky flipped through the booklet. "This is really cool. Thank you so much. We had no idea this even existed."

"My pleasure. Enjoy the rest of your holiday."

For a second, Becky thought she was referring to the Fourth of July, which was the next day, but her brain quickly translated holiday into vacation.

She and Noah went over to more closely inspect the door with its intricately carved lion and knights.

Noah explained, "King's Landing. Everything carved has something to do with King's Landing, which is where the Iron Throne was."

"The craftsmanship is simply outstanding." She'd known that some people really got into *Game of Thrones*, but she was coming to realize that it was a big deal in a lot of ways. The tourism dollars that poured into Northern Ireland from the show alone had to be staggering. "Let's get the binder and see what other doors we can find along the way."

They walked back to the car. Noah adjusted the driver's seat while Becky pulled out the binder and opened the map app on her phone. The passport booklet had a little map showing where each door was located. "Dang, it looks like we went right past most of them on our way to Coleraine. The next one is in Portaferry, which is about an hour away." She reached for her seatbelt.

Noah sat up straight and put a hand on her arm. "Wait. This is silly. I don't want to leave Belfast early when there are things you want to see. I didn't even know these doors existed and the last two days have been all about the *Game of Thrones* sites."

Becky was touched at his thoughtfulness. "Noah. It's only two hours early. Look." She pointed at the map. "Two of the doors are super close to Castle Ward, and the third is on our way back to Dublin. I may not have seen the show, but I have to admit, those stained glass windows and these carved doors? That's pretty cool and I want to see them. I promise, I'm not just grudgingly going along. I might not get all the nuance, but I can appreciate the artistry of what I'm seeing. Belfast is beautiful and I'm sure I could spend weeks exploring, but I also like the idea of finding something interesting and rolling with it."

"Are you sure?"

"Positive." She saw he was still hesitating. "We should get going."

The day was sunny and bright as they headed south to Fiddler's Green Pub in Portaferry, where they got a picture of door number two, which had a giant kraken at the bottom and crossed swords at the top. Becky snapped a ton of pictures, capturing every detail, while Noah bought a round for the sparse lunch patrons.

Ten minutes, and they were back on the road to the Portaferry Ferry Terminal, where they waited to board the ferry that would take them across the Strangford Lough.

"I'm so glad I'm not driving," Becky said. "I've never been on a ferry."

"I've been on a passenger ferry, but never one with my car. So this'll be new for both of us."

It was less nerve-wracking than she'd thought. The ferry slid into the dock, and then the line of cars was directed onto the boat, where three clear rows were marked. Noah simply followed the car in front of them, and aside from the unsettling loud clanging metal sounds, it was a simple process.

The ride across the lough was smooth, and faster than she'd anticipated. From the time they got on the ferry until they were driving off the dock, barely twenty minutes passed.

The GPS informed them that their next destination was less than a minute away. Sure enough, the pretty sage-green restaurant was very close. Becky snapped photos of the wagon full of red flowers and greenery, as well as the awards they had displayed on the wall.

As they went inside, she inhaled deeply. Whatever was on the menu had her attention. "Maybe we should just have lunch here?"

"I could eat."

A friendly hostess greeted them.

"Hi. We were planning to just see the *Game of Thrones* door, but something smells amazing, so we'd like to stay for lunch."

"Certainly. Right this way." The hostess led them to a table and pointed a short distance away. "There's the door."

Becky wasn't sure which to focus on, the door or the menu. She chose the menu. "This may shock you, but I'm not getting fish and chips."

"What? Who are you? What have you done with Becky?"

"I know, right? I'm going to try the seafood chowder and pan-fried Brussel sprouts and the flatbread with mozzarella and sundried tomatoes."

"Sticking with appetizers. Interesting choice. I'm going with the steak sandwich with garlic butter."

After they ordered, their server stamped their door passports and invited them to take pictures with the door depicting the map of Westeros. He even offered to take pictures with both of their phones so they could be in the photo together.

When they were back in the car, Becky said, "They were so nice. And those Brussel sprouts were amazing."

The GPS directed them to Castle Ward, only ten minutes away.

Chapter Thirty-One

Noah was more excited about this stop than anything else on the trip. To see the actual Winterfell-arguably the most important castle for the entire *Game of Thrones* series-in person was going to be the best experience ever.

Or maybe not quite so much.

Driving up to the majestic tower might have been awe-inspiring, if not for the double-decker tour bus parked in front of it.

"Okay, I knew a lot of it was CGI, but I hardly recognize it." He tamped down the rising disappointment as he tried to visualize the tv-show grounds in his mind against the reality. It would be better on the inside.

And it was. Mostly. They toured the castle and the grounds, but the best part wasn't the location itself. No, the best part was getting to meet two of the show's actual direwolves, Odin and Thor, who weren't wolves, but massive Northern Inuit dogs. They were real actors, having played Summer and Grey Wind in the show.

Noah could have gone home happy after getting to scratch the dogs' ears and give them treats.

As they walked away from the dogs' area, Becky nudged him. "Does that make up for the castle not being what you expected?"

"A hundred percent."

"I see something else you might enjoy."

He followed her to an archery station, where they were outfitted with bows and arrows and had a friendly challenge to see who was the better archer. It was Becky.

They went back to the car, and he felt a hundred times better about the experience than he had when they'd arrived.

He asked, "Alright, now we're on to the third door, right?"

"Ummm, I found a stop along the way I'd like to see, if you don't mind."

Of course he didn't mind. "Did you set the GPS for the new location?"

"Yup."

He followed the directions to a teeny tiny side road that led to an even teenier, tinier road that led to a beautifully maintained set of ruins with three giant peaked cathedral windows that looked vaguely familiar. "It's gorgeous. What is this place?" he asked as they crossed the beautifully maintained lawn.

"Inch Abbey."

He glanced over to see Becky grinning.

"Recognize it?" she asked.

He couldn't figure out what it was, even though it felt like he'd seen it somewhere before. "It seems really familiar."

"It's where Rob Stark was declared King of the North. I assume that means something to you." She laughed.

"Wow. Yeah, I see it." He was touched that she'd scouted yet another filming location for him to see.

She took pictures of the windows and all the tiny details that had withstood hundreds of years… and movie filming.

They finished up and got back on the road to the Percy French Inn, half an hour away. The folks there pleasantly stamped their door passports and let them take pictures.

Back in the car, Becky checked the binder and map. "I had a thought."

"Uh oh."

"I know, scary. I was thinking it might be nice to drive down the coast instead of on the main highway. It'd be an extra half hour and another ferry ride, so if you just want to take the highway, that's okay with me."

He was glad to make the change to the route. Driving along the coast would be nice. Doing something Becky wanted would be even nicer. "It's perfect. Set the GPS."

The road was narrow, but the scenery was breathtaking. Lush green hills on one side, vast blue ocean on the other, with plenty of cows and sheep dotting the landscape. The sun was still bright, so they rolled the windows down and breathed in the ocean air.

They passed through tiny villages and small towns until they came to Greencastle, where they boarded the Carlingford Ferry. This ferry was much larger than the first, and they were allowed to exit their vehicle and go up on an observation deck for the twenty-minute journey across Carlingford Lough.

The views of the surrounding mountains and ocean and coastline were stunning. Becky snapped pictures as the breeze whipped her hair.

Somewhere on the lough, they crossed the border from Northern Ireland into Ireland. From there, it took two hours to drive into Dublin and find their hotel.

It was just before eight o'clock when they wheeled their luggage to the reception counter to check in.

He let Becky go first, and as soon as the clerk typed her name into the computer, her face fell. "Oh, no."

"That didn't sound good. What's wrong?"

"Well, we have a situation."

He leaned closer to hear what the situation might be.

"We had a pipe burst and an entire floor is currently unusable. Unfortunately, we're completely booked with a conference and wedding guests, so we can't offer you a different room. What we can do is call one of our sister hotels to arrange rooms for you, if you'd like."

Becky asked, "Are any of those hotels in walking distance of St. Stephen's Green?"

"I'm sorry, no. The closest would be nearer the outskirts of the city." She typed something in the computer. "I see a second room was booked using the same credit card; are you traveling together?"

"Yeah."

"That room has two beds. If you're willing to share, I'm authorized to steeply discount the room rate for your inconvenience."

Oh, boy.

"We'll also include a meal voucher. I'm terribly sorry."

Noah said, "Can we have a minute?"

"Certainly."

He and Becky stepped off to the side.

"It's up to you," he said.

"I don't know. Would it be awkward?"

"Maybe?" Probably, but he wasn't going to say that.

She continued as though she hadn't heard him. "Undoubtedly it'll be a little weird, but taking all our crap back out to the car and finding a different hotel would be a pain, and then we still have to find dinner."

"That's true."

"Ugh. What do you think?"

He would do whatever she decided, but he was a little concerned about her already being tired and getting pretty darn close to hangry. Adding in a change in hotels would probably be worse than sucking it up and sharing a room. "I think it'll be fine. Separate beds, hard to beat the location. But probably a little awkward, especially if you snore."

She laughed at that. "Like a chainsaw."

"That's unfortunate."

"For you. I won't hear a thing." She tapped on the handle of her suitcase. "It makes more sense to take the room, doesn't it?"

"Entirely up to you."

She nodded once, firmly. "Okay. Let's just stay here."

"Okay."

They went back to the counter.

The clerk looked relieved as she handed over room keys and vouchers for the hotel's restaurant. "Thank you for your understanding."

"No problem. Thank you." Noah handed Becky her keycard and wheeled his suitcase toward the elevator. He wasn't sure how he felt about this turn of events. Not that sharing a room was going to end up meaning anything, but it had been good to have their own spaces to make their calls to home and handle their bathroom routines without needing to hurry up or quiet down.

Their room was more than adequate. Two queen beds dominated the room. At the window, a small coffee table was flanked by two upholstered armless chairs that looked rather comfortable.

"Oh, this is really nice," Becky said.

He joined her at the window.

She pointed to a park half a block away. "That's St. Stephen's Green. There's a bridge in the park from *Leap Year,* and we need to find the Temple Bar, which is where Declan got his mother's ring back from his ex-girlfriend. I also want to see the Book of Kells. Megan's husband, Eric, said the Guinness tour is great, but we should definitely do the Jameson Distillery cocktail class. And of course there are a bunch of museums and art galleries I wouldn't mind seeing."

He'd already gotten to see everything he wanted, so he was up for anything she wanted to do on their last day. "Do you want to order room service and we can make a plan for tomorrow while we eat?"

"You, sir, are brilliant." She quickly decided what she wanted from the menu. "Megan also said that we can get day passes for public transit, so we can hop on and off the busses and trams all day."

"That sounds better than driving everywhere."

They ordered room service, and Megan spread the binder on the coffee table and used the pad and pen the hotel provided to make a list of their must-do activities, and then their nice-to-do-if-we-have-time activities.

By the time their food arrived and they ate, they had a solid plan. Noah was looking forward to the Jameson tour, and Becky was most excited about seeing the Book of Kells, an illustrated manuscript of the four Gospels made by Irish and Scottish monks around the year 800. All in all, they had a wide range of activities that would fill the entire day they'd be spending in Dublin.

"I'm going to check in with home, if you don't mind," Noah said, gesturing to his phone.

"Not at all. I was just thinking about doing the same."

Noah texted Lincoln with a brief recap of the room situation and asked how the cats were. Then he tried calling Lilly, but as usual, his call went to voicemail.

"Hey Lil, just checking in before I go to sleep. I got to play with some direwolves today, can't wait to tell you all about it. Miss you. Love you. Give me a call."

While he was leaving his message, a text came in from Lincoln.

> IDK how to tell you this bro, but you're starring in your own romcom.

Chapter Thirty-Two

Becky texted Wyatt, her parents, and even Veronica, letting everyone know they were in Dublin for the entire day tomorrow. Only a few seconds later, her phone rang.

"Hello?"

"Hey, hang on a sec." Veronica's voice muffled as she moved around. "Sorry, I was going to call you later, but I figured you were near your phone, so it might be a good time to catch you."

"What's up? Is everything okay?" She was immediately on edge. Had something happened?

"Everything's great. I just wanted to run something past you."

"Okay?" Her pounding heart slowed to normal.

"My mom found this bus tour she's going to take the day after tomorrow to some Mayan pyramid site called Ickmil? No, wait. Uxmal. Here, I just sent you a link. My parents and my aunt and uncle are going, and they'd like to take Wyatt along because he loves that sort of thing. It's an all-day trip and I'll be honest, I have zero interest in riding a bus for four hours to look at another ancient pyramid. It's great and all, but not really my jam, and Joey's parents aren't going to this one, either."

Wyatt on a bus trip with only Veronica's family? Yikes. "I'm not sure I'm super comfortable with that."

"That's why I haven't said anything to Wyatt."

"What does his father say?"

There was a long pause. "I haven't said anything to him, either. If you say no, it's no, and that's that."

"Well, let me look at your link and I'll get back to you in a few minutes, okay?"

"Perfect. How's Ireland?"

"It's great. I'm a little bummed tomorrow is our last day. There's been so much to see."

"I can't wait to see the pictures. Oh! Speaking of pictures, I'm sending you one now. Let me know about the bus tour."

They hung up, and the phone dinged with the incoming picture. It was a picture of Wyatt and Veronica's nephew Kyle with a giant sand castle they'd built on the beach. Both boys were grinning from ear to ear. She missed him like crazy, but it was so good to see him smiling and making a new friend. It was also good to see the white streaks of sunscreen on his face and tips of his ears.

She looked at the link for the bus tour and read through several pages of reviews. She had a little twinge of not wanting to let him go, but she knew Veronica's mom would take good care of him. She texted back her permission and tossed her phone onto the bed.

Noah stretched out on his bed. "Lincoln said Tormund caught a grasshopper that somehow got in the house."

"Big day for Tormund. How's Lilly?"

"I haven't heard from her since yesterday's mall selfie. I swear she's been at the mall every day since she got there."

"I'm a little jealous. I used to love going to the mall. Now they're just slowly dying off and it's sad."

"How's Mexico?"

"Great, apparently. Veronica's parents want to take Wyatt on a bus trip to Uxmal. It's another Mayan site, and from the pictures, it's pretty impressive. Looks less touristy than Chichen Itza. Probably because it's a four-hour ride away from Cancun."

"That does not sound fun to me."

"Me, either. Wyatt, though? He'd ride a donkey for nine days to see this stuff without a peep of complaint. But a fifteen-minute trip to the grocery store? Torture." She got up and got her toiletry bag from her suitcase. "Do you need to use the bathroom? I like to shower at night, so I'll be in there a while."

"No, I'm good."

She showered and changed into yoga pants and a sweatshirt. She checked her phone and replied to messages from Wyatt, giving her super excited news about a trip to Uxmal, and from her mom, reminding her to pick up an authentic Irish wool blanket. Which she had already done back in Doolin.

Becky startled awake at the sound of the shower. It took a second to remember she didn't have her own room. She propped all her pillows behind her and took a few minutes to scroll through her phone until Noah was done in the bathroom.

He tiptoed out and froze when he saw her. "I'm sorry, did I wake you?"

"My alarm was about to go off anyway." She got up and

pulled the curtains open. The sky was clear and starting to lighten as the sun came up. "I hope it stays clear while we explore the park. I think everything else is pretty much indoors."

She hurried through her morning routine. "It seems really weird to leave our suitcases here for the whole day. We don't even have to take our backpacks." She stopped and put a finger to her bottom lip. "Speaking of which. I need to buy another backpack or tote bag or suitcase or something. There's no way all my stuff is fitting in my suitcase to fly home."

"Yeah, I was wondering how you planned on getting all those bags out of the car and onto the plane."

"I may have gone a little bananas with the blankets." And she had. She'd gotten blankets for Erin, her mom, herself, Wyatt, her grandparents, and small lap blankets for Megan, Sarah, Julie, and Phyllis. Not to mention all the other souvenirs like magnets and postcards and chocolate bars. And a gorgeous sweater she couldn't resist, even though it's July.

"I keep thinking I should get a blanket for Mom. She'd love that pastel plaid one you bought."

"I'm sure there are plenty of places to pick one up today. I want to check out the St. Stephen's Green Shopping Centre."

"Let's grab breakfast and get going."

They went to the restaurant in the hotel and filled plates from the extensive buffet.

She dug into her breakfast. "I'm going to miss the Irish way of having a huge breakfast to start the day, and then smaller meals later. It makes so much sense to front load fuel for the body heading into the day."

"I agree."

"I'm also going to make it a point to incorporate grilled tomatoes into breakfast at home. Maybe on weekends. This could be my new weekend thing. Massive breakfast followed by… whatever." She shrugged, spearing another tomato with her fork.

"Sounds good to me."

They ate quickly, anxious to get out and exploring while the sky was blue and clear.

St. Stephen's Green was a mere three-minute walk from the hotel. They crossed the road and went through the wrought iron gates to the park. It was seven o'clock, and the park only had a handful of visitors. Joggers and women pushing baby strollers, taking advantage of the beautiful morning weather.

They followed the paved paths, surrounded by lush greenery, stopping to read plaques posted at the statues that dotted the park.

Noah said, "I was—" just as Becky spotted the bridge and said, "There it is!"

"Sorry, I cut you off. What were you saying?"

He shrugged and said, "Let's go check out your bridge."

The small stone bridge arched over the pond.

"What happened here? In your movie?" Noah asked as they came to a stop at the top of the bridge.

Becky thought about it for a minute, then shook her head. "I really can't remember. They were talking, I think after the wedding they crashed. I just remember thinking it was such a pretty place to be."

Noah looked around. "It really is."

Ducks dotted the pond, adding an occasional quack to the conversation.

"So I was kind of thinking."

"Uh oh," she teased.

"I know how when we started this trip I had some, I don't know, preconceived notions about you, and how this would go, and I really appreciate that you set me straight on all that."

She stood still, just watching him and listening, having no idea where this was going.

"It was definitely eye-opening when you told me I don't know you, and you were so right." He looked out over the water and ran a hand through his hair. "I feel like on this trip we've gotten to know each other, and from my end it's been a great trip. They always say, if you want to get to know someone, take a road trip with them. I think a week-long road trip through two countries qualifies. Especially in a car the size of a cereal box."

"I should think so."

"I've had a really good time getting to know you. Like, the real you, not the you I had made up in my head. Wow, that sounds crazy. And I was thinking, maybe, if you're on the same page, we could continue getting to know each other when we get back home. If not, that's totally okay. I don't want to make our last day weird or anything."

"I would really, really like that. This trip has been amazing, and I wouldn't have wanted to be here with anyone else."

"Really?"

"Really."

His smile lit up his entire face.

She glanced around. By some miracle, they were alone on the bridge, in one of the most beautiful places in the world. "Are you going to kiss me now?"

"I would really, really like to."

Becky leaned up on her toes, her palms against his chest. He lowered his head and kissed her, and it was every bit as magical as she'd dared to hope.

Chapter Thirty-Three

Lincoln was right. Noah was living out a cheesy romcom, and he was here for every bit of it.

He kissed her again, and something in his chest just clicked into place. It wasn't the Becky he'd carried a torch for since they were kids. It was her. This woman in his arms. The Becky he'd gotten to know for real over the past week. The Becky he'd been stuffed into a tiny car with. The Becky who was patient and adventurous, but couldn't stand being late. The Becky who would eat fish and chips for every meal for the rest of her life–with grilled tomatoes for breakfast-if she could.

She was nothing like the girl he'd never actually known, but created in his mind.

No, she was better. So, so much better.

He had to hand it to the Ladies' Society. They had a knack for pairing people up.

"…center?"

"I'm sorry, what?"

She shook her head at him. "I said, do you want to walk over to the shopping center? Hopefully I can find a bag suitable for checking, and I bet you can find a blanket for your mom."

"Sounds good." He couldn't stop grinning like an idiot at the feel of holding her hand as they walked. Best Day Ever.

The shopping center was only a short walk away. Inside, Becky found a hard-sided rolling suitcase on clearance for cheap. It was the most obnoxiously Irish-touristy suitcase possible, with glossy shamrocks and depictions of the Cliffs of Moher and Celtic knot designs all over it.

"It's really tacky," she said. "But I kind of love it."

At one of the shops, he did find a pastel plaid wool blanket his mother would absolutely love, and he found a necklace for Lilly with a four-leaf clover pendant made with a Celtic knot design.

Just as he turned, a bracelet caught his eye. It was a dainty silver charm bracelet with a shamrock, a Celtic knot, a Claddagh, a tree of life, and a tiny map of Ireland and Northern Ireland. Between each charm dangled a round emerald-colored stone. It wasn't terribly expensive, but he wasn't sure if it was too soon or too presumptuous to buy jewelry as a gift.

He caught a glimpse of her across the shop, and he was sold.

They'd just left the shopping center with their purchases and were taking pictures at Fusilier's Arch headed back into St. Stephen's Green when his phone vibrated with an incoming call.

He grinned. "It's Lilly." He stepped off to the side of the pathway, realizing as he answered that it was only four thirty for Lilly. "Hey, sweetheart—"

"Daddy, I'm scared."

Her words ripped through him like a knife. "Lilly? What's wrong? What's going on?"

"I don't know what to do."

He let Becky steer him to a bench. "Where are you?"

She sobbed. "I'm at an airport."

"What?"

She started talking, but he couldn't understand a word she was saying through her tears.

"Lil, Lil, baby, slow down, I can't understand you. Take a breath. Are you somewhere safe?"

She choked a sob. "Yeah?"

"Do you know where you are?" His heart pounded and his fist clenched against his leg.

"I'm at an airport, but it's different than the one she picked me up at. It's so big and I don't know where to go. Daddy, I don't know what to do."

His heart shattered. She was scared, and he was four thousand miles away.

"Okay. Is it a big airport?"

She sniffled. "Yeah. It's so big I don't know where to go."

"Is there a sign? Maybe a security person or someone at a counter?" An idea suddenly came to him. "Hang on, baby, let me check the location finder for your phone." He tapped through his apps, praying the call didn't disconnect, and desperately glad he'd made it a non-negotiable requirement of Lilly having her own cell phone.

The app pulled up a map, zeroing in on her location.

"Okay, sweetheart, this says you're at the Miami International Airport. Does that sound right?"

She sniffled again. "Yeah."

"Why are you at the airport? Do you have a ticket? Do you have your ID?"

She choked out, "She just woke me up and said it was too much, she couldn't do it, so she told me to pack my stuff and I didn't know where we were going and we drove up and she just told me to get out of the car and I don't know what to do."

"Everything's going to be okay. We're going to get you home. Is your phone charged?"

"Yeah."

"Okay, let me find a map of the airport."

Becky had her phone open and unlocked. "Miami?"

He nodded.

She typed in the airport and pulled up a map. "Level two is where the ticketing and check-in is."

"Alright, there should be big numbers on the walls some-where that tell you what level you're on. I'm going to need you to go to level two."

"I don't see any numbers."

Before he could even think of it, Becky was searching for tickets.

"Is there a counter anywhere? With someone who works there?"

"Yeah, there's a lady working."

"Can you ask her how to get to level two?"

"Okay." Her voice was small, and he wanted so badly to transport himself there and take care of her. A moment later, she said, "Excuse me, how do I get on level two?"

A friendly voice said, "You're on level two, sweetie. To check in, you'll go down this hallway here and turn right. The check-ins are all the way at the end."

"Okay. Thank you."

"Good job. I'm seeing what tickets they have available and we'll get you home. Sit tight, okay?" He handed his phone to Becky, then scrolled through Becky's phone and found a ticket from Miami to Harrisburg with a layover in Atlanta that would take off at seven fifteen. Perfect.

Ouch. Not so perfect. The ticket to send Lilly to Florida was

$200. The ticket to get her home on such short notice? $1250. He pulled his credit card out of his wallet and tried to get his hands to stop shaking enough to purchase the ticket.

On the checkout screen, a little wheel spun and spun, then finally popped up with an "Ooops! Something went wrong!" message.

Immediately, a second call beeped on his phone.

Becky said, "The caller ID says Fraud department?"

"Shit." He accepted the call, which disconnected his call with Lilly.

"Hello!"

"Hello, Mr. Spencer. This is Mastercard fraud prevention with a courtesy call. Your card was just used for a major purchase in Miami, but our records indicate you are in Ireland. We've blocked the charge and will issue you a new card."

"No! It's a legitimate charge. This needs to go through." His entire body shook and he thought he might get sick.

"Sir?" The voice was confused.

"Yes. I am in Ireland. Yes, I am sitting in Dublin right now, personally trying to purchase a plane ticket from Miami. It's an emergency."

"Oh." Sounds of keyboard clicking filled the line.

He gave the website name he was buying the ticket from, the amount, and verified his identity, all while his phone vibrated with incoming calls from Lilly that he couldn't answer.

Finally, the charge went through. He hung up with the credit card company, and called Lilly back.

She was crying again.

"Lilly, I need you to put the airline's app on your phone."

When it had downloaded, he gave her the login credentials. "Next, make sure you have your phone and charger and passport and important stuff in your carryon, but no liquids and it can't be stuffed full or it won't fit the carryon measurements."

"My backpack just has my phone and tablet and stuff."

"Okay. You'll need to go to the ticket counter and show them your ticket in the app. They'll take your suitcase and then you'll go through security, just like you did at the other airport. Security will look at your passport and boarding pass on your phone." He'd feel marginally better once she was through security. Not that it was *safe*, but it was certainly safer than being in the lobby with people who hadn't passed through security.

"I'm in line."

"You're doing great, baby. I'm so proud of you."

By some miracle, she got checked in without a hitch and they directed her to security. He stayed on the phone with her until she found her gate. He double checked she was in the right place and said, "I need to call Grandma and Grandpa and let them know what's going on."

She burst into tears again. "No, no, please don't hang up."

"Okay, okay, I won't hang up. It's okay. I'll stay on the phone with you until you board." He hoped both their batteries would last that long. If the flight was at seven fifteen, they'd probably begin boarding at six thirty or six forty-five. Right now, it was only five thirty-seven.

Becky held her phone out. It was open to the keypad. "Use mine."

"Lilly, I'm going to call them on Becky's phone so I don't have to hang up."

Her crying was breaking his heart.

"I'm going to put Becky on with you for a minute, okay?"

"Yeah."

He swapped phones with Becky and dialed his parents.

Both of their phones went straight to voicemail. He tried again. Voicemail. Then he called his sister.

"Hello?" She sounded groggy and irritated.

It took a second to realize he wasn't calling her from his own number. "Nat, it's me."

"Noah? Do you know what time—"

"I can't get ahold of Mom and Dad. I need to talk to them like now."

The annoyance dropped from her voice. "What's wrong?"

"Lilly's at the airport in Miami. I got her a ticket home, but I obviously can't—" his voice broke. He sucked in a hard breath. He didn't have time to deal with emotion right now. "I need to…"

"What?! Where is she flying into? Harrisburg? Baltimore? Philly?"

"Harrisburg."

"No problem. When does she get in?"

For the life of him, he couldn't remember what time she'd be landing in Harrisburg. "I… she leaves Miami at seven fifteen, so I… Nat, I can't… it's here, hang on." He looked at the phone, but he was holding Becky's phone and the flight information was on his.

Natalie was moving around, and he heard clicking. "I see three flights coming in from Miami. One comes in at eleven fifty-two, one around two, and one this evening. Which airline?"

He told her and she said, "Does she have a layover?"

"In Atlanta."

"It's definitely this one, then, coming in before noon. Don't worry, Noah, we'll be there to get her."

He hadn't had time to worry about the end of the trip. He was still panicking about getting her on the first flight. And then getting her through the layover. "Thanks." He half-heard Becky making small talk.

"I'll keep my phone on me at all times. I'll try Mom and Dad, but they probably have their phones off until seven. You know what? I'll just get dressed and go over there right now. Keep me posted."

"Thank you."

"Love you. Try not to worry."

"Love you, too."

He hung up and swapped phones with Becky again. "Aunt Nat's going to get Grandma and Grandpa. They'll pick you up at the airport when you get to Harrisburg."

"Okay." Her voice sounded stronger and less tearful.

"You doing okay?"

"Better."

He wanted to interrogate her on what happened. No, that wasn't quite true. He wanted to go to Miami, find Lilly's worthless piece of crap mother, and… No use going down that road. He'd deal with her later. "You'll have to change planes in Atlanta. Do you know what you'll have to do?"

"I'm not sure."

He kept his voice calm and light as he explained what would happen in Atlanta. He hoped and prayed there were no delays on her Miami flight, because the layover was tight. She'd need to get to her next gate and on the plane quickly. He tried to emphasize that without making her any more nervous.

The air chilled, and raindrops began to fall, gently at first.

Becky popped open an umbrella and held it over both of them as he talked to Lilly.

In the background, he heard the first boarding announcement. It was six thirty-five, Lilly's time. Eleven thirty-five their time.

By six forty-five, Lilly was in her seat on the plane. He told her to put her backpack in the overhead compartment and fasten her seatbelt. She sounded much calmer now that she was on her plane.

She said, "I'll call you if I need help in Atlanta."

"Of course. Just remember to check your app as soon as you land so you know what gate to go to. Sometimes they change. You're doing great. I love you."

"Love you, Daddy." She disconnected the call.

The rain was turning into a downpour, drenching everything except the little circle they were huddled in on their bench. He felt bad about Becky's new suitcase getting soaked, but there wasn't much he could do about the weather.

It felt like there wasn't much he could do about anything.

/ Chapter Thirty-Four

Becky felt horrible as Noah hung up the phone and dropped his head into his hands. She did her best to hold the umbrella steady over both of them as the rain got heavier.

She let a few minutes go by, then said, "How about we take this stuff back to the room and get your phone charged?"

He nodded and took the umbrella so she could wiggle the new suitcase out from under the bench. She'd already put all their bags from the shopping center into it, so hopefully nothing had gotten wet.

They walked back to the hotel. Poor Noah looked shell-shocked, and Becky had no idea what to say to help him. They were in the elevator when his phone buzzed.

"Dad, hey. … Yeah, we're getting back to the room now. … I'll send you the flight info as soon as we get inside. … I have no idea, and Lilly was already upset enough. All she said was that her–*Danae*–said she couldn't handle it and dropped Lilly off at the airport. … No, I just got off the phone with Lilly and we headed back here to the hotel. … I appreciate it. … Love you too."

Becky unlocked the door and went over to sit on her bed.

"Thank God my parents can get her." He crawled onto his bed and plugged his phone into the charger. He leaned against the headboard and swiped across his phone. After a few minutes, he scowled. "There's no way to get home earlier. There's a flight that leaves before ours but it has a six-hour stop in Paris and gets in later than ours. I don't even have any way of knowing if her flight's on time or if she gets delayed until she calls me from Atlanta."

She gently told him, "There's a flight tracker app. You can see where the plane is in real time."

"Oh. Thanks." He installed the app and entered the flight information. "It says her plane is on time, on schedule."

"Did you text the flight info to your dad?"

"Doing it now. And the name of this app. I'm sure Mom'll want to keep an eye on it, too."

She plugged her phone in, too. Might as well keep them both charged, just in case. She wasn't sure what to say or do, so she just waited.

"Her flight is taking off."

"Great."

He sighed and ran a hand down over his face. "I guess it doesn't do any good to sit here all day. Did you want to go see whatever stuff was on the list?"

She knew his heart wasn't in it, so she decided to pivot away from the more fun, interactive places she'd wanted to see. "There's an art gallery and a museum right up the street. Maybe get some lunch and then hit those? I figure they're low key and we can leave if we need to."

"Sure."

They grabbed a quick lunch at KC Peaches, a charming little café half a block away, then walked to the National Museum of Archeology.

They were halfway through the museum when Noah checked the app and said, "They're landing right now. I'm going to walk outside and make sure I don't miss a call. You finish going through."

"Okay," she said, but he was already walking away. She walked around, half-heartedly looking at the exhibits. Twenty minutes later, she gave up and went out to find Noah sitting on a bench, talking to someone on the phone.

She hovered nearby, awkwardly trying not to look at him, but trying to keep an eye out for when he finished his call.

Eventually he did finish and waved her over. "She's on her connecting flight."

"Good. Now you can breathe easy."

"Easi*er*."

He seemed a little less stressed as they walked through the National Museum of Natural History, an odd little museum with taxidermied animals that had been restored from the Victorian era. Then they visited the National Gallery for a few hours, which housed some incredible artwork. Unfortunately, it was hard to appreciate with Noah's daughter in a tough situation.

They were most of the way through the art gallery when Noah's phone buzzed.

He quietly answered and immediately wilted in relief. "Oh, thank God. Let me talk to her." He walked to a corner where no one was looking at art.

Becky stared at the painting in front of her, but wasn't really seeing it.

Noah came back over to her and said, "She's with my parents. They're taking her to eat and then taking her home."

She could only imagine his relief. Words were inadequate, so she reached over and hugged him. He squeezed her back. "Can we still do the Jameson whiskey class?"

It was five o'clock.

"Yes, if we hurry." She ordered a taxi and twenty minutes later, they were being deposited at the Jameson Distillery.

The distillery was beautiful, done in stone and wood and steel, with glass cases housing row after row of green whiskey bottles. They even had giant 5-tier chandeliers made from the green bottles.

Noah was definitely subdued, but he seemed to enjoy their hour-long class on mixing whiskey cocktails. By the end, he was definitely feeling better, after sampling the cocktails he'd created.

Since they were both a little tipsy from the whiskey and it was getting late, they took a taxi to the Guinness Storehouse and got in just before closing time. They bought some souvenirs and then went to the Temple Bar, the iconic red pub that seemed to be a required stop in Dublin.

The pub was crowded. Musicians were on the stage, music filling the whole building. Becky was more concerned with Noah. He fidgeted, tapping his fingers on the table. His leg bounced with unspent energy and he kept glancing toward the door.

"Do you want to head back to the hotel?"

He didn't hesitate. "Yes."

The evening was clear, so they opted to walk instead of ordering another cab. Becky hoped it would help Noah burn off some of the adrenaline that was keeping him on high alert. They walked mostly in silence.

"Hey, there's a Starbucks. We can grab coffee there for the trip to the airport in the morning."

He grunted, "Sure."

"I need to grab the shopping bags out of the car so I can get everything organized in my suitcase."

"Okay."

"I have your stuff from this morning in my new suitcase. Oh, I need to fill out the luggage tag, too."

"Yup."

She sighed and went quiet. They walked to the parking area, got their bags from the hatch, and went to their room without a word. Noah looked like himself, carrying the bags and opening the doors, but it felt like walking next to a zombie. She knew she'd be a mess in his place, and she hated feeling helpless to make anything better.

Becky set Noah's things on his bed while he was in the bathroom, then carefully packed her suitcases and took everything unnecessary out of her backpack because it would be manhandled in at least five security checkpoints. She glanced over the binder, but there was nothing they needed from there now, so she packed it in her new suitcase, between layers of wool blankets.

She took her shower and mentally went through a checklist for the morning. She'd have to remember to grab her phone charger and her toiletries from the bathroom. They'd eat breakfast, check out of the hotel, and go to the airport. They could check in to their flight from their phones, so bypassing that step would save them some time at the airport.

When she came out of the bathroom, Noah was already in bed, softly snoring.

She was glad he was able to sleep. He needed it. She tiptoed around, turning off the lights and climbing into her bed. Sleep eluded her. So many thoughts and emotions swirled around her mind. She was sorry to leave Ireland, but she couldn't wait to be home. She was looking forward to getting to know Noah back in Hickory Hollow, back in their normal lives, in their normal spaces, but he'd seemed so distant today.

She brushed the thought aside. Of course he was distant and sullen today. If Wyatt was in trouble four thousand miles away, she'd be losing her mind, even after he was safe in the arms of her parents.

Once they got home and he saw Lilly, he'd be fine and they could have their first real date.

Chapter Thirty-Five

Noah picked at his breakfast.

"Better eat up, it's a long day with crappy airplane food."

"Yeah, I know." She was right. He forced himself to eat most of the food on his plate. He was just so anxious to get home. He wanted to be beyond the airport, in the plane, in the air, heading home.

They cleared their plates and went back up to the room. Becky walked through, double checking that they'd gotten everything. Noah couldn't care less if he forgot anything aside from his passport. He had one thing on his mind. Getting home.

They checked out of the hotel and loaded everything in the car.

Becky started the car and said, "Last chance to make any stops in Dublin."

"Nah." He knew he was being short and moody, but he just itched to be home. Not even so much *home*, but to see Lilly with his own eyes and know that she's okay.

He did his part to help navigate out of the city, stop to fuel up the car, and get the car back to the rental area. From there, they gathered their luggage and checked in on their phones. They found their kiosk, printed their boarding passes and luggage tags, deposited them onto the carousel, and made their way through two interviews about their trip, and what felt like a hundred security checkpoints.

Becky insisted on two bathroom stops along the way. He tried not to show his annoyance. It wasn't like they'd get on the plane any faster if they didn't make the stops.

Once they were through the final security checkpoint, Becky got them large iced coffees and a bag full of snacks for the flight home.

He kept checking his phone, but there was nothing. Which made sense. It was ten o'clock for them, but only five at home. No one would be up. Still, he resisted the impulse to call and hear Lilly's voice. He settled for sending her a couple of text messages to let her know he was getting ready to board the plane and probably wouldn't get messages for several hours.

The flight was long, tiring, annoying, but the worst part was the hour and a half layover in Philadelphia. Home was so close, and so far. He paced back and forth until they were able to board the little plane.

He was glad Becky had reminded him mid-flight to change his phone's SIM card back to his original one.

They boarded a plane that felt like a miniature toy compared to the flight across the Atlantic. Finally, FINALLY, they landed in Harrisburg at a few minutes before four o'clock. Nine, Ireland time, which meant they'd been traveling for eleven hours. And they still had an hour-long drive home.

Weary, they walked through the airport, toward baggage claim.

He asked Becky, "Did you need a ride home?"

"No, my parents are here." She held up her phone and wiggled it back and forth. "I got about six hundred texts the second I took my phone off airplane mode."

They made the turn to the lobby, and Noah jerked to a stop.

Lilly spotted him and sprinted at him.

He caught her in a bearhug until she told him she couldn't breathe.

Tears blurred his vision. "Are you okay?"

"Yeah."

He pulled her in to his chest and walked over to his parents.

Becky was hugging her mom. She gave him a smile and led her parents down the escalator to baggage claim.

Noah said, "What are you guys doing here?" Not that he was complaining. He was ecstatic to see Lilly, but he hadn't expected to see her until he got all the way home.

"I knew you'd be chomping at the bit to see her," his mom said.

"I have been." He smoothed Lilly's hair.

"Let's get your suitcase," his dad said. "Did you have a good time?"

"Yeah, it was a good trip."

His mom nudged his arm. "Do you have a new girlfriend we should know about?"

"No." Despite the conversation he'd had with Becky on the bridge at St. Stephen's Green, he had to be there for Lilly. He couldn't afford any distractions from being a father. He never should have taken this trip and been so far away from her.

And he never should have let her go to Florida. He'd never forgive himself for that.

Chapter Thirty-Six

Becky grabbed Noah's suitcase off the carousel, then her fabulously tacky new suitcase. Her regular one took the long way around, but it finally popped out of the chute onto the conveyor. Halleluia, they'd gotten all their luggage without incident.

"Thanks." Noah came up beside her and grabbed the handle of his suitcase.

She put a hand on his arm and gently squeezed. "I'm really glad they brought her to pick you up."

"Yeah. Kind of silly since now we have to take two cars home, but I'm so relieved." He hadn't needed to say that. It was clear on his face that he felt a thousand times better since he'd seen his daughter in person.

She had to admit there was a little twinge of jealousy because she would love to be hugging Wyatt right now. "Give me a call tomorrow and we can make a plan to grab dinner next week or whatever."

"Yeah."

She wasn't sure if she expected a quick kiss or a hug or an

awkward handshake. What she did not expect was for Noah to just nod and walk away.

His mom gave a little wave as they walked out the sliding doors to the parking area.

"We're up in the parking garage," her dad said.

"Okay," she said absently as he grabbed the handles of her suitcases. She followed her parents up the escalator and down the hallway to the parking garage.

Her mom hugged her again as her dad put the suitcases in the back of their SUV. "So? I'm dying to hear everything."

"I'm dying for some caffeine. They're really stingy with drinks on the plane and the flight from Philly was too short to even have drinks." She jumped in the back seat and marveled at how much room she had.

"Are you hungry? Do you want to stop somewhere and eat?"

"You don't mind?"

"Not at all."

"I'd love to eat. All we've had were snacks and a sad sandwich with questionable meat about seven hours ago." Her stomach was still on Ireland time, where it was almost ten. They'd have eaten dinner at least four hours earlier. "Getting back on my regular schedule is going to be such a pain."

"What's the time difference?" her dad asked.

"They're five hours ahead, so it's ten o'clock there."

"No wonder you're hungry. Brian, just go to Cracker Barrel. They're quick."

"Okay."

Her mom said, "What was your favorite part of the trip?"

"Wow, that's a hard question to answer. Everything about it was amazing right up until yesterday. We made a big loop around the entire country. Two countries, actually. Did you know the *Titanic* was built in Northern Ireland?"

"It was? I thought it was built in England."

"Me, too, but it wasn't."

Even though she was tired and wanted nothing more than to eat, go home, and crawl into bed, she kept herself talking and telling her parents about her trip. She needed to stay up until at least ten o'clock, which would be three a.m. to her confused body, in order to shock her system back to a non-jetlagged state. At least it was Friday, so she had the weekend to be miserable and sleep-deprived and force herself back on track.

"Did you guys get to see any fireworks yesterday?"

"They don't really care about the Fourth of July in Ireland, Dad."

Her mom snickered.

He shook his head and laughed at himself. "Go ahead, laugh at me. I guess they wouldn't, would they?"

After they dropped her off at home, she dragged the suitcases to her laundry room and unpacked all her clothes directly into the washing machine. Then she piled her blankets and souvenirs on the kitchen table, to be dealt with tomorrow. She checked on Cheeto and Dorito, sent Veronica a text to let her know she'd gotten home, and scrolled aimlessly through social media.

She made it to nine o'clock, decided it was close enough, and crashed into bed.

By four thirty, she was wide awake, and there was no point in laying in bed. So she got up, did laundry, sorted the blankets and souvenirs, and made a grocery list.

The morning was already very warm, a stark contrast to the cool days in Ireland. Before it got unbearably hot, she took her laptop outside to the patio and started going through her pictures.

Megan would be proud. There were some incredible shots in here, mainly because of the subject and not any particular skill she had.

She meticulously sorted the photos into folders by day, then into subfolders by each stop. She even loaded all the photos from her phone, which meant all the selfies of her and Noah. She knew he'd freaked out over the Lilly situation, but she couldn't figure out what was going on with him beyond that. He'd barely said two words to her on the flight home, and then just walking away in the airport?

She chalked it up to him being stressed and sleep-deprived and so relieved to see Lilly with his own two eyes. She understood it, she really did. If it had been her, she would have been a hot mess, so she was cutting him a lot of slack.

The best course of action was probably to send him a text and then step back and leave it in his hands. After all, he'd waited for her since high school, surely she could wait a few days for him.

Chapter Thirty-Seven

Around nine, Noah's phone vibrated with an incoming picture of grilled tomatoes and a message.

A smiley face punctuated the message.

Unfortunately, Noah wasn't smiling at all. His finger hovered over the phone's keyboard, but he had trouble being the complete coward he was intending to be. If he heard her voice or worse, saw her in person, he wouldn't be able to do what he needed to do.

He typed a message, backspaced over it, typed it again, and backspaced. A dozen times or maybe more. Tormund jumped up on the kitchen table and batted at his arm.

"It's for the best."

The cat didn't buy his explanation, and neither did he. But he sent the message anyway.

"Whatcha doing?" Lilly bounded into the kitchen.

He clicked the phone off and shoved it in his pocket. "We need to have a talk."

She rolled her eyes and got a bottle of water out of the fridge before flouncing onto the chair opposite him. "What?"

"I need to know what happened. Everything. Every detail."

She deflated, picking at the label on her bottle. "What's it matter? I'm home now."

"It matters, Lillian."

Using her full name snapped her attention to him. "Fine."

He softened his voice and leaned toward her a little, putting his elbows on the table. "I know you don't want to talk about it, so let's just rip off the band-aid and get it over with, okay?"

She peeled a piece of the label off and sighed. "The first couple days were great. Like, we went to the mall and got matching clothes and watched movies and it was super fun. Then she started dropping me off at the mall with her credit card. Like, fine, she had to work or whatever. Then her boyfriend came around and he was such a fake. Fake accent, fake tan, fake gold jewelry. He was so gross and didn't want me around, so, like, she went to his place the one night and got mad because I DoorDashed food because she wasn't home."

His neck heated. "One night? She left you by yourself overnight?"

Her eyes shifted.

"More than once?"

Lilly shrugged. "It wasn't a big deal. Like I said, I ordered food and watched tv."

His jaw clenched. He took a few breaths. He didn't want Lilly to think he was mad at her, but he was ready to explode. "Go on."

"So when she got home she said I couldn't stay all summer,

which was fine, because the mall was like the only thing to do and it's not like I had any friends down there."

"Okay."

"I figured she'd call you. But I guess her boyfriend wanted to surprise her with a trip or something and she was yelling at me and I guess I shouldn't have yelled back at her, but I did." Her chin quivered. "We went to bed like *big* mad and she woke me up the next morning super early and told me she couldn't take it anymore and I had to go. She made me pack my stuff in like five minutes and I didn't even have room for all the stuff I got at the mall and we got in the car and she just drove me to the airport and I was crying and couldn't even read the signs and I didn't know where I was and she just made me get out of the car with my stuff and she just like drove off."

Noah leaned back and put his hands under the table so Lilly couldn't see them clenched into fists.

"Then I called you. I didn't know what to do."

"You did exactly the right thing." He had no idea how he controlled his tone.

"I didn't know what time it was in Ireland, but I called anyway."

He put his hands on the table and leaned forward again. "Hey. Twenty-four seven, three sixty-five. I don't care what time it is, what day it is, where I am, or who I'm with. You can always, always, always call me. I'm your dad. That's my job."

Her eyes filled with tears. "But she's my mom. Isn't that her job, too?"

He rounded the table and got on his knees beside her chair. She leaned into him as the tears began to flow.

Her little shoulders shook as he held her. So many emotions swirled around. He was relieved and grateful she was home safe. He was anxious and scared for all the things that could have happened. And he was beyond livid and disgusted at his ex-wife.

As if summoned, Lilly's phone rang with an incoming call. Noah saw "Mom Danae" on the screen and snatched it up.

"Dad, wait!"

He said, "Lilly."

The firmness in his voice made her back down.

He stabbed at the phone as he stormed outside and closed the door behind him.

"Hey, Lil." Danae's chipper voice immediately infuriated him.

"What the hell is going on, Danae?"

She gasped. "Noah. This is Lilly's phone."

"You better tell me what happened. Now."

"What? Geoffrey wanted to go away for the weekend and Lilly had a massive attitude about it so I sent her home."

He pinched the bridge of his nose. "How exactly did that work, Danae?"

"Oh, come on. I knew she had your credit card. She was fine."

"Do you *have* a single functioning brain cell? You dropped a *child* off at a massive airport and drove away. Anything could have happened to her. Do you not see the news? Kids are snatched every day from situations just like this and trafficked."

"You're being a little dramatic. I waited until she was inside before I totally left."

"Dramatic?" He sputtered, struggling to grasp how stupid and clueless she was being.

"Clearly she got home just fine. You don't have to be an asshole about it. Let me talk to Lilly."

"Absolutely not, are you out of your mind?"

"Don't play with me, Noah. I'll drag you into court for full custody."

He was sure his head was going to explode.

"Now let me talk to my daughter."

"Over my dead body." The sheer audacity was stunning.

"You sure you want to do this? I'll show how you're keeping me from her. Parental alienation. Geoffrey's a lawyer. Put Lilly on the phone or you'll be a holidays-only dad so fast your head will spin."

Noah's teeth clenched so hard his jaw hurt. He ground out, "I dare you."

"What?" She clearly hadn't expected that response.

"I'd *love* to go to court and collect all that back child support you owe. In the meantime, why don't you get your lawyer boyfriend to explain how many felonies it is to abandon a child."

"Oh, is this how you want to do it?"

"Curtis Stroehman."

"What?"

"Curtis Stroehman. Write it down. He's my lawyer and from this moment on, since you threatened me, any contact you want to have with Lilly or me will be through him."

"You can't be serious. I can contact my daughter any time I want. You can't keep me away from her."

He recited Curtis's phone number.

She screeched, "Put my daughter on the phone. Now!"

"Did you get that number? You're gonna need it."

She tried a different tactic. "Noah, I'm sorry. I know it looks bad, but I knew she was okay or I wouldn't have left her. Do you really think I would have put her in danger? Of course I wouldn't. We don't really need to get the courts involved. I just want to talk to her. Maybe she can come back down for a week or two in August."

He could not possibly have heard those words. Before he could respond with a string of shouted curse words, he simply hung up. He blocked the number and deleted the contact from Lilly's phone. No more unsupervised contact.

He went back inside. Lilly was still at the kitchen table, glaring. She yanked her phone out of his hand. "What did she say?" She scrolled. "What did you do? You deleted her out of my phone? You can't do that! You have no right!" She screamed and sobbed and ran toward the stairs. He felt every stomped footstep in his chest, followed by a door slam that vibrated through the whole house.

He sat down and looked at his own phone. Becky had texted back with a single word.

Why??

He didn't have the energy–or the guts–to respond.

Chapter Thirty-Eight

The ten days before Wyatt's return crawled until it was finally the Tuesday of his return. She'd taken another vacation day to be home when he got back. Becky hadn't heard a single word from Noah. How ironic that he'd carried a torch for her for years and now she was the one with feelings and he was the one who was out of reach.

A door slammed in the driveway just before lunchtime. She yanked the door open and was across the porch and down the steps as Wyatt jumped out of the back seat and flew over to her. She opened her arms, and he flung himself into them. They squeezed each other so tight it was a wonder either of them could breathe.

"I missed you so much!"

He made a choking noise and pushed back. "You're squashing my guts."

She laughed and set him down. "Did you have fun? I can't wait to hear all about the ruins."

"It was so awesome! Veronica's mom knows a lot about the Mayans."

"That's great. I bet you two had a lot to talk about."

Veronica and Joey were out of the car, unloading Wyatt's suitcase and backpack from the trunk.

"I hafta go see Cheeto and Dorito."

Becky said, "Whoa, there, skippy. Say goodbye to your dad and Veronica."

He heaved an exaggerated sigh/groan, but hugged them both before sprinting into the house to check on his fish.

"How was everything?"

Joey's expression was stern. "Mostly good. But please keep in mind that I am Wyatt's other parent."

"What are you even talking about?" She had zero patience for his nonsense.

"You can't give permission for him to go off on a bus in a strange country without consulting me."

"Stop it. I gave my permission. If you said no, that would have been the end of it. Two yesses, one no. That's how this is supposed to work."

He snapped, "I just don't like the idea of you two going behind my back and having discussions without me. You're my co-parent with Wyatt, and she is my wife. There's no need for comparing notes or swapping stories about me or whatever."

Becky's face scrunched in disbelief. "This will come as a complete shock to you, but we don't discuss you at all. Every conversation we've had is about Wyatt. You and I are co-parents, but Veronica is his stepmom now, and that means she's part of Wyatt's team."

"Great. So you don't mind if he calls her Mom."

"Joey." Veronica said sharply.

"See? This is what I don't want." He flicked his finger back and forth between the two women. "The two of you ganging up on me."

"Oh, for crying out loud, knock it off. Veronica, glad you

had a nice trip." She grabbed Wyatt's suitcase and backpack and headed for the house. Best of luck to Veronica dealing with Joey's immature self-centered narcissism.

He called after her, but she ignored him.

She found Wyatt in his bedroom, his face barely an inch away from the side of the tank, talking to Cheeto and Dorito. She sat on his bed.

"I think they missed you."

The fish were close to the glass, their little mouths popping open and closed, watching Wyatt as if they were intently listening to him.

"I missed them. I saw a bunch of lizards and they were cool, but fish are better." He bounded over and took a flying leap at her.

She caught him, and they rolled backwards onto the bed, laughing.

"I missed you, too, Mommy!" He wrapped his little arms around her neck and squeezed.

"I missed you more."

"Nuh-uh. I missed you more."

"Nope, I missed you more." She blew raspberries on his neck, making him squeal with delight.

"Nooooo, Mommy, I missed *you* more."

They settled back against the pillows for a snuggle.

"What was your favorite part of your trip?" Becky asked.

"VeeVee's mom and I went on a bus for like a *thousand* miles to see Uxmal. It was even better than Chicken Itza."

She stifled a laugh at his mispronunciation. "What was better about it?"

He launched into a lengthy explanation of the two Mayan sites, but his real reason came at the end. "And there wasn't a bunch of people all over the place."

"Did you take lots of pictures?"

He nodded against her shoulder. "I took ten hundred million pictures. Did you take lots of pictures? Did you see a lot of castles?"

"I did see a lot of castles. But I only took six hundred million pictures. Maybe later we can put all your pictures on the computer so I can see them."

"Okay." He yawned.

"Do you want to take a little nap while I make lunch?"

"No. I'm not sleepy." He yawned again. His eyes were red and getting heavy.

She extracted herself from his arms and got off the bed. "I'm going to make lunch, you come down after you relax a few minutes."

He nodded, but was fast asleep before she made it to the door.

<h1 style="text-align:center">Chapter Thirty-Nine</h1>

"Dad, did you sign the permission slip?"

"For what?"

Lilly made an exasperated grunt and rolled her eyes, hard. "Field hockey. How many times do I have to say the same thing over and over and over?" She rolled her hands for emphasis.

It had been three weeks since the call with Danae, and Lilly still hadn't forgiven him for blocking her mother from her phone. Knowing it was the right thing to do was little comfort when faced with the sort of venom only a teenage girl can spew.

"Yes, your majesty, it's signed and clipped to the board, right in front of your eyeballs, if you'd care to look."

"Whatever." She ripped the slip off the bulletin board and shoved it into her backpack.

Noah shook his head. Great. Another weekend of slamming doors and eyerolls.

She stood by the door, tapping her foot. "Well? Are you taking me or what?"

"Taking you where?"

She sneered, "Um, hockey practice? Duh."

"Hey, take the attitude down a few notches."

"Whatever. I can't wait to move to Florida and have a little freedom."

He didn't take the bait. Florida was her new go-to for getting under his skin. He drove her to the school and gladly dropped her off for practice. She jogged across the field to where the other girls were congregating with their sticks and attitudes.

Good. Maybe a few hours of running up and down the field would help improve her mood.

He stopped by Caretti's Coffee Shop to treat himself to some sugar and caffeine. He deserved it, right?

"Hey, stranger."

He couldn't help but smile at his sister. Natalie was sitting at a small table, drinking coffee and doing something on her iPad. "Hey."

She moved her big purse off the chair for him to sit down with his coffee. "How's it going?"

"Not great," he sighed. "Lilly's still ticked. I don't get it. Danae dumped her, and she's mad at me for blocking her."

"It's a good thing."

"I don't see how."

Natalie leaned forward and put a hand on his arm. "It's safe to be mad at you. She's always on pins and needles with Danae. They had one small argument and Danae pulled that stunt. Lilly probably doesn't even realize it, but she's testing you. Seeing how mad she can be before you abandon her, too."

"I would never—"

"Of course not. How about I call her and offer to take her school shopping later? That'll get you out of each other's hair for a few hours."

"That's why you're my favorite sister."

"Yeah, yeah. Have you heard from Becky?"

He looked down at his cup.

"Noah. Don't tell me you still haven't talked to her."

His silence was answer enough.

Natalie shook her head. "I can't believe you just ghosted her. So what happened? She didn't live up to the imaginary Becky in your head from high school?"

"No." He scowled. "That's not it."

"Then what? You got to know her and it turned out you weren't that into her?"

He fiddled with his cup, trying to ignore her pointed stare.

"Oh, for Pete's sake. You got to know her on this trip, you're crazy about her, she's finally totally into you, and you ghost her because your psychotic ex dumped Lilly off, and now you have to be martyr dad."

His gaze snapped to meet his sister's. "Martyr?"

"Yeah. Martyr. You devote every waking moment to Lilly at the expense of yourself."

"That's kind of my job as a father."

"No." She shook her head. "Noah, you're an amazing father. Your job is to show Lilly what normal looks like. That yes, of course you put her safety and security first. But also that you're a person with interests and relationships. You've spent her entire life trying to compensate for the fact that her mother is a trash human being. That's a lot of pressure for a kid."

"Pressure?" That made no sense. He spent his life protecting her from that sort of pressure.

"I'm asking this with no judgment, just something to think about. Did you tell Lilly that you weren't going to see Becky because you have to focus on her?"

That stung because he'd definitely told her he was here for her, even if that meant not seeing Becky. "What does that have to do with anything?"

"From Lilly's perspective, she caused Danae to abandon her. And now from her perspective, she caused you to give up someone you really care about."

"That's not what it is."

"The mind of a teenage girl is a complicated thing."

"What are you suggesting?"

"Take a step back. Becky's a mom. She understands better than anyone that the kid comes first. But she was willing to make a little room in her life for you. Do you think that would come at the expense of her son?"

"Of course not."

"You should talk to her." Natalie sat back and took a sip of coffee. "Of course, it might not matter, considering the crappy way you've handled the situation. She might not even want to talk to you at this point."

"Thanks, Nat."

She shrugged. "Three weeks with no contact? I wouldn't answer a guy at this point. You've got yourself an uphill battle."

"Then why should I even try?"

"Because she's worth it." She leaned forward again and pinned him with her stare. "And so are you."

<h1 style="text-align:center">Chapter Forty</h1>

The second Saturday of August was clear and bright and hot. So very, very hot. Becky's sundress stuck to her as soon as she got out of the car. Her hair had been horribly uncooperative, so she pulled it back into a smooth ponytail. Not quite the look she'd wanted, but wearing it down wasn't an option when the mercury topped out at just over a hundred. At least her date didn't mind.

She'd gotten a brilliant idea and conspired with Erin to carry out her plan at the wedding. One of the Ladies was about to get a taste of her own matchmaking medicine.

Thankfully, the huge pavilion had ceiling fans that created a nice breeze. Filmy white curtains blocked the harshest bit of the setting sun. Rows of white chairs were set up facing the front of the pavilion. The back half was set up with tables and chairs for the reception dinner.

"I don't think I can keep this jacket on much longer," Thomas said.

Becky put a hand on his arm. "It's like a thousand degrees. Take it off."

"There she is." His voice was breathless.

"Here we go." Becky marched over to Ruth, practically dragging Thomas with her. She feigned innocence. "Ruth, I have someone I'd like you to meet."

Ruth turned and gasped. She quickly composed herself. "My goodness. Thomas. How lovely to see you."

"Lovelier to see you, Ruth."

Becky stepped back as the older woman blushed. "I'll let you two catch up."

From the way they were looking at each other, she was pretty sure neither had heard her.

Becky walked away and slid into a seat next to Sarah. They'd just spent the morning together at work. "Long time, no see."

"I'd give you a big sarcastic hug, but it's too flipping hot."

Rowan, Sarah's fiancé, fanned his face in agreement.

The chairs filled, and Becky caught a glimpse of Noah on the other side of the room. Her heart skipped a beat. She hadn't seen or spoken to him since they left the airport a month earlier. He looked *really* good. And he was alone. She wasn't sure how to feel about either of those things.

In a small break from tradition, everyone stood as Greg was walked to the altar by his parents. His dad looked healthy and strong, thanks to the kidney Greg had given him. A moment later, Erin was escorted to her husband-to-be by both of her parents.

Instead of attendants, their parents remained standing with them as they exchanged vows and became husband and wife. Applause erupted as they shared their first kiss as a married couple.

The small crowd was directed to the round dinner tables. Ruth and Thomas were seated together as Erin's contribution to the setup. Becky was seated next to Sarah on one side. The smile froze on her face as she read the card for the seat on her other side. It shouldn't have been a surprise that Noah was assigned that spot, and she knew full well Erin had planned that, too.

He hesitated before he pulled the chair back.

Sarah glared daggers in his direction.

"Hey," he said once he was seated.

"Hello."

"You look great."

"Thank you." She straightened the perfectly straight silverware in front of her.

"How have you been?"

Sarah muttered on her other side, "Laaaaaaame."

Becky lightly elbowed her. "Fine."

"How was Wyatt's trip?"

"Good."

"Did his soccer start yet? Lilly's field hockey started last week."

"Yes." She wasn't enjoying the short answers, but she didn't really feel the need to make the conversation easier on him.

Servers placed their roasted chicken meals in front of them. The other two chairs at their table remained empty, despite the name cards.

"This looks good."

She didn't answer.

"Not quite as good as fish and chips, though, huh?"

She poked at one of the tiny rosemary potatoes and kept her voice low. "Can we not do this?"

"What? Conversation?"

"Yeah. Conversation. Inside jokes like we're friends."

"Aren't we?"

Sarah snorted. "With friends like that," she mocked.

Rowan shushed her.

The glazed carrots were perfectly cooked, so she focused her attention on those.

They were halfway through the meal when the other two seats were occupied. By Millie and Gertie. Becky wanted to crawl under the table and hide.

Gertie sat beside Noah, and Millie took the spot beside her nephew, Rowan.

The servers hustled over with their plates.

Gertie shook her napkin out and placed it in her lap. "Tell us all about Ireland."

Becky waited for a beat, hoping for a meteor or maybe a drunken brawl to distract everyone. Nope. Nothing. She said, "Ireland was wonderful. One of the most beautiful places I've ever seen."

"Did you two have a good time?" Gertie pressed.

"It was an amazing trip," she tried to deflect.

"Very romantic, all that lush greenery and castles. The perfect place to fall in love."

That stung. Yes, Ireland had been the perfect place to fall in love.

Chapter Forty-One

Noah saw Becky go stiff. Did that mean…? Did she…? Had she…? No, surely not. It wasn't possible, was it? Blood pounded behind his ears. Was it actually possible that Becky had started falling for him in Ireland? He'd messed up even bigger than he thought, hadn't he?

"Excuse me," she said, getting up from the table.

Sarah glared at him.

He shifted uncomfortably as Gertie stared at him, waiting for an answer to a question he hadn't fully heard because his head was spinning. "I'm sorry, what?"

"I said it would be a lovely place for a honeymoon trip. Too bad Erin and Greg weren't able to use it. Although I suppose they might have chosen somewhere else."

"Sure. I…"

"It's wonderful that you and Becky could take the trip. Would have been such a shame for it to go to waste."

Sarah snorted again. He could physically feel her disdain rolling across Becky's empty chair at him. "Yeah, would have been a real shame for it to be *wasted*."

"Sarah," Rowan quietly said.

All around them, glasses clinked as guests tapped their silverware, demanding a kiss from the bride and groom. When the noise quieted, Erin's dad stood and raised his glass. He made a touching toast to his beloved daughter and the only man who could possibly be worthy of her. There was hardly a dry eye in the house, and by the time Greg's dad finished his toast about second chances and never taking the people you love for granted, even the staff working the event were in tears.

Millie dabbed at her eyes as Erin and Greg cut the cake. "And to think, the Ladies' Society had a hand in them getting together."

Gertie smiled at Rowan and Sarah. "We haven't gotten one wrong yet."

Sarah smiled at Rowan, then shot a glare at Noah. "There's always a first time."

Becky slid back into her chair. A moment later, slices of white cake with raspberry filling and creamy white icing were placed before them.

"This looks delicious," Gertie said. "Ruth outdid herself." She nudged Millie. "Did you see she's sitting next to Thomas?"

Millie beamed. "Oh, I definitely saw it."

As the cake disappeared, the music gradually got a little louder. While they had been eating, the chairs for the ceremony had been removed, clearing a dance floor.

Erin and Greg danced the first dance, then were joined by their parents and Avery and Alex, who'd been the behind-the-scenes maid of honor and best man. Then they invited the Ladies' Society ladies up to lead the Chicken Dance.

When the regular music started, Rowan nudged Sarah. "Let's dance."

She hesitated, looking at Becky and Noah.

"They're adults, babe. They'll be fine."

Sarah reluctantly got up and followed him, leaving Becky and Noah alone at the table.

They sat for a few long, uncomfortable minutes, watching the dance floor.

"I'm sorry," he said.

She looked at him, and his heart squeezed. He'd been selfish. Wrapped up in how long he'd carried a torch for her and she hadn't even known he existed, like that was her fault somehow. Then, when they went to Ireland and were getting to know each other, he hadn't considered she might develop feelings for him—not an old version of him she'd carried for decades, but feelings for the man he was today. Right now.

He had to make it up to her. If he was living in a romcom like Lincoln had said, he had to make a grand gesture and she'd forgive him, right? He could start with the perfect song. As if on cue, Madonna's *Crazy for You* blasted through the speakers.

"Would you like to dance?" He held out his hand. They'd dance, he'd explain how sorry he was, and they could start over.

Becky pulled her napkin off her lap and picked up her tiny purse. "No." She got up and walked away.

That was *not* how this was supposed to go.

Should he follow her? Chase after her? Grab the microphone and publicly declare his stupidity?

He drummed his fingers on the table. The DJ introduced the next song. As he talked, an idea began taking shape. He called Lilly, who helped him work out some details before she gave his plan her stamp of approval.

Sarah and Rowan came back to the table. Noah swallowed hard, steeling himself against Sarah's anger. "I need your help."

She glared and crossed her arms. "I'm listening."

Chapter Forty-Two

On Friday morning, as they opened the office, Sarah turned on the radio first thing. Becky raised an eyebrow. "You usually want the radio off. What are you doing?"

Sarah gave a noncommittal grunt.

Becky glanced at Julie, who shrugged and went back to the computer.

The first patient came into the office. Before Becky could greet them, Julie jumped up and waved them to her window.

Sarah reached over and slid Becky's window shut and turned the radio up a little.

"What is going on?"

Sarah pointed to the radio.

"Okay, folks, it's eight fifteen. News coming up at the bottom of the hour."

"What?"

Sarah pressed a finger to her lips. "I had nothing to do with this."

"With what?"

The DJ said, "Hollow 99 listeners, we get lots of song requests, but this morning we have a situation I've never had before. Noah has requested three songs for a very specific reason. Noah was very, very stupid–his words, not mine. After the trip of a lifetime, he ghosted, and I quote, 'the most amazing woman I've ever known.' Since he fully recognizes what he did, first up is *Unchained Melody* by the Righteous Brothers. For you young'uns out there, this is the theme song to the movie *Ghost*."

The song played while Becky sat, just staring at the radio.

The DJ came back on. "If you're just joining us, that was *Unchained Melody*, requested by Noah, who's trying to apologize for ghosting the perfect woman. Fitting for the situation, next up is Chicago's hit *Hard to Say I'm Sorry*. Mystery Woman, we hope you're listening."

While this song played, Becky stared holes into Sarah's head, but she refused to turn around and face her.

"Part three of this morning's saga, folks. Noah's third song request is one of my personal favorites from back in the day. Noah wants you to know he's sorry for everything, and he hopes you'll give him a chance to explain. If anyone has advice for Noah, head on over to our Facebook page and give us your ideas. Be nice. Here's the third song he requested. Good luck, buddy. Keep us updated."

Madonna's *Crazy for You* came on the air.

Becky's phone notifications went off like a machine gun.

"You were in on this?"

Sarah sighed and handed her the daily newspaper.

"What?"

"I had nothing to do with anything. I agreed to turn on the radio and hand you a newspaper. My involvement is done."

She scanned the front page of the newspaper. "What's the point of this?"

"Flip it over."

A full-page ad in bright green ink with a smattering of shamrocks declared, "BECKY, I'M SORRY. NOAH."

Julie gasped. "Do you know how much a full-page ad costs? He's going all out."

Just before noon, a delivery driver came in with two large pizzas. "Becky?"

"Yes, but we didn't order these," she argued.

The driver shrugged and set the boxes on the counter.

Sarah snagged the boxes and carried them to the break-room. "I'm not turning down pizza, even if I'm still mad at the guy. We *are* still mad, right?"

One of the pizzas was mushroom and olive, Becky's favorite. The mushrooms were placed on the pizza in the shape of a heart, while the olives made a shamrock.

The other pizza was pepperoni, which Sarah was already eating. "Mushroom and olive? That's disgusting."

Julie came in and grabbed a slice of pepperoni. "Smart, though. No one will ever steal your pizza."

"Are we going to call him?"

"No." She ate a slice of pizza. "I'll wait until—"

"You better come out here," Julie called from the front.

Becky and Sarah both rushed out to find a bouquet of shamrock balloons in the corner of the waiting room.

Sarah muttered, "He can lay off the Ireland theme. We get it."

Julie elbowed her. "It's sweet."

"Speaking of sweet, look outside." The Caretti's Coffee Shop van had pulled to the curb. Megan hopped out and got a box from the back. She brought it in and handed it to Becky with a huge grin.

The top of the box was a cellophane window, giving a perfect view of gourmet brownies and caramel squares that looked an awful lot like the ones they'd gotten at the Route 85

Drive Thru. He must have shown Jody pictures to have her replicate them.

The afternoon passed without any other deliveries. By the time they locked up at five o'clock, Becky had over a hundred messages. She shook her head and shoved her phone into her purse. She'd deal with them later.

Julie grabbed the balloons while she balanced the brownie box on her arm. Sarah locked up behind them.

They rounded the corner to the parking lot, and Becky stopped short. Noah was parked beside her car. He leaned against his car, one ankle crossed over the other, his hands in his pockets.

Sarah grabbed the brownie box, newspaper, and her keys from her hands. She worked with Julie to get the stuff into Becky's car, then they made a hasty exit. Which was hilarious, because Becky knew they were dying to see what was happening.

"Hi," she said.

"Hi." His mouth quirked up in a tentative smile. "Um, you might have heard that I'd like to apologize to you."

"Yeah, I think there was something about that. I'm not sure though, I was so busy today."

"I wanted to give you these myself." He reached into his car and pulled out a vase with a colorful bouquet of gerbera daisies.

"Thank you. These are my favorite."

"I asked your mom."

"My mom? You've involved the entire town in this."

"Not quite. I missed the guys who were filling potholes on 322 and I'm pretty sure the cashier at Prescott's wasn't listening at *all*."

"Maybe they heard it on the radio this morning. Or saw the paper."

He lifted his hands and crossed his fingers, then stuffed his hands back into his pockets. "Becky, I'm sorry. It hasn't been easy figuring out how to be a good dad and still having a life of my own. I had the best time in Ireland, and that's because I was with you. We made a great team, and I think we'd be a really good team here at home, too. Odds are very good that I'll screw up again somewhere along the way, but I can promise you that I won't ever ghost you or shut you out again."

She tucked a stray lock of hair behind her ear.

"Oh. And before you say anything, I have something I want you to have, regardless of how this goes." He leaned into his car and came back out with a small box that he handed her. "I got this at the shopping center in Dublin. I was going to give it to you on the bridge at St. Stephen's Green, but everything went to crap."

She lifted the lid and sucked in a breath. A delicate silver charm bracelet rested on a piece of tissue paper. "It's beautiful."

"Whatever happens, I want you to know that I loved our trip and spending time with you. I'm grateful you gave me the opportunity to get to know you and I'm really sorry I screwed it up when we got home."

She stared at the bracelet. "I like to think that if the situations were reversed, I would have handled it better. That I'd be super mature and do everything just right. But I think I'm just fooling myself. I'd have been clawing at the walls, trying to get home, and once I got back to my kid, everything else would get shoved by the wayside. It's not like we had made any kind of commitment to each other. We just vaguely talked about maybe dating once we got home. So I can understand how it all went the way it did. I don't ever expect to be *the* priority for you, but I do expect to be *a* priority."

"Done."

She looked up and met his gaze. She read his sincerity and his uncertainty. "Do you remember what I said to you on the bridge at St. Stephen's Green?"

"You said a lot of things. Refresh my memory."

She stepped closer to him. "I said, 'Are you going to kiss me now?'"

A smile spread across his face as he repeated his answer. "I would really, really like to."

She went up on her tiptoes and was very happy to discover that their second kiss was just as magical as their first.

Epilogue

July, Two Years Later
  Inishmore, Aran Islands, Ireland

The Doolin Ferry docked and the passengers spilled off, most of them shaky from the rocky ride. Becky was glad to get onto solid ground. Quite a few of the other travelers had unfortunately tossed their breakfasts overboard along the way. Thankfully, neither she, Noah, nor the kids had gotten sick on the journey. Hopefully when the ferry came back to pick them up at four, the seas would be calmer.

Noah rushed them off the dock and to the Aran Bike Hire before the rest of the group swarmed the establishment. A bit later, they were outfitted with bikes, helmets, and a map of the island.

"Here's the plan," he announced confidently. "We'll bike to the Poll na bPéist, then the Aran Sweater Market, check out some views along the way, then loop around back to eat and be back to the ferry."

Lilly groaned and stuck her tongue out. "I don't even know what that is."

Becky stifled a snicker as Noah described how Poll na bPéist, also known as The Wormhole, was a natural rectangle stone formation that filled with water. His explanation did not make it any more appealing to Lilly, but Wyatt thought it sounded pretty cool.

They rode almost half an hour before they had to park their bikes and follow red arrows spray painted on the rocks for another fifteen minutes to find it. Lilly, as expected, was underwhelmed. Wyatt was excited to see people actually swimming in the hole.

Noah seemed antsy. Even though this was his idea, he kept glancing back toward the way they came.

"Nobody's going to steal our bikes," she chided him.

He reached over and pulled her close. "Nah, I think I'm just paranoid about missing the ferry."

She gave him a kiss and tapped the tip of his nose. "Unlikely. You've got the day mapped out so we're back at a restaurant near the dock in good time."

"Let's head out anyway."

They trekked back over the stones to their bikes, both kids complaining the whole way.

Noah checked his map. "About ten minutes to our next stop."

They rode for a while, then Noah announced they were almost to their destination.

"I thought we were going to the sweater market next?"

He hopped off his bike and grinned as he held out a hand to her. "Detour. I thought Wyatt would like to see this."

"What is it?" Wyatt asked.

"Dún Aonghasa. It's an ancient fort."

Wyatt looked it up on his phone and let out an excited,

"Wow! It's over three thousand years old. Oooh, it's also set to get official status as world heritage site."

Lilly sighed. "Whatever that means."

Wyatt snarked back, "It means it's important, so pay attention and learn something."

Both kids walked away from each other.

"Stay away from the edge," Becky warned.

Noah held her hand as they walked over the uneven rock formations. "Do you know what else this site is famous for?"

"No."

"Really? I'm surprised you don't recognize it. Look around."

She turned and looked out over the ocean, at the stunning horizon and the equally breathtaking cliffs. It was stunning, but she couldn't think of why she should recognize it. When she turned back, Noah was down on one knee, holding a ring. "Noah," she breathed.

"This spot is where Declan proposed to Anna."

She put a hand over her mouth, immediately realizing he was correct.

"And this is where I'm proposing to you. Becky Reed. Will you marry me?"

Tears blurred her vision. "Yes, of course, yes!"

Noah got to his feet and wrapped his arms around her. The ring caught on her jacket and slipped from his hand. "Oh, no!" It bounced on a stone and disappeared.

The ground all around them was rocky and uneven. They both went to their hands and knees, searching the cracks and crevices where it had fallen.

Both kids joined the search.

Noah huffed a sigh of relief and said, "Got it," just as Lilly held up a ring and said, "Is this it?"

Noah put the ring on her finger before they lost it again.

The ring Lilly found was a silver Claddagh ring, which she handed to Becky. "Just like the one Declan gave Anna."

Later that evening, back at Kate and Mary's bed and breakfast in Doolin, their hostesses were beside themselves at the news. They were already talking about the best time for Becky and Noah to come back for their honeymoon.

Becky half-listened, her head buzzing a little from the champagne and excitement of the day. She sat at the table, stuffed full of homemade treats and overflowing with happiness. Noah's arm was strong and warm across the back of her chair.

The past two years hadn't been easy, but they'd been worth every second. Wyatt and Lilly got along for the most part. Not an easy feat for an eleven-year-old boy and fifteen-year-old girl. Wyatt was a great big brother to Joey and Veronica's son Eli, and he was excited about the daughter they were expecting in four months' time. Now that Joey had a new family to occupy his time, he'd become much more tolerable as a co-parent. And Veronica? Becky loved her to pieces and now considered her one of her best friends.

Lilly was thriving, thanks to a wonderful family counselor who helped Lilly tremendously in learning that Danae's shortcomings weren't her fault or responsibility. Danae wasn't happy about only having supervised contact with Lilly, but honestly, Lilly was fifteen. If she wanted to have more contact, she could. Instead, she kept Danae at arm's length for her own mental health.

Becky took a page out of Veronica's book in dealing with Lilly. She stayed in her lane with anything that had even a whiff of parenting, and put her energy into getting to know

Lilly. Becky introduced her to the best romcoms (especially *Leap Year*, of course) and Lilly shared her love of anime and K-pop. They had their moments, but overall they got along very well.

"You awake?"

She nodded her head. "Just thinking about the difference two years makes."

Noah kissed the top of her head and squeezed. "Gotta hand it to the Ladies' Society. They knew what they were doing when they gave us two tickets to paradise."

The Ladies' Society's matchmaking track record was intact. Becky had to laugh, though, that they'd been the ones to turn the tables and reconnect Ruth and Thomas.

She sighed and corrected him. "No, they gave us two tickets to Ireland." She gestured to the kids and looked up at him. "And now we have four tickets to paradise."

Enjoyed this trip to Hickory Hollow? Keep it going with Book 8 in the series, Bad Advice.

When shy, anxious Lincoln has trouble dating, Gretchen steps in to help him out. Just a few practice dates between friends. One problem: doesn't practice usually come before the real thing?

Hickory Hollow. Get comfy, stay a while!

You don't want to miss news of my upcoming books, events, and behind-the-scenes sneak peeks. Sign up for my newsletter today at carriejacobs.com!

Author's Note

Dear Reader,

Ireland is one of those places that has been on my bucket list forever! It's such a beautiful country with so much history and so many breathtaking locations. After writing this book, I almost feel like I've been there. Almost.

I can't tell you how grateful I am for today's technology when it came to research for Two Tickets! (Sorry, card catalog, I do not miss you.) I spent a lot of time on Google Maps and Google Street View, making sure I got the details right for this trip. Full disclosure: I do know that the travel times Google Maps lists are best case scenario and may not line up with reality. But since I couldn't hop on a plane to Ireland to drive the route myself, it's the best I could do, and I think the timeline is mostly realistic.

There's also a little bit of me in this story. I would LOVE to visit the *Game of Thrones* film locations, and *Leap Year* is one of my favorite movies.

Thank you for taking this trip with me.

If you enjoyed Becky and Noah's story and have a moment to spare, leaving a review online would be very helpful to me. (Even if you didn't buy it online, you can still leave a review.) If you'd like to hear more from me, sign up for my newsletter! You'll get exclusive sneak peeks, behind-the-scenes info, notice of upcoming releases, and all that jazz. (Sign up at carriejacobs.com)

You can also follow me on Facebook (facebook.com/writer-carriejacobs) for notice of upcoming events and more importantly, pictures of my furry editorial assistants.

Best,
Carrie

About the Author

Carrie's love of storytelling began in early childhood and never wavered as time marched onward. She reads in pretty much every genre imaginable, but found her writing happy place in small town contemporary romance and romantic comedy.

From that love came Hickory Hollow, a mashup of her hometown and places she's either visited or would like to. Her favorite part of Hickory Hollow? The residents don't have to drive an hour to get to Target, like she does in real life.

Carrie lives in beautiful central Pennsylvania with her family and very spoiled furry editorial assistants.

Connect with Carrie through her newsletter or social media!

Website: carriejacobs.com

facebook.com/writercarriejacobs

instagram.com/carriejacobsauthor

goodreads.com/carriejacobs

www.ingramcontent.com/pod-product-compliance
Lightning Source LLC
Chambersburg PA
CBHW061534210726
48287CB00006B/1952